"You're not to interfere with my daughter anymore," Wade said

"You're her 4-H leader, not her mother," he added.

"As though I'd want to be, since that would mean being married to you." Tess wasn't quite sure where that comment had come from. Actually, she'd love to be Macy's mom...if only she came without her dad.

Wade looked stunned by her words. "Well, I reckon there's not much danger of that." He downed the rest of his beer and set the bottle on the countertop. "I'd throw the bottle away, but I imagine you'd like to recycle it," he told her sarcastically, thinking of her do-good ways.

"Oh, I don't know," she said, crossing her arms as she got up from the table. "Maybe I'd rather break it over your thick skull." She flashed him a mock smile.

To her surprise, he laughed. "I do like your spunk, Miss Tess Vega," he said. He pointed a forefinger. "Just remember. You're Macy's 4-H leader, and that's all." He tipped his hat. "Night, spitfire."

"Good night yourself," she said to his departing back. "Jackass."

Dear Reader,

I think one of the most common questions asked of an author is, "Where do you get your ideas?" Sometimes that's easy to answer and sometimes it isn't. Ideas come from many sources, often simply out of the blue, and at times sparked by an incident, a newspaper article or perhaps a conversation. I like to take my ideas and toss them into a mental slow cooker and let them simmer awhile.

The one for this book was sparked by an Alan Jackson song. When I heard Alan's sexy voice crooning "WWW Dot Memory," I knew instantly that I needed to write a book in which the hero is a cowboy who runs some type of Internet business. I tossed it into my slow cooker and let it stew for several months. Imagine my surprise when I opened the lid and discovered the story of Wade Darland (Macy's dad from *Sarah's Legacy*), which had cooked itself up while I wasn't looking.

When Wade decides that ranching is simply becoming too tough to make a living at these days, combined with the fact that he wants to spend more time with his kids, he comes to the conclusion that he needs to go a little high-tech—well, for a cowboy, anyway—and put up a Web site for his new tack and leather business, "Cowboy Up." He's confident he's got his world under control, his family neatly tucked into a protective circle where no outsiders are allowed—most especially a woman.

Little does he know he's about to butt heads with Tess Vega, Macy's new 4-H leader, a vegetarian and rescuer of abused and neglected horses. I had a great deal of fun writing Wade and Tess's story. Come with me, dear reader, and join Wade and Tess on their journey in search of love and commitment.

Brenda Mott

P.S. I love to hear from my readers. My e-mail address is BrendaMott@hotmail.com. Please reference the book on the subject line.

Cowgirl, Say Yes
Brenda Mott

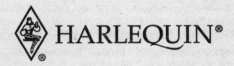

TORONTO • NEW YORK • LONDON
AMSTERDAM • PARIS • SYDNEY • HAMBURG
STOCKHOLM • ATHENS • TOKYO • MILAN • MADRID
PRAGUE • WARSAW • BUDAPEST • AUCKLAND

ISBN 0-373-71127-1

COWGIRL, SAY YES

This edition published by arrangement with Harlequin Books S.A.

® and TM are trademarks of the publisher. Trademarks indicated with
® are registered in the United States Patent and Trademark Office, the
Canadian Trade Marks Office and in other countries.

Visit us at www.eHarlequin.com

Printed in U.S.A.

To my own cowboy husband, David—for your loving support and for putting up with all my critters.

I'd like to thank the following people for their help in providing information that went into this book.

D'Ann Linscott-Dunham— good friend, fellow cowgirl and 4-H leader.

Dr. Mark Flinner.

Brenda Schetnan, R.N., and Mary Jane Hangs, who have both cared extensively for Alzheimer's patients. Also, Katie Lovette, fellow member of Smoky Mountain Romance Writers and author of *Loving Care for Alzheimer's Patients.*

Tom Anderson, who owns the real "Cowboy Up."

And last, but definitely not least, the folks of Colorado Horse Rescue and Terri Shell, Kitty and Bucky of Dream Catcher Farm Horse Sanctuary, for graciously answering my questions and for the wonderful work they do. May God bless you for saving our four-legged friends.

CHAPTER ONE

Tess Vega opened the Mother's Day card and signed her name at the bottom. Then she reread the note she'd penned moments earlier.

Dear Mama,
Sometimes it helps me to put words down on paper. Words you don't understand anymore. I hate that Alzheimer's took you away from me and Dad, Zach and Seth. But even more, I hate that it took you away from yourself. The disease is so unfair. But then, I guess so is any other disease people suffer....
All week, I've seen ads on TV for greeting cards with sentimental verses, and for buying just the right Mother's Day gift. I want to give you a perfect gift, Mama, but material things no longer hold any meaning for you. They really don't for me, either. All I want is a way to wind back the clock to how it used to be for us. I miss you, Mama. I'll visit you today and bring you flowers and balloons. You may not recognize me anymore. But sometimes I think you can sense things deep down. If so, you'll know this: I love you with all my heart.

Tess folded the note in half and reached for the glue. She squeezed a thin line of it around the edges of the paper and sealed the note shut. Then she slipped it in the card and glued that shut, as well. The words she'd written were for her mother only, not for anyone else's eyes. And while sealing notes that no one would ever read inside a card might seem foolish, it gave Tess some peace.

She'd been writing such notes for years, tucking them away in a greeting card on each and every holiday. Raelene might not be capable of reading them, but she enjoyed holding the cards, and Tess felt great satisfaction at knowing the words that came from her heart were there each time, hidden inside.

Tucking the card into its envelope, Tess rose, then gathered up the balloons and flowers she'd purchased and headed outside to her truck. Birds sang in the quiet surrounding her farmhouse as she slid behind the wheel. She placed the balloons and flowers on the seat beside her. They filled the cab of the pickup with cheer. Tess clung to that cheer as she drove toward town and the County Care Facility.

Determined to make this day the best she possibly could for her mother.

WADE DARLAND STEERED his horse toward Windsong Ranch, worried about his daughter. It wasn't like Macy to disappear without telling him where she'd be. But then, at the age of ten—almost eleven—she'd taken to doing things her own way of late, behaving like an alien creature. A creature called *woman*. He sure found it easier to relate to his twelve-year-old son, Jason, though he loved both his kids equally.

Sighing, Wade shook his head. Maybe Bailey would have an idea where Macy was, though even that was doubtful. His daughter hadn't been hanging out at Bailey's place as much as she used to, before it became the main location of Windsong Ranch—before Bailey and Trent married and started a family of their own.

The Murdocks were Wade's closest neighbors in the small mountain community of Ferguson, Colorado, and raised Arabian horses on the eighty-acre farm just two miles from the Darlands' Circle D ranch. They also owned the adobe-style ranch house that rested on an adjoining three hundred sixty acres—the place Trent had called home before he and Bailey got together. Macy, who no longer had her mother to turn to, had found a friend and mentor in Bailey the moment she'd met her. President of the local bank, Bailey was an animal lover, and Macy had spent a great deal of time the first summer Bailey moved to Ferguson, tagging at her heels, hanging out at her farm.

But now, with twin babies to occupy their time, the Murdocks had little to spare. Because Wade himself kept busy trying to make a living ranching—which wasn't easy these days—he knew Macy was at a bit of a loss without Bailey's fairly constant company. With nine days to go before school let out, Macy had begun to neglect her homework. Spring fever taken into consideration, Wade still kept a firm hand on both her and Jason, making sure they stayed focused. Not always an easy job for a widowed man.

All the more reason to reconsider ranching full-time, Wade thought. The Circle D simply took too much away from his kids.

Focusing on the here and now, he turned his blue roan gelding up the driveway of the white frame farmhouse and let the horse break into a trot. The ground beneath Dakota's hooves squished, dampened by last night's rain. Overhead, the leaves on the massive cottonwoods fluttered in the breeze, calling out a lazy invitation for all and anyone to enjoy the dappled patches of sun and shade on the grass below.

Trent sat sprawled in a chair on the front porch as Wade approached. He wore faded jeans and a T-shirt with what appeared to be a trace of baby vomit down the front of one shoulder. He broke into a wide grin when Wade pulled Dakota to a halt at the foot of the steps.

"Howdy, neighbor." Trent moved as though to rise, but Wade motioned him to stay put in the chair.

"Don't get up on my account." He grinned back. "You look tired, hoss. What's wrong? Are the twins keeping you up nights?"

Trent swept a hand through his cropped blond hair and nodded. "More like they're keeping us up round the clock. Austin's got colic, and Cody cries in sympathy."

Wade chuckled. "Better you than me. I'm glad those days are behind me."

Trent quirked his mouth. "Yeah, I'd forgotten how this routine goes." His words were bittersweet, and Wade knew he still missed his little girl, Sarah, who would've been nine now, had cancer not taken her young life. But Trent had a new family with Bailey, and seeing his friend so happy did Wade's heart good.

"Hey, have you seen Macy?" Wade asked. "I thought she might be up here pestering Bailey."

"She stopped by earlier," Trent said. "I'm not sure, but I think she went up to the ranch." He indicated the place on the hill above the farmhouse.

"What's she doing up there?" Wade asked, glancing toward the dividing fence between the properties.

"Tess Vega leased the ranch from me. I thought you knew that."

"No. I heard she'd taken over Macy's 4-H group, but I wasn't aware she was living at your ranch." Tess's father owned the local feed store, and Wade had been acquainted with the Vega family in that regard for a number of years now. When Macy's 4-H leader had married and made plans to move away, Tess had been an ideal replacement. She had connections in the community through working at the feed store and was well acquainted with most of the 4-H kids and their parents, who bought supplies from Lloyd Vega. Plus, she ran a horse sanctuary for abused and abandoned animals, funded by donations. The county agent had been more than happy to accept her when she'd volunteered for the vacated position.

Trent nodded again. "I leased the house and twenty acres to her for her sanctuary."

Wade really hadn't given much thought about Tess's non-profit organization—Western Colorado Horse Rescue—until now. But things suddenly clicked at Trent's comment. Macy loved animals, and Bailey no longer had enough time for her. No wonder his daughter was drawn to Tess Vega.

Just then the screen door creaked open and Bailey

stepped out onto the porch. She closed the door behind her with exaggerated care to mute the squeak. Motherhood had done nothing to diminish her attraction. She might be wearing a loose flannel shirt because her waistline was not quite back to normal, but she looked good. And happy.

Wade smiled. "Hey, Bailey. How're the boys? I hope Macy's not getting in your way too much."

Bailey smiled. "Are you kidding? She's my best helper." She bent and gave Trent a peck on the cheek. "Next to you, sweetie." She winked and Trent covered her hand with his as she rested it on his shoulder. "At least, when she's here she is." Bailey narrowed her eyes. "Is everything okay, Wade? Macy doesn't come over as often as she used to."

"Yeah. I think she's just feeling a little ousted by the twins."

"Then I'll have to make sure she knows how much I miss her," Bailey said. "Want to come in and take a peek at the boys?" She motioned toward the door. "I put them down for a nap, but if you're quiet you can have a look." She had the typical proud expression of a new parent, and Wade was moved by her happiness. She and Trent had been through a lot in their pasts. He was truly glad they'd found each other.

For a brief moment, loneliness squeezed at his heart. *God, how he missed Deidra.* The five years since her death had passed in a blur. Yet he still had a hard time coping with Mother's Day, which he'd always tried to make special for her even while she was pregnant with Jason. He shrugged the gloomy feeling aside. He'd learned to live for his children.

Mother's Day had come three days ago, and he'd spent it with Macy and Jason, playing horseshoes, barbecuing hamburgers. Not dwelling on the fact that Deidra was no longer with them.

"Thanks," he said in answer to Bailey's invitation, "but I better go find Macy. She needs to do her homework and finish her chores."

"Oh, well, I think she's up at the ranch," Bailey said. "With Tess Vega."

"Yeah." He nodded. "Trent mentioned it. Guess I'll ride on over there and see."

"Don't worry," Bailey added. "Tess is really a nice person. She loves animals." She beamed as though this was the best quality someone could have. "But then, I guess you know her from the feed store."

"Yeah." But not well. Funny how a person could do business with someone for years without really delving into her social life. He supposed if Tess was going to be involved with Macy, he'd better make it a point to get to know her better.

Wade looked around, noting the many pets Bailey had gradually added to her farm, beginning with a stray dog, a half-blind horse and a rogue tomcat. The dog and cat now lay curled at one end of the porch—Buddy, the blue heeler mix, too lazy even to bark; the battle-scarred tomcat content to soak up the comfort of the dog's sun-warmed fur. In a nearby cage, several rabbits hopped around, nibbling at a handful of alfalfa not far away, and a trio of ducks waddled across the lawn on their way to the children's wading pool, located in one corner of the yard.

"I'll head on over to her," Wade repeated.

Another animal lover.

Another mother figure for Macy to attach herself to.

Lord have mercy. He didn't need this at all.

"ARE YOU SURE your dad wants Amber to come live
at the sanctuary?" Tess eyed the little palomino
mare that stood with one hip cocked at the hitching
post in the driveway. The horse looked well cared
for, without a worry in the world. Not her normal
rescue case. Why on earth would Wade Darland not
allow his daughter to keep her own horse? What
kind of father was he?

She'd seen him around town plenty of times, and
often talked to him at her father's feed store, where
she worked part-time, but she didn't really know the
man. And because she'd only recently taken over as
Macy's 4-H leader, she hadn't yet run into Wade at
a meeting.

"Uh-huh," Macy said in answer to Tess's question. Then she quirked her mouth. "Well, I'm pretty
sure, anyway. I've been talking to him about it."

"I see. Macy, why doesn't he want to let Amber
retire at your ranch?"

Macy started to answer, then turned, instead, to
see who was approaching on horseback.

Tess looked, too, and her stomach knotted as
Wade Darland himself rode up the driveway on a
pretty, blue roan quarter horse. Macy's comment left
her with the feeling she was in for a confrontation.
As though agreeing, her dogs trotted along the driveway, barking a warning.

"Uh-oh," Macy said, grimacing. "I think I forgot
to finish my chores. And my homework." She

moved toward her horse as her dad halted in front of her and Tess.

"Hi." He tipped his well-worn cowboy hat, and Tess was treated to a glimpse of hair the color of rich brown soil. Then the horse shifted, putting her gaze directly in line with the sun.

Tess shielded her eyes and looked up at Wade. "Hi," she said. "Macy just remembered her homework."

"That, and you've got chores to do, young lady." He frowned, but he didn't appear genuinely angry. Maybe he wasn't such a bad guy after all.

His next words shot her last thought to the ground.

"Macy, what are you doing here? You know better than to take off without telling me or leaving a note."

It wasn't the note business that nettled Tess. It was the "what are you doing here" part, with emphasis on the *here*.

"I am Macy's new 4-H leader," Tess said.

"I'm aware of that," he replied. "But that doesn't excuse my daughter taking off without leaving word." He turned once more to Macy and repeated his question.

"I'm sorry, Dad," Macy said, not looking so at all. "I just wanted to go for a ride and see Bailey's twins again."

"And?"

Wade seemed to know his daughter better than she thought.

Macy shifted from one foot to the other, clutching Amber's reins.

"And talk to Tess about Amber," she muttered,

staring down at her feet as she scuffed the toe of her boot against the gravel driveway.

"What?"

"And talk to Tess—" Macy began, speaking more clearly.

"I heard you." Wade frowned. "Macy, we've already been over this." He glanced Tess's way. "Now's not the time. We'll talk some more when we get home."

"But, Dad…"

"Macy." Wade gave her a firm look. "You heard me. Come on. Get on your horse and let's go."

He focused on Tess, turning the blue roan so that the sun was no longer in Tess's eyes.

"Sorry if Macy's been pestering you," he said. "We'll be going."

"Hold up a minute." She laid her hand on the roan's muzzle, stilling Wade's pull on the reins. "Macy isn't pestering me. She came over here to talk to me about giving Amber a permanent home."

The sun-bronzed color in his face deepened, along with the scowl creasing his forehead. He was a good-looking man, she'd give him that, but right now his expression did nothing to add appeal to his charmless demeanor.

"She shouldn't have done that," he said. "I told her not to."

"Why?" Folding her arms, Tess challenged him with the single word.

"What do you mean, *why?*" He scowled some more. "There's no reason for asking, that's why. We've got a ranch of our own, and when the horses can no longer serve a purpose, they'll go to the sale barn."

Now it was Tess's turn to scowl. "The sale barn? Wade, you know what happens to horses that go there. At least the ones past their prime."

He shot her a glare that said she'd overstepped her boundaries, but she didn't care. Idiots like him made her rescue work necessary.

"I'm not going to argue with you on this, Tess. It's none of your concern."

"Is that right?" She frowned at him. "I'd say it is my concern when your daughter comes to me practically in tears because you aim to ship her horse off to the kil—to the auction."

"I said I wasn't going to argue with you." He spoke the words evenly, but his hazel eyes showed irritation at her. "Come on, Macy, we're burning daylight."

"Burning daylight?" Tess scoffed. "You've been watching too many John Wayne movies, Wade. Maybe you ought to spend less time with your remote control and more time finding out what's truly important to your daughter." As soon as the words were out, she knew she'd overstepped. She really didn't know Wade well enough to speak to him that way, but when people acted as though animals were disposable—useful today, dumped tomorrow—it made her furious.

He clenched his jaw. "What did I say?" he reiterated. "The horse is none of your concern, either. Macy, come on!" Without waiting, he thumped his heels against the roan's sides, making the gelding jump into a trot.

Tess scowled after him, her heart breaking when she saw the expression on Macy's face as she followed her father down the driveway. From the back of her palomino, the little girl gave a sad little wave, then faced forward.

Tess wanted to run after the man and yank him from the saddle. Maybe knock some sense into his head or, better yet, start on the other end with a cowboy boot to his butt.

She watched her dogs, who circled her feet, sensing something had upset her. Duke, her German shepherd, growled, and Bruiser, her miniature pinscher, trotted briskly down the driveway, looking right then left. His high-pitched bark warned he just might mean business if something was amiss. Only Sasha, the Australian shepherd, wagged her stubby tail, her red-speckled body wriggling along with it.

"You're too late, Duke," Tess addressed the German shepherd. "You should've bitten him while you had the chance."

"MACY, why did you do that?" Exasperated, Wade sat at the table, looking at his daughter. Her eyes filled with tears, making him feel every inch the creep Tess Vega obviously thought he was. "Why did you lie to Tess and tell her I said she could have Amber?"

"Because," Macy said, swiping angrily at her tears. "I don't want Amber to go to the sale barn."

"But, honey." Wade softened his tone, reaching out to put his hand on Macy's shoulder. He gave her a gentle squeeze. "If you don't sell her, then you won't have any money to put toward a new horse. Amber's getting too old to do barrels and poles. You know that, don't you?" The barrel-racing and pole-bending events Macy competed in required a lot of running, coupled with sharp turns around three fifty-five-gallon drums set in a clover-leaf pattern, or six poles placed in a row. To compete on a regular basis took a lot of physical effort for a horse.

Macy sobbed, no longer able to hold back. ''I know. But I *love* her!'' She said the word as though it was foreign to him, making him feel ten times worse. He'd never meant to make his daughter so upset.

''Baby, don't cry. I'm not trying to be mean. I'm just trying to be practical. You know, Grandpa Darland was always the same way when I was growing up. Horses get old, Macy. It can't be helped. Just like we all do. And when they're too old to use, then you've got to be sensible and ship 'em to auction. Replace them with new ones. You'll find another horse to love.''

''You don't ship people off to auction just 'cause they're old,'' Macy snapped, some of her spunk returning. She sniffed loudly. ''If so, Grandpa Darland would've been hauled off long ago.''

Wade let out a chuckle and rumpled Macy's hair. ''Better not let him hear you say that.'' He sighed, searching for a way to make her see reason. ''Macy, it's not the same thing at all. Horses aren't people.''

''Amber's people to me. And if you won't let her stay here, then I want her to go live with Tess.'' Her lip trembled, but she bit it, fighting for control. She'd always been a tough little cuss, which broke his heart all the more.

''Honey, it's not that I don't want Amber to live here. I was only trying to help you see the smart thing in selling her so you can have a new horse. I can't afford the purchase price of one right now,

with my leather business just taking off.'' A good
4-H horse could run into the thousands, and Wade's
new business selling tack and leather belts was not
yet well established. "You understand, don't you?''

She frowned at him. "I understand that part of it,
but I still don't want to sell her.''

"Okay," he said, holding up one hand in surrender. "You don't have to. Nobody's trying to force
you to sell your horse. I just thought it might be a
good idea, that's all...." He let the words trail away.
Had he given Macy the impression he was trying to
force her to sell her mare? If so, he hadn't meant to.
He simply didn't understand her way of thinking,
any more than he understood Tess's.

A horse sanctuary, for God's sake. Who would
ever dream up such a crazy thing? Horses weren't
pets the way dogs were. He could see the sense in
an animal shelter, but a *horse sanctuary?* He'd
grown up on a working cattle ranch of over six thousand acres, and all the cowboys on the place, including his own father looked at the horses they rode
as working animals...part of the operation, just like
the tractors that furrowed the hay fields and the
pickup trucks that delivered the bales. When horses
broke down, it was time to get rid of them and replace them with something newer, something better.

But his daughter, it seemed, had different ideas,
in spite of being raised on a working ranch herself.
He blamed people like Tess for that, even Bailey
Murdock. Oh, sure, he liked Trent and Bailey both,
but they weren't native to the area. Trent came from
California, where things were viewed differently,
and Bailey was from the city—Denver. Not that he

had anything against folks from California—or from the city, either, for that matter.

It was just…well…take Trent's fancy horse. Arabians. For the life of him, Wade couldn't figure why anyone would pay thousands of dollars for a hotheaded horse that wasn't good for much, as far as he could see, except prancing around, looking pretty.

And Bailey had gotten Macy all fired up about pets and saving stray animals.

More than ever, Wade wished Deidra were still alive. Trying to fill the role of father *and* mother wasn't easy. Sometimes he made the wrong choices. Apparently this was one of them.

Pulling his thoughts back to the immediate situation, Wade wrapped his arm around Macy's shoulders and drew her into a hug. "You can stop crying," he said. "Amber can stay."

"She can?" Her blue eyes wide with hope, Macy looked up at him, wrenching his heart.

"Yeah, she can. But that means no new horse until we get some more money somehow."

"I don't care." A smile lit her face. "As long as we don't have to send Amber to the sale barn."

"Fine. Now, finish your chores, then do your homework." He picked up the milk glass and cookie plate that sat empty in front of Macy. "I'll get your dishes this time." He gave her a wink.

Macy slid her chair back, stood and wrapped her arms around his waist. "I love you, Daddy." Then she raced out the door.

"I love you, too, baby." Wade spoke softly, the words echoing in the empty kitchen.

He moved to the sink, rinsed the dishes and

stuffed them into the already overcrowded dish-
washer. Absentmindedly, he added detergent and
flipped the switch. The machine whirred to a start,
quickly filling the kitchen with the scent of hot water
and lemon.

Wade opened the fridge and took out a package
of hamburger, ground from their own beef on the
Circle D. How on earth was he supposed to make
ends meet with what the ranch was bringing in? Yet
if he sold the cows and got out, they'd no longer
have the luxury of eating as many steaks a week as
they wanted. He'd seen the price of beef in town,
and it angered him beyond words that the rancher
and the farmer weren't the ones making money off
the meat and produce sold in the supermarket. The
middleman was, and without the homegrown beef
to supplement their food supply, they'd be hard-
pressed to eat well.

Wade shaped the burger into patties while his
mind raced.

Still, his leather business was gradually picking
up, and he did have the new Web site nearly up and
running. Cowboy Up could turn out to be a bigger
hit than he'd imagined. There was a lot to be said
for the World Wide Web, and working in the house
rather than out in the barn or elsewhere on the ranch
would give him a lot more time to spend with Jason
and Macy.

Yet he still couldn't decide whether to sell the
cattle. Maybe he'd just sell part of the herd. *Maybe
Tess Vega could start up a cow sanctuary,* he
thought dryly.

The screen door banged open, then shut, interrupting his thoughts as Jason flew into the kitchen

like a tornado on the heels of a hurricane. "Hey, Dad! When's supper? I'm starvin'." Lanky for his age, Jason was always hungry, and seemed to outgrow his jeans as fast as Wade could buy them. The boy moved to the sink to wash his sun-browned hands using the dishwashing soap, then hastily wiped them on a paper towel.

"Son, don't waste the paper towels like that." Wade tossed him the dish towel and Jason gave his hands another swipe. "Dinner will be ready shortly. Why don't you help me out...peel a few potatoes."

"All right." Jason moved to the potato bin, his light-brown hair peeking out from beneath his ball cap.

"Take your hat off."

Whistling, Jason flipped it at the rack by the back door, missed and scooped it up, then aimed once more. This time the John Deere cap found its mark. Jason grinned at him, then pointed. "What's that on your head, Dad?"

"What?" Wade reached up to touch his head, and his hand bumped against the brim of his worn, gray Resistol. It was such a part of him he hadn't even realized he still had it on. He laughed, then hung it on the peg next to Jason's cap. "Silly of me, huh?"

"Hey, Dad," Jason said, sitting at the table and running the peeler over a large russet potato. "Did you know that Tess from the feed store moved into Trent Murdock's place?"

"I heard," Wade said dryly. "Your sister was up there this afternoon."

"Wondered where she'd gone off to," Jason said. "She was supposed to help me with the bucket calves." Every spring they ended up with a few calves that needed supplemental feeding for one reason or another. A bucket with rubber nipples attached inside served as a surrogate mother.

"I know. I lined her out." Wade grinned and Jason grinned back. They both realized his idea of firm discipline was little more than a lecture. Most often, he found reasoning with his kids worked just fine, but today there'd been no reasoning with Macy.

His thoughts turned again to Tess. He'd seen her on numerous occasions at the feed store, but he'd never really noticed until today that she was a good-looking woman. At least, she could be, if she'd learn how to wear something other than bib overalls, and if she'd take her flame-red hair out of those silly braids.

Braids like a kid. Hell, she wasn't much more than a kid. Probably about twenty-four, he thought. Or maybe twenty-five. He wasn't sure. These days anyone under thirty seemed young to him.

At thirty-three, Wade already felt every one of his years in the aches in his joints and muscles when he lay in bed at night after a hard day putting up fence or pulling calves during calving season or whatever else was required to keep the Circle D running. His days of affording hired help were long past, and trying to keep things up with only Macy and Jason to pitch in had been hell lately.

Deidra had been his right arm as well as his best friend. A strong, hard worker and practical to the bone. Nothing like Tess, with her batty ideas about rescuing old horses.

Horse sanctuary.

"Dad?" Jason waved a hand in front of his face. Wade blinked. "What?"

"Did Tess work her charms on you, too?" Jason teased.

"Hardly." Then he frowned. "What do you mean 'too'?"

"Nothing." Jason chuckled. "She's hot, ain't she?"

Wade knuckled his son's hair. "You're not supposed to be noticing things like that yet."

"Dad! I'm almost *thirteen*." He said it as though the age equaled manhood.

Wade grinned. "Yeah, I guess you are. And I guess she is. Hot, that is," he added. "But she's sure irritating."

"Yep." Jason nodded as though he held the wisdom of the world in his mind. "Women usually are."

CHAPTER TWO

TESS SHUT the refrigerator door a little too hard, and the magnetic calendar that didn't seem to stick right anymore slid off and plopped on the floor. She picked it up and noticed her upcoming birthday marked with pink Hi-Liter—Macy's doing. Six more days and she'd turn twenty-seven. Twenty-seven and still married to her job.

She shrugged off the thought. Only her run-in with Wade was making her think that way. Any other time, she knew she was better off sharing her home with no one but her animals. Heck, she had all the kids she needed in her 4-H group. And Lord knows she'd had enough of being a family caregiver to last a lifetime. Not that she would ever begrudge the time she'd devoted to her mother. Instead, she treasured it.

Raelene Vega had developed familial Alzheimer's disease—FAD, a rare form of Alzheimer's—at the age of forty-one. As the years passed, she'd required Tess's ever-increasing care. It wasn't her fault, no more than Tess's dad and two older brothers were to blame for being men—which translated to help-less half the time.

Tess had been the primary caregiver, maker of meals and soother of colds, flu and broken hearts since the age of sixteen. Her father had insisted that

Raelene, the woman he'd thought would be his life's partner, stay at home for as long as possible. With the progress of time came progress of the disease. Tess had quickly grown to hate FAD. Not for what it put her through, but for what her mother suffered.

Once a vibrant, intelligent woman who took pride in the three kids she'd chosen to adopt, she'd taught them how to ride a horse, how to build a barn and what to do when a member of the opposite sex called for the first time on the phone. But in the grip of Alzheimer's, Rae's mind had quickly deteriorated. Her condition had worsened to the point that although Lloyd Vega and all three of his children visited Rae regularly at the County Care Facility, she rarely knew who they were anymore.

Tess tried not to think about that part.

And she tried not to be selfish and thank God that, even though she felt like Rae's flesh and blood, she wasn't. Tess's birth mother had abandoned her and her brothers when they were small, fading from their lives without so much as a second thought. Raelene had married Lloyd a short time later, and adopted Tess and the boys. FAD ran in generations, and if Tess, Zach and Seth had been Rae's biological children, they would have had a fifty-fifty chance of inheriting the disease.

Angry at herself not for the first time for letting such a thought come to mind, Tess slapped the calendar back up on the fridge, opened the door and peered inside. An assortment of fresh vegetables and cheese greeted her, and her stomach growled. She'd given up meat ten years ago, when her love for animals dictated she do the right thing. Reaching into the fridge, she chose a cluster of fresh broccoli and a chunk of Monterey Jack, both of which would go nicely with the ziti she'd purchased yesterday. She'd also treat herself to a good, ice-cold beer. Tess rarely drank the stuff, but the day she'd had today warranted one.

First there'd been the call she'd gotten at work…a summons to a boarding stable located ten miles from town. The caller had been a concerned neighbor, and the tale she'd told had been familiar. One that never failed to twist Tess's stomach into a knot. An abandoned horse, neglected because the owner no longer cared and had found better things to spend money on.

Tess had driven out immediately, to find a bone-thin gray mare standing in a stall full of manure. Mane and tail matted, hooves curled like elf shoes, she had a dull expression in her eyes that said she'd given up hope. Crud caked her once-pretty dappled coat, and flies buzzed around the stall in excess. The entire barnyard looked as though it hadn't been cleaned in a millenium.

Furious beyond words, Tess had offered the idiot stable owner, who now "took care" of the abandoned mare, fifty dollars for the animal, knowing he'd ask for more. He hadn't disappointed her. Two hundred dollars later, she'd left with the gray safely stowed in the two-horse trailer behind her Dodge Ram. The poor creature had loaded without much fuss, especially once she laid eyes on the flake of grass hay waiting for her in the trailer's manger.

Back home, Tess had promptly called Doc Baker, who came out as soon as he could and examined the mare. He proclaimed her salvageable, gave her wormer medication and a vaccine to guard against tetanus, influenza and sleeping sickness, and recommended a top-notch farrier to trim her grossly overgrown hooves. Tess's own farrier, married to Macy's former 4-H leader, had moved away last week.

With the mare under Doc's watchful eye, Tess left the barn long enough to call the number on the business card he'd given her. To her delight, the ''Johnnie'' Blake who answered the phone turned out to be a woman. She promised to drive out the next day and take care of the mare. Tess applauded the fact that her new farrier was female, especially since the gray would require some extra-special attention and Tess stubbornly refused to believe that any man could have as big a heart as a woman when it came to needy animals.

Back in the barn, she found the old mare down. Heart in her throat, she watched Doc Baker tend to her with gentle hands and a soft voice. He'd quickly reassured Tess that the horse was fine. She simply suffered from exhaustion and had spent the reserve of her energy for the day. Still, he stayed with the animal for the better part of an hour to be certain she was indeed okay. Before he left, he told Tess not to hesitate to call him in the middle of the night if necessary, blowing her theory of insensitive men all to hell.

Then Macy had ridden over, begging her to give Amber a home. Next had come her argument with Wade Darland.

Twisting the cap off a longneck bottle of Coors Light, Tess leaned back in a kitchen chair, propping her booted feet on its neighbor.

Now, there was a man who was enough to drive

any woman to drink. Good-looking as all get out, he nevertheless irritated her beyond words with his attitude. Lord, what was wrong with him? Upsetting poor Macy that way. What did he plan to do? Ship her horse off to the killer? That was likely the only buyer he'd get for a mare in her twenties. The horse was still ridable, but not so fit for speed events anymore. Macy thought Amber was about twenty-three, but she wasn't sure because the mare wasn't registered.

Tess took a swig from the longneck, then rose to check on her boiling pasta, sidestepping one of her cats as he laced himself between her ankles with a plaintive meow, begging. "You won't eat pasta, Champ, and you know it."

The sound of a truck in her driveway sent her to look through the screen door. Her heart did a dive. Wade Darland climbed from behind the wheel of a battered Ford pickup, his gray hat dusty, his boots scuffed. What did he want now?

The last of the sun's rays made a backdrop against his shoulders as he headed up the sidewalk. Duke lunged at him, taking a snap at his heels, and Wade shouted. Tess opened the screen and gave a sharp whistle that had all three dogs retreating to the porch. Wade hesitated halfway up the walk, eyeing Duke. At a hundred and five pounds, the shepherd looked like a canine version of Arnold "I'll be back" Schwarzenegger. Or maybe more of a "make my day" kind of dog, as he showed Wade his teeth and the length of hair rising on the back of his neck.

"You're okay," Tess called out. "He won't bite now."

Wade appeared skeptical but strode up the walk

anyway, then waited while Tess took hold of Duke's collar before coming all the way up the steps. "Be nice, Duke," she said.

"Duke?" Wade raised one eyebrow. "You've been watching too many John Wayne movies, Tess."

She laughed in spite of herself. "All right. Maybe I deserved that one." She nodded toward the screen door. "Go on in." Only after he was safely inside did she let loose of Duke's collar. "So what's up?" she asked, closing the screen behind her. "Did you come here to lecture me on the evils of horse rescue, or were you planning to drive splinters under my nails until I agreed to give up my quest?"

He glared at her. "That's a fine way to treat a neighbor, Tess." He nodded at the beer. "Got another one of those?"

She huffed out a noise that let him know she found his manners sorely lacking, then opened the fridge and extracted a longneck. On the stove, the pasta boiled wildly. She checked it and found it almost ready.

"Have you eaten yet?"

"Yeah. I feed my kids every Wednesday, whether they need it or not."

Tess turned and shot him a glare, only to find him grinning at her behind her back. The tension in her neck eased, and she allowed herself to return his smile, but only briefly. She couldn't let his looks disarm her.

"So, why did you come out here?" she asked, pretty sure she already knew the answer.

"I wanted to clear up a couple of things," he said, taking a pull from the beer bottle. Tess watched his long, strong fingers curl around it, noticed the way his lips covered the brown glass as though he were about to kiss it...and licked her own. He was enough for her to indulge in a fantasy. Enough to make her stupid.

Again, she dragged her thoughts from that direction. Who needed a man, anyhow?

"Clear away," she said, turning to dump the pasta into the strainer, not caring if it was completely cooked or not. She topped it with broccoli and some chunks of jack and sat down at the table, gesturing Wade toward a chair. "Sure you're not hungry?"

He scooted out the chair, revealing her black cat, Inky, who lay curled on the cushion. The cat gave Wade an indignant stare at having been moved from his resting place, not offering to budge from his perch. Unceremoniously, Wade lifted Inky from the cushion and set him on the floor, the expression on his face telling her all she needed to know of his opinion on cats. One she'd already heard from Macy. Tess glared at him, but he didn't seem to notice.

He eyed her plate. "You call that a meal? Where's the meat?"

"Where it's supposed to be," she said. "On the hoof, not in the freezer."

"Oh." He laughed. "Oh-ho-ho, I might've known. A vegetarian." He said it as though being a vegetarian was a felony. She supposed to a cattle rancher, it might as well be.

Narrowing her eyes, she poked a broccoli floret with the tines of her fork. Pretending it was Wade's fat head. Arrogant jerk. What kind of man didn't like cats? "What's it to you, Darland?"

"Darlin'?" He raised his eyebrows and shot her a grin. "And here I thought you didn't like me."

Tess felt her lips twitch in a near smile. "You know that's not what I said." Then she stabbed another piece of broccoli. How did he do that to her? Make her anger run hot, then ooze away, cold, as though he'd dumped a bucket of chilled honey on it.

"Does your daddy know you're a traitor?"

"Excuse me?"

"That's right. He supports the cattle and sheep ranchers around here, keeping their livestock in grain products. And all the while you're shunning meat, eating vegetables like some do-good yuppie."

Tess let her mouth fall open. She couldn't help it, and was glad for the fact that she'd already swallowed her bite of ziti. "In the first place, I'm sure my dad is quite aware of my meal preferences. And in the second, I can't believe you're sitting in my kitchen, drinking *my* beer and throwing insults at me! Maybe I ought to call Duke in here."

"Won't be necessary," he said. "I'm not staying any longer than it takes to tell you what's on my mind." He set the beer down and leaned forward in his chair. "It's about Macy."

Immediately, Tess sobered. Had he punished her when they'd gotten home? Had the child retaliated in some way?

"Is she okay?"

"Yeah, she's fine, no thanks to you."

"Oh, pardon me, Mr. Beef-eating Rancher, but I

wasn't the one who threatened to sell her mare to the glue factory.''

"I never threatened anything." Wade's scowl was back, darkening his hazel eyes to a stormy near green. "I simply tried to get Macy to see the sensible side of things and— Oh, what am I trying to explain it to you for? You sure don't get it."

"No, Wade, I think you're the one who doesn't get it. You're breaking your daughter's heart. What would it hurt you to let her keep the horse? You've got about five zillion acres between you and your old man, yet you can't find room for one retired mare?"

He made a huffing sound. "Dad's not ranching anymore. He sold most of his place to some developers last month so they could subdivide it and make more room for yuppies to move into this valley." He glared at her as though she were personally responsible.

"Well, don't look at me. I'm against all the development happening, but what are you going to do to stop it?" The question was a rhetorical one.

"Imagine that." Wade drew back, startling her with his smile. He raised his beer in toast. "We actually have something in common, Miss Veggie."

"Don't call me that." Tess scowled at him, then shook her head and gave in to the laugh that bubbled up inside her. She raised her own beer bottle, clinked it against his, then sobered. "But really, Wade. You can't sell Macy's horse."

"I already know that."

She'd been prepared to argue further. His agreement took her by surprise. "You do?"

"Yeah, I do. I didn't realize I'd upset Macy that

much.'' He shook his head. "She sure doesn't think things through the way her mama did. Anyway, that's one of the things I came to tell you. The other one is, you're not to interfere with my daughter anymore. You're her 4-H leader, not her mother.''

"As though I'd want to be, since that would mean being married to you.'' She wasn't quite sure where that comment had come from. Actually, she'd love to be Macy's mom…if only she did indeed come without her dad.

Wade looked stunned by her words. "Well, I reckon there's not much danger in that,'' he said. He downed the rest of the Coors Light and set the bottle on the countertop. "I'd throw that away, but I imagine you'd like to recycle it,'' he said. His posture and manner of speech reminded her of Woody Harrelson in the movie *The Cowboy Way*. Just as much class, she thought with sarcasm. Even more good looks, she admitted reluctantly. And twice as much trouble.

That, she was sure of.

"Oh, I don't know,'' she said, crossing her arms as she got up from the table. "Maybe I'd rather see if it will break over your thick skull.'' She flashed him a mock smile.

To her surprise, he laughed. "I do like your spunk, Miss Tess Vega,'' he said. He pointed a forefinger. "Just remember. You're Macy's 4-H leader, and that's all.'' He tipped his hat. "'Night, spitfire.''

"Good night yourself,'' she said to his departing back. "Jackass.''

HER PHONE RANG in the middle of the night, and for a minute Tess thought it was the alarm clock. Disoriented, she sat up in bed, then scrambled from beneath the covers to answer.

"Hello?" Heart pounding, Tess realized it was 3:45 a.m.

Her mother.

Please, no.

"Tess, it's Joy Isley. I'm so sorry to wake you at such an ungodly hour, but we've got some horses loose out here, and you were the first person who came to mind."

Shaky with relief, Tess ran a hand through her rumpled hair. "It's okay. Where are they?"

"They've raced up my driveway from the road, and they keep circling the yard and outbuildings. My dog's barking woke me up. There're three of them— the horses, that is. I was going to pen them and call the sheriff later, but I can't catch them. Bobby's trying to keep them from running back out on the road. I'm really not all that good with horses. Shoot, maybe I should've just called the sheriff and not bothered you."

"No, it's no bother, Joy. I'll be right there."

Tess hung up the phone and hurried to the bathroom. She splashed some water on her face to help her wake up and ran a comb through her hair. Minutes later, she was dressed and heading down the road toward the Isleys' place with a bucketful of grain and three halters and lead ropes. A single mother, Joy was a regular at the feed store. Her son, Bobby, raised rabbits and pygmy goats. Tess doubted their pens could hold a horse.

A short time later, she pulled her truck into Joy's driveway, carefully bypassing twelve-year-old Bobby, who stood in the glare of the headlights, waving his arms anytime the stray horses drew near. Tess angled her truck across the driveway to help block their path and climbed out. She didn't recognize any of the geldings. Two sorrels and a bay, they bore no distinctive markings or brands to differentiate them from the dozens of other horses Tess saw daily in neighboring pastures.

Excited by their strange surroundings, along with the darkness, wind and the bleating goats, the geldings raced in circles, threading their way between outbuildings and the house. One managed to escape onto the road, nearly running over Bobby in the process. Tess gathered two lariats from her truck and strung them from the pickup's mirrors to the fence posts on either side of the driveway, foiling the escape attempt of the remaining geldings.

Wishing for her team-penning mare, she gave chase on foot after the bay, shaking the grain bucket in his wake. Once he realized his buddies weren't joining him in his wild escapade, the horse circled back. All three horses bugled loud whinnies into the early-morning air, snorting and running until their coats were damp with sweat. By the time she managed to catch them and help Joy lock them inside some makeshift stalls in the barn, it was after five-thirty.

"I'll place some calls and see if I can track down the owners," Tess promised. "Maybe Dad will have an idea who they belong to."

"Thanks so much, Tess," Joy said. "I've got to go to work, but if you need help with the calls, I can do some on my lunch break."

"It's okay. I'll phone you later and let you know what's going on." Tired, eyes burning, Tess undid the ropes from the fence posts and tucked them back behind the seat of her truck once more before driving away. She started to head home, then decided she might as well grab a bite of breakfast on her way through town. Why not? Ferguson lay halfway between Joy's place and her own.

Yawning, Tess pulled into the parking lot of Audrey's Café. The cowbell on the door clanged as she entered, but accustomed to the sound, no one looked up.

No one, that is, except Wade Darland.

To Tess's surprise, he sat at a table with Macy and Jason. She hadn't noticed his truck in the parking lot, but at any rate, she never would have figured him for the sort of father who would take his kids out to breakfast on a school day. He looked at her in a way that suddenly made Tess aware that her barely combed hair was stuffed under a ratty ball cap.

In a way that also made her notice he was even better-looking than she'd remembered.

Oh, brother.

She really needed to go home, go back to bed and start this day all over.

CHAPTER THREE

WADE NEARLY CHOKED on a piece of bacon when he glanced up and saw Tess walk into the café. He couldn't believe that he'd run into her again so soon after their little talk last night. Had she seen him driving through town and followed him?

The expression on her face quickly dispelled that notion. She hesitated at the door, as though unsure whether to wave or simply take a seat. Her gaze scanned the crowded room, and she frowned when she saw that nearly all the tables were full. Before he could decide if he wanted to wave at her, Macy took matters out of his hands.

"Tess!" she called, motioning. "Over here."

"Macy, I don't think—"

"What's wrong, Dad?" Jason grinned around a mouthful of blueberry pancakes. "Don't you want her to sit with us?" The teasing spark in his son's eyes said he was enjoying the opportunity to give his old dad a hard time.

"I don't care one way or the other," Wade said, ignoring Jason's smirk as Tess approached the table.

"Hi, Macy," she said. "Jason." Then she turned to him. "I'm surprised to see you out and about today."

"Why's that?" Wade cut a slice of pancake with the side of his fork.

"I wouldn't have thought you'd be here on a school day."

"Why not?" He slid the pancake into his mouth and chewed deliberately, letting her squirm, though he'd pretty well figured what she meant. She didn't consider him the sort of dad who would go to the trouble of waking up extra early to take his kids out to breakfast on a morning when getting ready for school was hectic enough in itself.

But before Tess could reply, Jason spoke up. "It's $1.99 pancake day. Dad says it's smart to take advantage of such a good deal."

Wade squirmed. That made him sound cheap, but dang it, a single father had to cut corners wherever he could.

"It's $3.50 if you get a side of bacon," Macy added. Then she grinned. "But I guess you don't have to worry about that, huh, Tess?"

"No, I guess not." Tess folded her hands over the back of the empty chair next to Wade. "Mind if I sit down?"

"Go right ahead." He gestured with his fork, feeling a little guilty for not having offered before she could ask. But only a little. He really didn't relish the idea of sharing with Tess Vega his weekly morning out with the kids.

The waitress spotted Tess and hurried over. "What can I get for you, hon? Today's our $1.99 pancake special. All you can eat." She nodded toward the buffet table centered in the room. "Bacon or sausage is extra."

"Just the pancakes will be fine. And a glass of orange juice, please." Tess smiled, and Wade noticed she had dimples.

Well, it wasn't as if he hadn't noticed them before. It was just that he'd never paid attention to how cute they made her look. He grimaced inwardly. *Cute.* Tess was that, all right, in an immature sort of way. Today her braids were gone, but it didn't much matter. She'd crammed a ball cap over her hair, which looked as though it hadn't seen much time with a comb of late, and she wore her usual bib overalls with a blue tank top underneath.

He'd just begun to study the freckles sprinkled across her nose when she turned and caught him staring. Quickly, he averted his gaze and focused once more on his breakfast. He said the first thing that came to mind. "So, what are you doing out and about so early?"

"I got a call from Joy Isley this morning. She had some stray horses wander onto her place." Tess described the geldings. "Any idea who they might belong to?"

Wade shrugged. "Beats me. A lot of folks have bays and sorrels. Why don't you ask your dad?"

"I intend to, and Doc Baker, as well. I just thought you might know." She took a drink from the glass of water the waitress had set in front of her. "But, of course, I forgot that horses are simply working animals to you. I doubt you'd ever see the individuality in one."

Wade sipped his milk, giving himself a minute to do the mental ten-count thing. It was too early in the morning to be arguing with a redheaded woman who was suddenly doing funny things to his stomach and his head. "Now, there's where you'd be wrong," he said, setting his glass back on the table.

"Oh?"

"That's right, Miss Smarty-Pants horse rescuer. I've owned plenty of horses with what I'd say was individual personality in my time."

"Really?" Fighting a smile, Tess braced her elbows on the table and leaned her chin on laced fingers. "Tell me about them."

"Let's see." He poured more maple syrup over his pancakes, which seemed to suck the stuff up like sponges. "There was Winchester..."

"No, Dad, tell her about Ace." Jason smiled broadly at Tess. "He saved Dad's life."

"No kidding?" Tess drew back, looking impressed.

Wade felt his face warm. He didn't like to think about that day he'd fallen through the ice. He'd been a dumb kid, not listening to his dad.

He eyed the empty place in front of Tess. "Don't you want to get some pancakes?"

"In a minute. First I want to hear about your hero horse." She waved her hand in a hurry-up gesture. "Go ahead."

Wade told her about Ace, the six-year-old black gelding that had been his father's best working ranch horse. One winter, when Wade was ten, he'd decided to try his hand at ice fishing. There was a huge pond, almost lake size, in one of the pastures not far from the house. Fed by the river, it was a great place to catch trout, and Wade had decided his dad's warnings of the dangers of thin ice were not warranted.

A freak warming trend in January had left the ground thawing, the ice beginning to melt. But he'd been certain it was thick enough to hold him, and had sneaked away while his dad was busy splitting firewood. As he used a saw to cut a hole in the ice, it cracked around him, and he fell through into the frigid water.

Ace was one of the horses on pasture in the enclosure around the pond. When Tom Darland looked up from his task to see his best horse running in circles, snorting, eyes fixed on the pond, he'd known something was amiss. Tom trusted the gelding's sharp senses.

"Dad ducked through the fence and spotted me before he was halfway across the pasture. He yelled for a ranch hand who happened to be riding in from mending fence." Wade glanced at Tess and saw her deep green eyes focused on him raptly.

He nearly forgot where he was in his story.

"Tell her about the rope," Jason encouraged.

"My dad's quite a hand with a lariat," Wade went on. "Which was lucky for me. He grabbed that cowboy's rope and ran for the pond. Threw a loop around me and hauled me in. I was dang near froze to death."

"Dad didn't get a spanking, though," Macy added. "Even though Grandma Darland thought he ought to. Grandpa said being half-frozen was punishment enough."

"But he never tried to ice fish again," Jason finished. "And Ace became the hero of the Bar D."

"Wow." Tess sat up straight in her chair and eyed him. "Who would've known? So you cowboys don't *always* think of ranch horses as just working animals, right?" She held his gaze, eyes full of feigned innocence.

Wade shifted in his chair. "Well. Mostly we do. But Ace was special."

"Whatever happened to him?"

"Uh—he's still around."

"You mean you didn't take him to the sale barn?"

"No. He wasn't my horse to sell."

"And your dad didn't take him, either?"

He could see the corners of her mouth begin to quirk with amusement, and from the way her eyes sparkled, he could tell she was trying her best not to break out in a full-fledged grin.

Busted. "No, actually, he didn't."

"'Course not." Jason turned to Tess. "Grandpa sold off most of the Bar D, but he still has Ace. He's twenty-nine years old now. The horse, not Grandpa." He grinned.

Tess laughed. "I'm impressed." She scooted her chair back. "Let me get some of those pancakes, then you can tell me about Winchester."

A SHORT WHILE LATER, Macy and Jason headed out the door to walk to school with their friends who lived in town. Ferguson Riverside, which went from kindergarten to grade eight, was only a mile from the café, and Thursday was the one day Macy and Jason didn't have to ride the bus.

Wade knew he should leave, too, and get to his chores. But as he and Tess settled into talking about various horses and other things he'd begun to enjoy his conversation with her. He discovered that she'd agreed to take on Macy's 4-H group because it was a "horse only" club. None of the kids in the group raised meat animals, such as sheep, steers or hogs. Before Wade could have a chance to let that comment rile him, the conversation led to one that had him even more up in arms.

"I've been thinking about something," Tess said. She pushed her empty plate away and cupped her glass of orange juice. "If you're unable to buy Tess a new barrel-racing horse right now, why not look into adopting one from the sanctuary? The fee is minimal."

Wade bristled. Who was she to determine what he could and couldn't afford to buy? That her statement was true didn't make him feel any better.

"Who says I can't buy one?"

Tess raised her eyebrows. "Then you were trying to get Macy to sell Amber only because you don't want an old horse around anymore?"

He scowled at her and opened his mouth to explain it all again, then shook his head. "I told you before—it's none of your concern."

She held up a hand in surrender. "Okay. You're right. I didn't mean to be nosy. It's just that all my rescue cases aren't necessarily crippled and old. I frequently get an animal that's suffered from malnutrition or abandonment, nothing else. As a matter of fact, my own mare was a rescue animal. I'd be happy to adopt a horse out to Macy the next time I run across one that might be suitable for 4-H." She frowned back at him. "That's all I meant, Wade, so you can just tamp down your male pride and smooth your feathers. There's no reason to be so pigheaded."

He let out a huff of air, then scooted his chair away from the table. "I'm hardly the one who's pigheaded, Tess. Look, it was nice having breakfast with you, but I've got work to do." He scooped up the check for his and the kids' meals, then reached for the one the waitress had laid near Tess's elbow. Before she could protest, he held up one hand. "I've got it." He touched the brim of his hat. "See ya around."

"Thanks," Tess said dryly.

Ignoring her, he walked to the cash register to pay. He did his best not to look back at her over his shoulder. For a whole minute.

Unable to resist, Wade cast a casual glance toward their table. Tess hadn't wasted any time in leaving. The cowbell clanged as she closed the door behind her. But not before he saw her watching him, as well. Quickly, he averted his gaze, paid the tab and strode outside. He'd parked on the street near Audrey's. In the parking lot, Tess sat behind the wheel of her Dodge truck.

He expected to hear the engine crank over. Instead, the small ticking of a bad starter reached his ears. Tess's lips moved as she mumbled in frustration and gave the Ram another shot. Nothing.

Wade walked toward her, telling himself he couldn't very well drive off and leave her stranded. "Engine trouble?" he asked, leaning his elbows on the door frame above her open window.

She glared at him. "Nope. I just like the view here." Then she rolled her eyes in a good-natured way. "I think it's the starter."

"Can I give you a lift? I was going over to your dad's feed store, anyway."

"Actually, that's not where I was going. At least, not right now."

"Yeah?"

She hesitated, looking uncomfortable. He wondered briefly if she'd been on her way to see a man. The thought that she had someone in her life hadn't occurred to him for some reason, which was stupid. Just because he had no social life didn't mean she wouldn't.

"I understand," he said.

She gave him a puzzled frown.

"Hey, if you've got someone to meet, it's okay by me." He blurted out the words like a high-school boy, then immediately felt foolish. What was he doing? "That is—"

She cut him off. "I'm not exactly meeting some-one." Again, she hesitated. "I thought I'd stop and see my mother before I headed home."

He stared blankly at her for a moment before what she said registered. *Of course.* Tess's mom lived at the County Care Facility. Years ago, he'd heard Raelene Vega was ill, but he'd never paid much at-tention to town rumors and hadn't been nosy enough to come right out and ask Lloyd what was wrong with his wife.

"Oh." He clamped his mouth over the question that now threatened to spill out. It was none of his business. For some reason, though, he suddenly felt compelled to ask.

As if reading his thoughts, Tess spoke. "She has Alzheimer's. I try to visit her at least twice a week."

"Oh," he repeated. "I had no idea. I heard people around town talking about your mom being sick, but I didn't know…uh…isn't she a little young to have Alzheimer's?" He wasn't really sure how old Rae was. But Lloyd appeared to be about fifty-something, and Raelene would likely be close to his age.

A look of pain crossed Tess's face, then was gone. "Yes, she is. Mom developed a rare form of the disease when I was a teenager."

"I'm sorry to hear that." He held her gaze, and suddenly, a picture of what Tess's adolescence must have been like flashed through his mind. A sick mother. A dad on his own. Wade could certainly relate. "I'd be happy to drive you over to see your mom," he said.

"There's no need. It's not that far. I can walk." She pushed open the door of her pickup and stepped out.

She felt small to his six foot two. The urge to reach down and take the ball cap from her head gripped him as they stood toe to toe. He'd never before seen her hair out of braids. He wondered what it looked like beneath that cap, what it would feel like trailing between his fingers.

Man, those pancakes must've weighed down not just his stomach but his mind, as well.

"It's a good two miles or so," he argued. "Let me drive you."

She lifted a shoulder, but he saw the pulse at the base of her throat jump. He wasn't the only one aware of how close they were standing to each other.

"All right. Thanks." Tess closed the pickup's door, leaving the window down. Not many people around town bothered to lock their vehicles.

She walked beside him toward his Ford, and he felt like her date as he held the door for her and gave her a hand up into the four-wheel drive. Her palm felt soft, yet he could detect a row of calluses that told him she worked hard. Her arm was tanned, slender and well formed beneath her tank top, and just a peek of a pale-blue sports bra greeted his view as he let his gaze roam her body.

What would she look like in a pair of Rockies jeans?

Wade shook off the thought. He had to stop it. This was crazy. She was Macy's 4-H leader, for heaven's sake.

Letting out a sigh, he moved around to the driver's side and climbed into the pickup. After firing the engine, he pulled out of the parking lot.

A picture came to mind as he drove toward the County Care Facility. One of Tess as a stubborn child, refusing to eat her hamburger casserole, but gaining points as a good little girl for finishing all her broccoli.

He laughed without fully realizing it.

"What's so funny?" Tess stared at him, a soft smile on her face. The sort of smile a person has when he or she isn't sure what the joke is.

Even with her rumpled hair and her tattered ball cap, she was pretty. He found himself picturing her in the Rockies once more.

"Nothing." He faced forward and concentrated on the road. "Nothing at all."

THE MINUTE WADE DROVE AWAY toward the County Care Facility, Tess began to wish she hadn't accepted a ride from him. Would he want to come in with her? Or would he simply be satisfied with dropping her off? She hoped for the latter. Seeing her mother so sick was difficult enough. It wasn't something she wanted to share with Wade—or anyone else, for that matter. She even found it hard to visit her mom in the company of her own father. The look in his eyes of a haunting, continual loss was usually more than she could bear.

When they pulled up in the CCF parking lot, Tess opened the door before Wade could get any more chivalrous ideas about doing it for her. "Thanks for the ride," she said, stepping out onto the pavement.

"Do you want me to come in with you?" he offered. "Or wait here for you?"

"Neither. I'll call Dad to come get me."

"You sure?" He studied her.

"Uh-huh." She nodded, feeling a little bad about turning down Wade's kindness. "Thanks again." Closing the door, she gave a wave, then quickly turned to head for the building's front entrance.

The nurses greeted her by name as she entered. Molly, her favorite, smiled and fell into step beside her. She spoke in a husky, nearly gruff voice that belied the tender care she bestowed upon her patients. "I was just getting ready to take your mom a little treat," she said, indicating the tray in her hand. A small bowl of tapioca pudding rested on it. Her mother's favorite. Or at least, it had been when she could remember things like that. "She wasn't real happy with her oatmeal this morning."

Tess managed a smile. "That's sweet of you, Molly. I'm sure she'll like that." She hesitated. "How's Mom doing today?" Lately, Raelene's days went from not so good to worse. Tess wondered how much longer her mother could cling to life, existing this way. The black thought made her stomach churn.

"She's doing pretty good," Molly said. Her face creased with sympathy. "I admire the way you come see Rae all the time, hon. She may not really be aware of who you are, but…well, it's nice that you're here."

"I could never abandon her," Tess said. "She's my mom."

Molly nodded, her short, salt-and-pepper curls bobbing. "May God bless you for that, my dear." Together, they entered the room where Raelene sat in a chair near the window.

"Raelene, look who's here," Molly said. "It's Tess."

Rae's face lit up, and she smiled. "Yes."

Tess's chest gave a little hitch. For the briefest moment, Rae almost looked normal. But Tess knew better. Rae might recognize her briefly, but in the span of a heartbeat, she'd once more have no idea who Tess was. Where was the justice in that? Why did God allow such things to happen to such a good person?

With no more answer to her question now than she'd had eleven years ago, Tess pasted a smile on her face and walked over to stand beside Rae. "Hi, Mama. How are you today?" Rae held the card Tess had given her for Mother's Day, twisting it in her hands. The edges were bent and one was torn, but it didn't matter. As long as Raelene got some enjoyment from it. Tess reached to stroke her mother's hair, which had once been dark and silky but was now gray and brittle.

"I've brought you some pudding," Molly said. "You want Tess to feed it to you?"

Rae appeared confused. She opened her mouth as though trying to answer. Then she spoke, looking directly at Tess. "Those cows ate my shoes before I brushed my hair."

"I see," Tess said, feeling the familiar lump rise in her throat. To know that the sentence made perfect sense to her mom was the hardest. She picked up the pudding and spoon from Molly's tray.

Molly patted her wrist. "Call me if you need anything, hon." She left the room, shoes padding softly against the linoleum.

"How about a little pudding, Mama?" Tess scooped a small bite onto the spoon and held it out in offering.

Rae took it, the effort for her to swallow just as great as if she'd been chewing on a chunk of solid food. "I heard you didn't like your breakfast earlier."

"Yes." Rae opened her mouth for another bite of pudding, and Tess knew she'd already forgotten the oatmeal. Rae ate the pudding, then focused on Tess's face, forehead creased, eyes worried. "I need to put the goats to bed."

"It's okay, Mama. They're already in for the night."

Rae stared at her. Then suddenly, she slapped the spoon out of Tess's hand. It bounced against the floor. "No!" She shook her head over and over, arms flailing. The Mother's Day card fell to her lap, then slid onto the linoleum.

"Mama," Tess soothed. "It's all right." She rose from her chair, knowing she was probably going to have to call for Molly.

"Goats," Rae insisted, her mind fighting to communicate the words she so desperately needed to speak.

Tess knew she was fixating on a time in the past, when Raelene's own mother had a herd of Nubians.

It had been nine-year-old Rae's job to make sure they were put up in the barn for the night, safe from coyotes.

Gently, Tess placed her hands on her mother's shoulders in an effort to still her motions. "The goats are fine, Mama. You did good. You got them in safe for the night." Eyes burning with unshed tears, she gave her mother a tender squeeze. "I promise."

Moisture filled the corners of Rae's eyes, and thankfully, the irritation drained from her like air from a balloon. She slumped briefly in Tess's arms, then turned to stare out the window, lost once more in her own silent world.

"Mama, do you want any more pudding?" Tess asked, her hands still resting on Rae's shoulders. "I can get you a clean spoon."

"Yes." But the word held no true meaning, and Tess knew the pudding was a lost cause.

She picked up the fallen greeting card and set it on the nightstand, then placed a kiss on top of Rae's head. "I love you, Mama." Sniffing, she wiped a stray tear away and managed to hold back the rest. She'd cried so many tears for the unjust disease that had robbed Rae not only of her mind and body, but of her true self.

"I'll be back soon," she said.

Rae didn't answer as Tess walked quietly out the door.

CHAPTER FOUR

TESS ALWAYS LOOKED forward to Thursdays as one of her days for working at home, and even though this one hadn't started out on quite the right note, at least everything had ended up okay. She'd easily located the owner of the three stray geldings—Darlene Johnson, who lived about a mile and a half from Joy Isley's place. Darlene had been frantic with worry over her missing horses and had stopped by the feed store to tack a Lost notice up on the bulletin board.

A loose latch on her corral gate had allowed it to blow open in the night, releasing the horses onto the road while she slept, unaware. Lloyd Vega had talked to Darlene prior to driving out to tow Tess's truck to the family ranch for repairs, and he'd given her Darlene's phone number. Tess put her in touch with Joy, helped her dad with the Dodge, then had him drop her off at her place. She'd spent the rest of the day at her computer, then done her chores, fixed a bite to eat and climbed into the shower to get ready for her weekly 4-H club meeting.

Now Tess stood under the spray of hot water, looking forward to the meeting, which was the main reason Thursday had recently become her favorite night of the week. She loved kids, and had quickly found that working with her group of 4-H children took the edge off the stress she faced in dealing with other aspects of her life. She spent three days a week, plus alternate Saturdays, at the feed store. On her days off, Thursdays included, she worked in her home office, a spare bedroom in the back of the rental house, where she did bookkeeping for her father's ranch and feed store, along with other data processing jobs that came in from a temp service in town. Working at home relaxed her and gave her ample time to spend with her rescue horses. It also allowed her to be readily available should her mother need her in any way. Tess found comfort in knowing she could set her own hours and therefore go to Raelene's side at a moment's notice.

The only dark spot she could possibly foresee this evening was that Wade, according to Macy, usually drove his kids to 4-H. Having taken over the group just last week, Tess had been in charge of only the one meeting thus far. On that particular evening, Macy had ridden Amber to the arena, where the riding meetings were held. But as Tess chatted with her new group, she learned that Macy's dad rarely missed 4-H. At the time, she'd found that admirable. She knew Wade was a widower, and she'd thought it nice that he made the effort to attend his kids' 4-H meetings. Jason belonged to a group that met on Tuesdays, with boys and girls his own age and older. That group had projects that involved meat animals. Absolutely not for Tess.

Still, Tess took joy in seeing the local kids grow through their accomplishments. 4-H was a youth organization in which volunteer leaders like her taught skills that included everything from cooking to animal husbandry. The majority of the kids in Ferguson and its surrounding areas participated in projects that involved the raising and showing of livestock. Horses were very popular, and Tess thoroughly loved working with Macy and the other children.

Climbing from the shower, Tess reached for an oversize mulberry-colored bath towel and wrapped it around her body, then wound a smaller one around her hair. She needed to call Seth, her youngest brother, to see if he'd give her a ride to town. As if on cue, the phone rang. Gripping the bath towel with one hand, Tess hurried to answer.

"Hello?"

"Hi, Tess, it's Macy."

"Macy, what's up?" Tucking the phone under her chin, Tess reached to scratch behind the ears of the white cat curled on the back of the couch. Immediately, Champ leaped onto the cushions to vie for Tess's attention.

"Dad said your truck was broke down. Do you need a ride to 4-H?"

Tess grabbed for the phone as it slipped from beneath her chin. "Your dad offered?"

"Well, sort of. I asked him and he said yes."

Tess smiled to herself. She could just picture Macy conning Wade into giving her a ride. Sure, he'd offered her one in town today, but it had been the polite thing to do, under the circumstances. Somehow, she couldn't picture him willingly volunteering to act as her chauffeur.

"That's really nice of you, Macy, but I was just about to call my brother for a ride."

"You don't have to," Macy insisted. "I mean, we're going to the meeting anyway. And your house isn't far from ours."

"True." Tess curled the phone cord around her finger, picturing the way Wade had looked that morning in his cowboy hat and faded jeans. He was trouble she didn't need and didn't have time for. Still, accepting a ride from him would be handier than bothering Seth. Her brother's place was five miles away, versus two to the Darland ranch. "Okay, Macy, I'll take you up on that."

"Cool! We'll be there about five forty-five."

The meeting began at six. "Sounds good. Be sure to tell your dad thanks for me."

"I will. See ya!" Macy hung up and Tess chuckled.

At their first club meeting, it hadn't taken long for her to feel truly drawn to Macy. She'd known the little girl from Macy's occasional visits to the feed store with Wade and Jason, but having her in 4-H had given Tess the opportunity to get better acquainted. Macy was spunky and tough, though she seemed to harbor some hidden feelings about her mother's death. Tess couldn't help wanting to reach out to her, and wished Macy would open up and talk about Deidra. Maybe with time.

Tess could tell the kid missed having a woman around. It was why Macy went on and on about Bailey and the things they'd done together over the past year. And Tess was pretty sure it was why Macy seemed to be taking a strong liking to her, as well, which was fine with Tess.

She thought of her own birth mother. Tess had been in kindergarten, Seth in first grade and Zachary in third when their mother had taken off. The despair that had washed over her all those years ago still had a way of working itself into the pit of her stomach now and then. Though Jacqueline Vega hadn't died, she'd still left Tess feeling orphaned. Lloyd had done his best to fill the empty space his wife had left, yet Tess had plunged into a state of withdrawal, closing herself off from everyone.

The comfort she found in caring for her many pets had cushioned her, and she'd reached out to them, wrapping their presence around her like a cloak. She'd taken to nurturing every stray cat and dog, every fallen bird she could get her hands on, somehow needing to reverse her role from child to caregiver. To act as mother to creatures more innocent and helpless than her.

Lloyd had immediately picked up on what his daughter was doing. With kindness and love, he'd joined Tess in caring for her critters, gradually pulling her from the dark place where her little soul had gone to hide. He called it "getting back her sunshine," and he'd worked hard to make sure that her emotional needs were properly cared for, as well as those of his two boys.

And then Raelene had come along, and Tess had felt loved twofold as Rae stepped so naturally into the role of mother. Unable to have kids of her own, Raelene rejoiced in her new family and thanked God on a daily basis—out loud, right in front of Tess and her brothers—for the children he had brought into her life.

And that was the reason Tess would never, ever abandon Rae. No matter what. Her mother needed her, and she could think of nothing she'd rather do with her time than be there for the woman who'd stood by her and loved her throughout her childhood. No matter how much Rae's state of mind deteriorated, nothing could ever take away the bond they'd shared. A bond Tess still clung to.

Shaking her thoughts back to the here and now, Tess readied herself for the 4-H meeting. She dressed in a clean pair of bib overalls and a T-shirt, then combed her damp hair into two braids. Adding a ball cap to her attire, she stepped outside just as she heard Wade's Ford pull into the driveway.

When she opened the truck's passenger door and locked eyes with Wade, it was the first time in as long as she could remember that she regretted not having taken more care with her appearance. She'd had little time for dating, what with looking after her mother. Not to mention the awkwardness she'd striven to avoid by not bringing a boy home. She didn't want anyone, not even her girlfriends, to witness Rae's deteriorating condition. Ashamed of her attitude now, which had been somewhat self-centered back then, Tess nevertheless still harbored some of those feelings. Only, presently they were on her mother's behalf. If Tess were been in Raelene's shoes, she wouldn't want strangers staring at her, wondering about her disease.

And as far as the opposite sex went, a fling with one of her father's ranch hands when she was nineteen had left Tess wary of repeating the experience. She simply had better things to do with her time. And fussing with hair and makeup wasn't one of them.

At least she wasn't in the disheveled state Wade had caught her in this morning, with her hair barely combed and lack of sleep puffing her eyes. Still, she felt like Cinderella after midnight as she slid onto the seat beside Macy.

Wade was dressed in a white Western shirt with silver metallic threads woven through the material, and shiny pearl snaps. His freshly pressed jeans looked new, and his dark hair seemed neatly combed beneath a black hat that wasn't at all battered and worn. His feet were encased, not in his usual scuffed Tony Lamas, but in a highly polished pair of round-toed, black cowboy boots with a riding heel. A whiff of sage-scented cologne floated her way across the truck's interior.

"Wow," Tess said without thinking. "Where are you going all spiffed up?" Did he have a date? Maybe he planned to drop Macy at 4-H and leave. The idea left a strange, sour feeling in the pit of her stomach, though it shouldn't have. Wade could spend his time any way he wanted.

"What do you mean—where am I going?" Wade practically growled the words as he put the truck into gear, but a playful look in his eyes diluted the force behind them. "I thought we were picking you up for 4-H."

Self-consciously, Tess fingered the bill of her ball cap, which read Have You Hugged Your Cat To-day? "Yep. That's right." Groping for something to ease her discomfort, she shot him a crooked grin. "I just wasn't aware it was a formal occasion."

"What, this old thing?" he teased, holding out his arms as he looked the front of his shirt up and down. Then he winked, and Tess's heart did a crazy little flop.

"Dad," Macy scolded, giving him a shove. "You know those are new clothes." She turned smugly toward Tess. "He's being modest. He doesn't want to shout the fact that he sold his first saddle today, just one hour—" she held up her forefinger "—after our Web site was up and running."

"Really?" Tess tilted her head in pleasant surprise. Her dad carried some of Wade's leatherwork in the store, but she hadn't been aware he was making saddles.

Wade eased off the clutch, focusing on the road ahead as he pulled from the driveway. He glanced at her. "It took me totally by surprise. The guy e-mailed me and it turned out he lives in Deer Creek." The neighboring town lay ten miles west of Ferguson. "He drove right out and bought the saddle."

"Congratulations," Tess said.

"Dad got enough for the saddle to get each of us new shirts and jeans," Macy said. Her voice rose with excitement. "And, to put some money away toward a new barrel horse for me! I might be able to get one this summer after all."

"Say…" Tess drew back in exaggerated admiration. "Now, *that* is something to celebrate." She smiled at Macy, then addressed Wade. "You realize her project horse has to be registered with the extension office by June 1, don't you?" Each 4-H member had to declare in writing which horse they planned to use for the year's events, which included horse shows and gymkhanas.

The smile he'd worn slipped from Wade's face, to be replaced by his typical scowl. "I know that." He stared straight ahead. "I guess she'll just have to use Amber for another year."

"If you're sure," Tess said, letting him know that she still had a way around that if he wanted to take it. "She can have more than one project horse, you know."

Now he did glance at her. "I'm aware of that, and yes, I'm sure," he emphasized.

Tess barely suppressed the urge to stick her tongue out at his profile as he faced the road. "Stubborn," she muttered.

"What's that?" he asked. Macy raised her eyebrows and cast a questioning look from one to the other.

"Stubborn...stains." Tess brushed at a nonexistent spot on her clean overalls. "I always spill when I eat ice cream, and it looks like I'm wearing a spoonful of my dessert." She reached out to give Macy's arm an affectionate shake. "How about you, kiddo?"

"Sometimes." Macy wrinkled her nose.

"Wanna test ourselves? I'm for a banana split after the meeting if you are. My treat." She glanced at Wade. "You can even bring your grumpy old dad if you want."

Macy giggled. "Okay by me. Dad?"

"We'll see." His scowl darkened, but Tess couldn't help thinking it was partly an act.

Why on earth was the man so determined to put up a tough front when anyone could plainly see how devoted he was to his kids? Though she had to admit she'd been taken a little by surprise to discover it, Tess also had to admit that this quality in Wade appealed to her. Not that she'd ever want to go out with him or anything. Not really. Her plate was already full enough. Sure, he was good-looking, but still, she knew she'd be better off avoiding him. A tough, arrogant cowboy, he'd made it clear that he didn't have a whole lot of use for a woman like her in his life. A woman with an independent way of thinking. She was sure he'd prefer a meek little rancher gal who would bake him pies and bread and cook steak and baked beans for supper.

Yep. Tess was positive that if the two of them ever got together, their relationship would read like a romance novel gone bad. *The Cattle Rancher and the Runaway Vegetarian.* She smothered a giggle.

Minutes later, they pulled into the parking lot at the fairgrounds. A few cars and pickups were already in the lot, and Tess's attention immediately snagged on one of the 4-H mothers, Sharon Jenkins. Her normally tanned face was devoid of color, and her hands shook as she waved for Tess's attention.

"What's wrong with Sharon?" Macy asked.

"I don't know." Tess rolled the truck's window all the way down and leaned against the door frame.

Sharon ran toward her, breathless. "Tess, thank goodness. You've got to come with me." She glanced at Macy. "It's…urgent."

Instantly, Tess's heart dropped. "It's not one of the kids…?"

"No. Not the kids." Sharon looked at Wade. "Actually, Wade, we could probably use your help, too. Can Macy stay here with Kelly and Lori?" Kelly was Sharon's daughter, a year younger than Macy; Lori, Kelly's best friend.

"Sure," Wade said. Concern lined his face. "Do you want me to park or drive?"

"Drive," Sharon said. "My sister-in-law's here. She'll take care of the kids for a while." Pam Jenkins taught agriculture at the high school and often attended the meetings with her family.

Sharon gestured. "Macy, honey, Kelly's over there. Why don't you keep her company until we get back."

"What's wrong?" Macy asked. She turned to Wade for guidance. "Dad?"

"It's okay, honey. Run along with Kelly. We'll be back shortly."

"Okay." Reluctantly, Macy climbed from the truck as Tess moved out of her way.

Tess slid once more onto the seat next to Wade, allowing Sharon to climb into the passenger side. The thought that she now sat up close against him barely registered as she focused on what Sharon told them while they drove from the parking lot.

"It's awful, Tess." Sharon clamped a hand to her heart. "Kelly and Lori went riding after school today. They stayed at Lori's afterward, getting their record books squared away. These were the notebooks in which each child recorded every detail of his or her 4-H project. Then they rode back to our house just before supper. When they passed Clem McMurty's place, the girls heard a scuffle in the round pen." She ran her hands up and down her arms as though ridding herself of goose bumps.

"That damn Clem had his pretty liver chestnut tied to a post and was beating him! The girls rushed to our house and I called the sheriff's office right away. A couple of deputies went out there, but when I phoned back to check on what happened they said that the horse had no visible welts—only some vague marks—and that there was not much they could do about it since using a whip on a horse isn't illegal. They said it wasn't a clear case of abuse. Can you believe that?" Her dark eyes flashed with anger. "Clem claimed the horse had gotten out of hand and kicked him, and that he had to line him out. Anyway, the girls were really upset and so was I. All of us were worried about the horse.

"I went out there on my way over to the fair-grounds. You can see the round pen from the road." She looked from Tess to Wade and back again. "The gelding is lying flat on his side, snubbed to a post. He's not moving."

"That scumbag!" Tess clenched her hands as her blood pressure peaked. "Wade, hurry!"

ANGER TIGHTENED Wade's gut as he sped toward the McMurty ranch. While he didn't believe in cod-dling horses the way Tess seemed to, neither did he approve of abusing them. When he pulled into the driveway, Tess and Sharon were out of the truck and flying toward the round pen before he could bring the Ford to a complete halt.

Wade parked and walked up the sidewalk to knock on the front door. "Clem!" he called. "It's Wade Darland." He rapped with his knuckles once more. No one answered. Descending the steps two at a time, he hurried toward the round pen, more worried about the horse and Tess's frame of mind than he was about trespassing. He knew she hadn't given the matter so much as a thought, especially since Ferguson was a small town where neighbors were usually welcome. Not in this situation, how-ever, he'd wager.

Behind him, the sound of the back door finally creaking open reached his ears.

"Who's out there?" Clem called gruffly.

"Wade Darland, Clem!" Wade repeated, tossing

the words over his shoulder. He reached the round pen, and the sight before him sickened him beyond belief. Apparently, Clem had taken his spite out on his horse once the sheriff's deputies departed.

The liver chestnut lay on his side in the dirt of the enclosure, eyes closed, three of his legs bound with a stout cotton rope. The gelding's side rose and fell as he drew strained breaths, grunting in pain and resignation. Welts lined his chocolate-colored coat, some of them caked with blood. His head, restrained by a strong nylon halter and rope, was tilted at an awkward angle where he'd fallen while dallied to the post dead centered in the pen. It was a wonder the animal hadn't broken his neck.

Cursing, Wade ducked through the fence rails and dropped to one knee beside Tess. He laid his hand on the gelding's neck. The chestnut's skin was clammy to the touch. Wade cursed again and stood, simultaneously pulling his pocketknife from his jeans.

"Cut him loose!" Anger choked Tess's voice, and her hands shook.

Wade sliced the rope in a sawing motion, taking care to ease the colt's head gently to the ground as the rope gave.

"Hey!" From outside the corral, Clem McMurty shouted.

Heavyset, shoulders wide, he moved quicker than one would have expected for a man his size. He had a good seventy pounds on Wade, but Wade had him in height by about three inches. Fists tight, Wade rose and pivoted on the balls of his feet to face Clem as the man roared forward like an enraged bear.

"What the hell do you think you're doing?"

Clem demanded, climbing into the corral. "You're trespassing. Get away from my horse!"

Wade pressed his mouth into a line, holding his temper with every ounce of restraint he possessed. More than anything, he wanted to haul off and pop Clem in the face. But as satisfying as he knew hitting the jerk would be, he also knew it wasn't the way to handle the situation.

"I'd say you're the one who needs to get away from the horse," Wade told him. His pulse pounded in his ears. "Maybe I ought to tether you to that pole and give you a go-round with a buggy whip so you can see how it feels!"

"You want a piece of me?" Clem's eyes glowed with anticipation and a smirk pulled his mouth out of shape. He stood knees bent, arms extended, and motioned for Wade to come closer. "Come on, Darland, let's go."

Tess's kick to the seat of his pants took Clem totally by surprise. The sole of her booted foot connected with his backside—none too gently—and he tumbled forward, pitching to the dirt on his hands and knees.

Instantly, Tess was in his face. Bent at the waist, she pressed her nose all but up against his. "You want a piece of someone, try me." Her voice was calm, level, all the more riveting than if she'd shouted the words. "You lowdown, son-of-a-black-jackal. You want to charge me with trespassing? Why not add assault and battery while you're at it, you scumbag, pond-sucking jerk." She moved even closer, her forehead a gnat's hair away from Clem's. He'd risen to his knees, and now he lost his balance once more and tumbled backward. He landed on his butt with an "Oomph."

"Geez, lady, take it easy." He glared at Tess. "I ain't gonna fight no woman." His eyes shot daggers from her to Wade, but Wade could see Tess had taken at least some of the wind out of his sails.

"No," Tess said, "and you aren't going to lay one finger on a helpless animal again, either." She stood over him with booted feet spread and planted, arms crossed. "How much?"

"What?"

"You heard me. How much for the horse? And don't try to gouge me, or I'll go ahead and let the sheriff handle this. You and I both know he won't be leaving with a warning this time."

Clem looked as though he wanted to protest. He glanced over at the chestnut, who remained lying on his side, though Tess and Sharon had already freed the horse's legs from the rope.

Sharon spoke, quiet anger lacing her voice. "You don't have to pay this rattlesnake for anything, Tess. You know when the authorities come out, they'll take possession of the gelding. You'll end up with him anyway."

"She's right," Tess said to Clem. "Only, I don't feel like waiting for the wheels of justice to roll. That horse needs me now, so I'll ask you again. How much?"

"Oh, I don't think old Clem wants much at all for this gelding," Wade said, moving to stand beside Tess. "As a matter of fact, I'm thinking that by the time you figure in the cost of vet bills, feed, et cetera..." He waved a hand in the air, as though calculating. "Why, I'm pretty sure this check ought to cover it." He slid his checkbook from his pocket and scribbled out a good portion of what he'd gotten for the saddle that day. "I mean, considering the fact that if we do call the sheriff out here, you're going to be facing a mighty stiff fine besides having your horse taken from you...well, you get my drift, don't you, Clem?"

Clem's face turned the shade of a purple cabbage. "Yeah, I get your point," he said. He stood and dusted off the seat of his pants.

Wade signed the check and tossed it at him. "I trust you'll call the brand inspector in the morning." According to Colorado state law, no sale of a horse could be complete without the brand inspector examining the animal. "Oh, and one more thing." He pointed a finger at Clem's chest. "If I ever hear so much as a whispered rumor about you treating another animal like this, you're gonna find out what abuse really means."

Turning his back on the man, Wade knelt beside the chestnut. The horse's breathing seemed to be coming closer to normal, but he still made no effort to rise. "Hey, fella," Wade soothed, stroking the gelding's neck. "You're going to be all right." He looked up, straight into Tess's eyes. Her expression was a mixture of anger not yet spent and gratitude.

"Thanks," she said. Then she turned to Sharon. "Would you mind calling Doc Baker? You might have to go to the neighbor's house."

"I have a cell phone in the truck," Wade said.

Sharon nodded and headed in that direction. Clem stomped back to the house and slammed the door without another word.

"Want to help me see if I can get this poor horse

to stand?'' Tess asked. Her green eyes filled with concern and compassion and Wade's heart raced. He'd figured her for the type of woman who had spunk, but seeing it firsthand…

"Sure thing." He stepped up beside the chestnut and took hold of the halter, steadying the gelding's head as Tess tugged gently but firmly on the severed lead rope.

"Come on, boy," she coaxed. "You can do it."

"Up you go, fella," Wade said. He gave a pull, and between their efforts, the gelding scrambled to his feet and stood looking around, wary, shaken.

"Attaboy," Tess crooned. Sadly, she petted the horse's neck, being careful not to touch any of the welts that lined his body. "I still can't believe anyone could treat an animal this badly. No matter how many cases of abuse and neglect I witness, it never fails to make me sick to my stomach."

Wade stepped up close to her and tilted her chin with one forefinger. "Remind me never to make you mad," he said. His pulse skittered, both with the aftermath of his anger at Clem, and with the feelings Tess stirred in him.

She fixed her eyes on his, and he studied the look in them, imagining what it would be like to lower his mouth to hers and brush a kiss across her lips. A kiss that might deepen and turn to something more serious. A stroke of tongue against tongue, Tess's body pressed against his. Warm and firm…

Wade swallowed. His pulse throbbed in his temples with the finesse of a snare drum, and his brain seemed to have gone numb. He pulled back and lowered his hand, pleased by the flicker of disappointment he thought he saw in Tess's eyes for a brief moment.

"You saved one more, and I'm betting that's something that never ceases to make you feel good." Talk about feeling good, he couldn't think of a time he'd felt better…and it had nothing to do with the horse.

Tess pursed her lips as though tasting the kiss he'd imagined, and the idea that she possibly shared his fantasy set him on fire all over again. For a moment, he thought she was going to say something to him like *Make sure you keep your lips to yourself, cowboy—and your lustful thoughts, too.*

Instead, a smile tugged at the corners of her mouth, and she reached up to touch her bottom lip in a way that he found sexy. He wanted to grab her wrist and kiss those slender fingers of hers, one at a time. *Lord help him.* He had to stop this. He cleared his throat and forced his thoughts back to the horse and the conversation at hand. "That's what drives you to do this work, isn't it?"

"You've got that right, cattleman," Tess said. Then her smile widened. "Looks like Macy has herself a new horse."

The full realization of what he'd done hit him. Macy was going to go nuts. Wade grinned. "Looks like." He continued to eye Tess.

A new horse for Macy. And for him, a bad and definite case of the hots for his daughter's 4-H leader.

CHAPTER FIVE

MACY WHIMPERED in her sleep.

Her arms and legs felt heavy when she tried to move them. Why wouldn't they work right? She needed to run. Had to warn her mother of the danger that lay just around the bend.

The train tracks crossed the road above, stretching as far as she could see both ways. In the distance the engine's whistle blew—a ghostly sound that made her shiver. Fighting to get her arms and legs to work, she moved through the thick grass of the field below the tracks. Her ankles caught in each tuft, toes snagging, causing her to stumble. She had to reach the road in time....

Her mother's blue car grew closer, headed for the railroad crossing. Macy could see her behind the wheel, though her face wasn't clear. What she saw in detail was her mother's hands, knuckles white as she gripped the steering wheel. She was focused on nothing more than getting home. She seemed unaware of the train.

The car picked up speed. The same car Macy rode in with her mother when they went to the grocery store to pick out cereal and cookies and the big red apples Macy loved. The car she liked so much because it had a huge back seat where she could bounce...up...down...up...while her mother piled bags of groceries all around her until she felt safe and concealed, where she pretended to be a soldier hiding in the jungle of paper and plastic. And the seat belt—when her mother said, "Buckle up, cupcake"—that was really the safety strap that belted her into her fighter jet.

But she wasn't in the car now, and this wasn't a game. Macy saw her mother pull up to the railroad crossing and gradually slow. *Yes!* Macy tried to shout. *That's it. Stop. Just stop, Mommy, please.*

She could make out her mom's long, blond hair, scooped up in a ponytail, just like her own. And then, behind the blue car, a pickup truck came to a halt. Clem McMurty climbed from the truck, his face scrunched and mean-looking. He clenched a buggy whip in one big fist, and he began to snap it in the air as he walked toward her mother's car. "Go!" he shouted. "Just go."

No! The word caught in Macy's throat.

Fearfully, her mother looked over her shoulder at Clem, then back at the railroad tracks. The warning lights began to flash above, bells clanging, hurting Macy's ears. The black-and-white striped barrier trembled, prepared to lower.

And Mommy stepped on the gas. Sped onto the tracks.

The train whistle blared. The engine was no longer in the distance. It was there. Right there. Bearing down.

The train slammed into the car with the horrible screeching of metal upon metal.

"No!" Macy screamed, and sat up in bed. Her hands shook. Beneath her the sheets lay damp with sweat. Tears burned her eyes. Her stomach churned.

She hadn't dreamed about her mother's accident in a good long while.

"Macy?" From the hallway, her dad called out to her. He rapped on her door, then pushed it open. Light flooded the room as he flicked on the switch. He wore a pair of pajama bottoms and a T-shirt, and his hair stood up. He looked worried, and at that moment Macy loved him more than anything in the world. He was always there for her. Always.

"Honey, what is it? Are you sick? Did you have a bad dream?"

She nodded yes to both. Her stomach felt horrid, but she knew the churning would stop as soon as the bad dream faded. She hated the nightmares when they came. Sometimes she had good dreams of her mom and of Sarah: she and Mommy holding hands, walking through a field of wildflowers...she and Sarah riding their horses in the sunshine....

But sometimes, like tonight, they were bad. Sometimes in the dreams Sarah was sick, her hair gone from the cancer medicine. And when those dreams came, they were often followed by ones of the accident that had taken Macy's mother from her. The accident that had been her fault, though no one knew it but her. Doing what she always did when the thought pushed its way into her head, Macy blocked it. *No, no, not my fault. Not my fault...*

But it was.

Her dad sank onto the edge of the bed and wrapped his strong arms around her. He gave her a squeeze and rested his chin on top of her head. "It's okay, sunshine. It was just a bad dream. I've got you. I've got you." He ran his hands up and down her arms, warming the goose bumps. Then he pulled back and gave her a sad little smile. "You want some water or something?"

Macy felt silly. She wasn't a little kid anymore. In the dream, she'd been small, but in reality, she was almost in middle school. Too old to cry out in the night for her daddy. "I'm okay," she said, pushing her hair out of her eyes.

"You sure?" He sounded worried.

She nodded. "I'm sure."

Still, he hesitated. "You want Smokey or Bandit to sleep in here with you?"

Now she knew he was worried. The red heelers were working cow dogs, and they stayed outside, where, according to her dad, they belonged. The only times he'd ever let them stay in was five years ago, right after the accident, when Smokey and Bandit were pups and they'd slept in a box, one next to Macy's bed, one beside Jason's.

And again when Sarah had died.

Macy quirked her mouth in a smile. "I'm not *that* upset, Dad." She let her grin widen. "But if you really want to let Smokey and Bandit in, that's okay by me."

He chuckled and rumpled her hair. "Maybe I overreacted a tad." Then he frowned. "What was your dream about, honey?"

She sobered. "Mom. And Clem McMurty."

"Clem?"

"Yeah. I guess it was sort of a dumb dream. He chased Mommy with a whip and made her...made her drive onto the train tracks."

"Oh, Macy." Again, her dad held her, giving her a bear hug of a squeeze. He looked at her, his expression serious. "You're upset about what Clem did to the horse. That's what made you have the dream."

"It was really mean," she said.

"It was. But Clem's not going to hurt Diego anymore. He's your horse now. You named him and everything." He smiled.

Warmth spread through her tummy. "Yeah, I did. And I'm going to show him how to not be afraid."

Her dad kissed her forehead. "Good. And you don't be afraid, either, 'kay?"

She rubbed her nose with the palm of her hand. "Okay."

He rose. "Want the hall light on?"

"No. I don't need a *night-light*."

"All right." He pointed one finger at her. "But no more bad dreams, you hear?" He gestured toward the powder-blue dreamcatcher that hung over her bed. "You let that do its job." He put his hands on his hips. "Wait a minute. I know what the problem is." Reaching up, he took hold of the dreamcatcher with both hands and blew a huge puff of air across it. Cheeks bulging, he did it again. Then he grinned and stood back. "There."

Macy giggled. "What are you doing?"

"Blowing off the dust and cobwebs," he said. "That was obviously why your dreamcatcher wasn't working right. It got clogged up. But it's fixed now." He gave her a wink.

"It's supposed to catch the bad dreams in its web, Dad."

"Yeah, but not on a spiderweb."

Macy giggled again. "Thanks."

"'Night." He headed for the door. "Call me if you need anything."

"I will." He started to close the door.

"Dad?"

"Yeah, honey?"

"Can you leave it open?"

"Sure." He pushed it wide and winked once more.

Macy smiled. "Good night."

"TESS!"

Macy's shouted greeting drew Wade's attention, and he glanced over his shoulder and spotted Tess's Dodge heading up the driveway.

Turning her back on him and Jason, Macy ducked through the fence rails of the round pen and ran toward the truck, calling to Tess through the open window. "Hurry! Come look."

Her excitement stemmed from the fact that Diego had begun to warm up to her. The liver chestnut now stood in the center of the round pen, lead rope attached to his halter, ears shifting back and forth as though to determine what new and possibly dangerous event might be in store for him. Wade soothed the horse with reassuring words and a gentle hand, then shook his head and grinned.

In spite of her undying loyalty to Amber and love for her, Macy had already grown attached to Diego. She'd come unglued when she'd heard what Clem had done to the chestnut, but her anger had turned to excitement when she found out the horse was now hers. Still, it bothered Wade that the incident had given his little girl nightmares. He had to admit he'd had his doubts about whether he'd done the right thing, not in rescuing the horse but in buying him for Macy.

After Doc Baker's initial examination two days ago, things had seemed a little shaky. The four-year-old horse wasn't in bad health, other than needing a good worming and an update on vaccinations, but he'd been abused to the point where he was jumpy around any sudden movement. Macy was allowed to handle him only under Wade's careful supervision. But she didn't seem to mind.

Now, as Wade saw Macy's excitement when as she ran toward Tess, his doubts began to fade. Maybe Diego would be as good for her as she already appeared to be for him.

Tess parked, got out of the truck and walked toward the round pen, her arm draped across Macy's shoulders. The two of them made a picture that left a fluttery feeling in the pit of Wade's stomach—something he hadn't felt in so long it seemed foreign. He tried not to think about the way he'd nearly given in to the impulse to kiss Tess two days ago. He still fantasized about that imagined kiss, and could practically taste it at times when he lay in bed at night alone.

Wade licked his lips and forced himself not to dwell on things better left unexplored.

Tess lifted her free hand in greeting as she and Macy drew closer.

"Hi, Tess." Jason grinned at her like a lovesick calf.

"Hi there, Jason. Wade." She ducked through the fence rails, then nodded toward Diego. "So, how's he doing?"

"Not bad overall. I think he just needs a lot of time and patience."

"He's already starting to like Macy," Jason offered, earning a frown from his sister for spoiling her surprise.

"Watch, Tess," she said. Slowly, so as not to startle Diego, she retrieved a bucket of sweet feed from where she'd left it near the fence and approached the gelding. "Hey, baby, baby," she crooned. "It's okay. You want a treat? Huh? Do you?"

Seconds before, Diego had stood warily on the end of the lead rope, muscles tense; clearly, he was ready to bolt at the slightest indication that Wade posed a threat. But for some reason, the horse trusted Macy. With a soft whicker, he took a cautious step her way, then another, ears still flicking, eyes focused on the bucket of grain.

He stretched his neck toward her, and Macy crooned some more. "Attaboy. Come on. There you go." Shedding the last of his resistance, Diego stepped closer and thrust his nose into the bucket to snatch a greedy bite of sweet feed.

Tess laughed. "I see it didn't take long for you to charm him."

"Told you," Jason said. He shook his head. "She's gonna have him as spoiled as Amber."

Ignoring him, Macy grinned at Tess. "I think we've bonded." She reached out and entwined her fingers in the gelding's cream-colored forelock, stroking the flaxen strands.

Tess's smile widened. "I'd say so." She moved up quietly beside the horse but made no immediate effort to touch him. Not until she'd spoken to him in a soothing voice that had the fine hairs on Wade's arms standing straight up.

"Sweet boy," she soothed. "Can I pet you? Uh-huh?"

Wade cleared his throat. "He—uh—he might let you." *And so would I, if you asked nice.* Shaking off the ridiculous thought, he offered her the lead rope. "He tolerates me some, though not the way he does Macy."

Tess took hold of the rope and passed it to Macy. "Then she ought to be the one to hold him, don't you agree?"

The gooey, lustful thoughts Wade had entertained immediately shifted to familiar irritation. "I don't know. I'm not sure I trust him with her yet. He got quite a beating from Clem, and I doubt it was the first time. I don't want to take a chance on her getting hurt."

"And neither do I." Tess stared back at him, her eyes full of mischief. "We're right here."

Wade sighed inwardly, looking from her to Macy. "Fine." He pointed a cautionary finger. "But be careful."

"I will." Macy gripped the rope with confidence and crooned to the chestnut. "You won't hurt me, will you, boy?" The lead in one hand, she kept hold of the bucket with the other, balancing it on one knee while Diego continued to munch. The chestnut closed his eyes in bliss, easing Wade's concern somewhat.

"Guess I'll go do some chores," Jason said, as though he'd had enough of Tess and Macy's girly horse talk.

Wade knew he ought to do the same but felt compelled to stick around, instead. And if he was totally honest with himself, he'd have to admit his motives weren't entirely driven by his concern for Macy's safety. Dang it, ever since the other night, he'd found himself thinking about Tess more than he ought to. He needed to stop it. He knew better. He had his reasons for staying single and he had to stick to them.

As Jason clambered through the fence rails and headed for the barn, Wade groped for a change of subject. "So, how's everything at the feed store? Is your dad ready for some more bridles?" It had been almost a month since Lloyd Vega had taken some of Wade's leatherwork on consignment.

Tess nodded. "As a matter of fact, that's one of the reason's I came over. Dad said he could use another half dozen if you've got them. They're selling really well." She reached in her pocket and pulled out a check. "He sent this over for you."

Satisfaction filled Wade as he glanced at the amount of the check before putting it in his wallet, as he grinned. "Thanks, Tess. I wasn't sure how they'd do."

"Well, worry no more. I'd say Cowboy Up is off and running." She eyed him in a way that made his pulse pick up speed once more. "I checked out your Web site yesterday. It looks good."

Warmth spread through him, though he felt like a fool. Her words shouldn't please him so much, but they did. "Thanks," he said again.

"I'd say you've got reason to celebrate," Tess added. "Are you and the kids up for a little party?"

"Maybe. You got one planned?"

"My family does." She gave a little shrug. "Tuesday's my birthday. Dad's throwing a shindig tonight at the ranch. I thought you and the kids might want to come. We can toast your leather business while we're at it, and you can bring some more bridles for the store if they're ready. Some belts, too.''

He nodded. ''I've got some.''

A birthday party. Wade could hardly keep himself from asking which one. He still thought Tess looked young. Then he recalled the expression he'd seen in her eyes when she'd told him the other day about her mother's illness. *Mom developed a rare form of the disease when I was a teenager.* Her words suggested she'd experienced things beyond her years. Coping with Raelene's condition must have been hard on the entire family. Sad.

But then, life was full of sad and unfair things. Like two kids losing their mother.

The thought was enough to continue to remind him that he'd vowed to focus on raising his children alone. Deidra had been a good mother; his partner in life. They hadn't shared the kind of red-hot, passionate love depicted in the chick flicks she always managed to talk him into watching, but they had had a tender, caring partnership. He'd been happy with her, and it had taken him a long time to pick up the pieces of his shattered life and find a way to carry on alone. And now that Deidra was gone, he couldn't see anyone taking her place. Plus, he'd managed so far to plug along on his own. He didn't need anyone's help now, and he certainly shouldn't be letting Tess put his hormones in an uproar. He'd be better off keeping his distance.

But before he could come up with an excuse to give her the bridles and belts now and decline her invitation, Macy spoke.

"A party with cake and everything?"

"You bet," Tess said, giving one of Macy's braids a tug. "Think you can handle helping me whip up a batch of homemade ice cream? Since we didn't get to go for those banana splits the other night."

"You better know it." Macy turned eagerly toward him, still holding on to her beloved gelding. "Dad? Can we?"

"We'd love to have you," Tess said. "My dad is quite a cook, believe it or not. That's one thing he did help me out with after..." She hesitated as though she'd said more than she'd intended, then finished her thought. "After Mom got sick."

"What's wrong with your mom?" Macy asked.

Tess folded her arms and ran her palms up and down them. "I'll tell you another time, honey. Tonight let's focus on happy things, shall we?"

Macy nodded. "Okay." She looked at him once more. "Dad?"

Wade sighed. He could hardly turn down the invitation now. Telling himself he wasn't making up excuses to spend more time with Tess, he nodded. "Why not. When do you want us?"

"Seven o'clock. Dad's barbecuing."

"Is that right? What are *you* having—roasted zucchini?"

"How'd you guess?" She shot him a wink over her shoulder as she turned to face Macy. "Let me show you a little grooming trick Diego will love. You'll have him following you around in no time, just begging for attention." Again she glanced back at Wade. And gave him a wicked smile.

His heart thumped.

He wouldn't mind doing a little begging of his own. No matter what his better judgment dictated.

"I think I'll go help Jason with his chores," he said gruffly. He stalked away, ignoring the sound of Tess's laughter, which seemed to float behind him on the spring breeze.

Laughter that had him second-guessing his decision to avoid having a woman in his life.

"HEY, CINDERELLA, you look good."

Tess glanced up at the sound of her father's voice. He'd come through the back door and now stood in the kitchen, a stainless-steel bucket of milk in hand. In addition to the herd of four hundred–odd head of Suffolk sheep he raised, he kept a half-dozen Guernsey and Jersey cows, which he milked by hand.

Tess smiled at him. At fifty-four, her father still seemed as handsome as he did in the wedding photo she held in her hand. After setting the framed picture on the armoire that rested against the dining-area wall, Tess moved toward the kitchen. "I thought I'd better clean up a little bit, since you're throwing me a party and everything." She slipped her arms around his middle and gave him a hug. Lloyd towered over her, a big bear of a man who had always made her feel safe.

He placed the bucket of milk on the counter. "Careful there, hon, you'll get all dirty. I need to shower off this barn grit and get ready myself." He removed his cowboy hat, exposing a head of hair that remained thick, though more gray now than red, and hung the hat on a peg near the door. Then he reached for the bar of grainy soap on the sink and scrubbed his hands.

Wistfully, Tess watched him, remembering all the times she'd done so as a child. Something about the olive-green soap gave her a warm, comforting feeling. She'd forever associate its clean, no-nonsense scent with her father and his hardworking hands. And with times when her mother was still well.

"Something bothering you, sweet pea?" Lloyd asked, snapping Tess from her daydreams.

Tess sighed. "I was remembering the days before Mom got sick." She chewed her bottom lip, knowing she was ruining her lipstick, not caring. "I miss her so much, Dad. I just wish she could be here tonight, that's all."

Lloyd rinsed his hands and reached for the dish towel. "I know, honey. I wish she could, too." Then he frowned. "Did you realize Zach hasn't been going to see her much lately?"

Tess's frown deepened. "No, I didn't. Since when?" She and her brothers rarely got the chance to visit Raelene together; still, she'd thought they always made time for their mom on whatever days of the week they had free.

"Since around the anniversary date of your mom's hospitalization."

Her dad always called it that. *Hospitalization.* The big, strong man with the cream-puff heart couldn't bear to acknowledge the place his beloved wife resided in as a nursing home or even a care facility.

Tess didn't have to think twice to recall the date they'd been forced to turn Raelene's care over to the nurses. March 20, the first day of spring, and she remembered well how sad it had been to put her mom in such a place when spring was breaking open the cold fist of winter and daffodils were poking up through the last of the snow to greet tender shoots of grass. New beginnings for the world...an end of a way of life for her mother.

"Nearly *two* months?" Tess spoke the words in shock. "Why?"

Lloyd lifted a shoulder, his expression worn. "I'm not sure. I guess he's just tired of seeing her in the shape she's in. And getting married probably has a lot to do with it."

Zachary had recently eloped with a woman he'd met at a horse sale three months ago. Donna had a daughter, Becky, who was ten, and Zach had seemed to adjust well to his ready-made family. So what was the problem?

"What do you mean?" Anger filled Tess. "Are you saying Donna is keeping him from Mom?"

"No, no." Lloyd waved the thought away. "Donna's a better person than that. All I'm saying is, having his own family now has made your brother see some real good in life. I think he's doing the ostrich routine. If he doesn't notice any sadness, then it isn't there."

"That's ridiculous." Tess frowned. "Not to mention totally unfair. Are you sure that's the reason?" But deep down, she knew her dad was likely right. Of the three of them—Tess and her two brothers—Zach had been the one who'd had the hardest time accepting Rae's illness early on. Still, he'd always gone to visit her.

"No, honey, I'm not positive. I'm just guessing. I know folks handle things in different ways, but I've got to tell you, I'm deeply disappointed in your brother, and I mean to have a long heart-to-heart with him when we're alone. But today's not the day to talk about that.'' He gave her a one-armed hug and a smile. "We've got some celebrating to do. My baby girl's turning twenty-seven. Practically over the hill." He let out a boisterous laugh and Tess poked him in the ribs.

"Over the hill! Speak for yourself, you geezer." She laughed. "You'd better get dressed. We've got plenty of company coming, and you're in charge of the grill."

Lloyd flapped his arms comically, as though preparing to bolt. "Ooo-ee, doggies, I'd better get right on it then. I've got some special veggie shish kebabs marinating in the fridge for my birthday girl. All your favorites on 'em, kid. They're about four feet long." He held out his hands to demonstrate.

Tess laughed. "Go on, then. I'll watch out for the guests."

Lloyd hurried up the stairs that led to the enormous bedroom he'd once shared with Raelene, and Tess walked over to the armoire once more and looked down at the framed photographs covering its surface. Next to her parents' wedding photo was one of her dad as a young man, and another of Raelene, holding hands with Tess and her brothers. Tess stood to her right, with Seth beside Tess. And on Rae's left was Zachary, grinning a missing-tooth smile at the camera. His red hair stood up on end, damp with the lake water where he'd been wading. Her dad had taken the photo on the first camping trip they'd gone on as a family, the summer Tess was six.

Happy, carefree times.

She longed for them still.

Both furious with her brother and disappointed in

him, Tess made her way to the living room. She
hoped he came to the house soon.

She had a thing or two to say to him, party or
not.

CHAPTER SIX

"DAD." Macy poked her head around the corner of the open bedroom door.

Wade still stood in front of the closet, where he'd been for the past five minutes, trying to decide which shirt to wear—something he normally never thought much about. What in thunder had gotten into him? He reached for one, slipped it from the hanger and slid his arms into the sleeves. Black was always good.

"Yeah, honey, whatcha need?"

She stepped into the room and closed the door behind her, which struck him as odd. "I don't want Jason to hear," she explained, apparently noting the perplexed look on his face. "I have to talk to you about something. Something…well…kind of womanly."

A lead Frisbee landed in his stomach, then flew to his throat. Surely not…surely she was too young to start. He groped for total recall of the pamphlet he'd quietly snagged from the doctor's office one day not too long ago. On the subject of telling his little girl all about the process of becoming a woman and the bodily changes she'd face. What age had the pamphlet stated? Was eleven too young? Macy's birthday was next month.

Wade closed his mouth. "Uh. Okay." Swallowing, he cleared a space on the bed among the shirts he'd tossed there minutes ago.

Macy sat down and looked at him with her big blue eyes. Oh, God. *Deidra, what do I do?* He shot a quick prayer heavenward that he might not botch this. Not too badly, anyway.

"Daddy, some of the other girls at school, well, they're starting to—"

Oh, Lord, he couldn't do this! Calling himself a coward, a rotten dad and a dirty rat fink to boot, Wade hastily interrupted his daughter. "Honey, hang on a second." He chewed the inside of his cheek. "I know what you're about to tell me."

"You do?" Macy frowned.

"Yes. And, um…well, I'm thinking maybe it would be better if…well, if I'm not the one you ask about this."

Macy looked confused. "Why not, Dad? You've always said Jason and me can talk to you about anything."

"Jason and I," he corrected, grasping, stalling. "And I know, honey, but…" What in thunder was he doing? This was his little girl, for crying out loud. He couldn't let her down. He was all she had. She had no mother, no woman in her life to…

Tess. Her name came to mind so naturally, it scared him. Maybe he ought to have Macy talk to Bailey, instead. But then, she was busy with the twins. *Oh, Lordy.*

"I did say that, honey," he went on. "And you can talk to me if you want to. But…well, wouldn't you feel more comfortable discussing this with another girl? I mean, with a woman?" He gestured, groping for reason. "Maybe you could ask Tess about it." And maybe he was a total jerk, pushing off a talk of tampons and sanitary pads and what to do for cramps on a woman who was merely an acquaintance and Macy's 4-H leader.

A woman he'd almost kissed.

But to his surprise, Macy brightened. "I'd love to talk to Tess about it, if you're sure that's okay with you." She laid a hand on his knee. "I just didn't want you to feel left out."

Relief filled him, and he let his shoulders sag briefly. "It's fine with me, honey." Guilt gripped him once more. "That is, if you're certain you're comfortable with that idea. I mean, we don't really know her all that well. Not really."

Again, Macy looked puzzled. "I think I know her well enough."

"Well, okay then."

Macy rose to her feet. "Can I call her about it right away?"

"Call her? On the phone?"

"Ye-ah." She drew the word out in two syllables, looking at him as though he'd lost his mind. Which he had.

"Are you sure it's not something you'd rather discuss with her in person?"

"Well, that would be a lot more fun," Macy said, her forehead creasing as though the thought hadn't occurred to her until now.

Fun?

"But I'm sort of in a hurry," she added.

"Oh." Good gosh, was it that urgent? Never mind Tess. He'd drive his daughter to the store, or go for her. He'd meant to buy something ahead of time; only, he hadn't thought "ahead of time" would come this quickly, and the prospect of picking out tampons...

Wade shuddered.

"I could drive you to the store," he said, feeling his face warm. He hoped she wouldn't want him to go in with her. Would she know what to choose? Hell, come to think of it, he wouldn't have a clue anyway. "To, uh, get what you need."

Macy smiled. "That's really nice, Dad, but it would be a lot better if I talked to Tess first."

Again, he inwardly heaved a sigh of relief. "Yeah, you're probably right. But I will go with you if you change your mind." He wanted to be a good father. No matter what that called for. He reached for his wallet. "Hold up a minute, honey." He pulled out a twenty and handed it to her. "Is that enough?"

She frowned at the money. "Enough for what?"

"Well, I mean, if Tess ends up taking you to the store instead of me, is that enough?"

Macy took the crisp bill. "I'm sure it is. I'll bring you back your change."

"No worries," he said. "Get whatever you need."

"Gee, thanks, Dad," she said. "I can't wait to tell Becky."

"Becky?" He knew who she was—Macy's new classmate whose mother had recently married Zach Vega. Yes, he supposed his daughter would want to talk to her friend about this sort of thing. Women were like that, and they had to start at some point.

"Yeah. She told me you'd never let me wear makeup yet. At least not until middle school started, and even then she figured you'd say no, because that's what her dad said.''

''Makeup?'' Wade tried not to let his mouth fall open.

''Yeah. You know…mascara, eye shadow, lipstick.'' Macy frowned as she stuffed the twenty in the pocket of her jeans. ''What did you think I was talking about?''

The lead Frisbee was back. ''Nothing.'' He forced a smile and snapped the pearl fasteners on his shirtsleeves. ''Just, you know. Lipstick and all that.'' He gestured, then scratched the back of his head. Actually, he *hadn't* planned on letting her wear makeup quite yet. But what on earth could he possibly say now?

Oh, brother.

''Thanks again, Dad,'' Macy said.

''Uh, Macy.''

''Yeah?''

''Try to stick with something tame, will you? No ruby-slipper-red or anything, huh?''

She grinned. ''Don't worry.''

''Sure.'' He waved as she left the room. ''No worries.''

Lipstick.

Good grief.

And here he'd been rattled over tampons.

TESS HADN'T WORN her hair down, without a hat, in so long it felt strange. Self-consciously, she flipped a strand of it over her shoulder and met Wade's eyes as he entered the room. He looked at her as though he'd never seen red hair before, and for a minute, the charcoal-gray dress slacks belted at her waist, coupled with a ruffled, mint-green Western blouse, left her longing for her familiar bib overalls. Then she watched the expression in Wade's eyes go from surprise, to pleasure, to longing, and she decided that his look was well worth discarding her bibs for a day.

It had been a while since a man had stared at her that way—like a sweet piece of candy he couldn't wait to taste—and she hadn't realized until now how much she'd missed it. Dating had been difficult at best when Tess was in high school, given her feelings about bringing a boy home. Her priorities had lain in taking care of her mother and keeping up with homework and household and ranch chores. Somehow, the pattern had continued after graduation.

Time moved on, with her not making much for seeing men. She had gotten to the point where she simply didn't care about men one way or the other. Yet she recalled the days when she *had* taken more care with her appearance—when she'd made the mistake of letting a cowboy get into her head and her heart. She'd dropped her guard and gotten involved with Lorenzo Juarez, who'd worked on her father's ranch.

He'd taught her a lesson she'd never forgotten, and when he left town after taking her virginity and breaking her heart, Tess quickly discovered that hiding beneath a John Deere cap and a pair of bib overalls was a great way to fade from view. She'd focused on other things, and soon Lorenzo was barely a memory. Her mom, her horse sanctuary and now her 4-H kids filled Tess's every need.

Still, she'd chosen to dress up for her party tonight, makeup included, and it felt both right and good. Wade was enough to make her forget all things negative. Enough to leave her glad she'd reapplied her lipstick moments ago.

A pleasant feeling curled through her stomach as Tess set a platter of hors d'oeuvres on the buffet table. With trembling fingers, she reached for a toothpick-speared olive sandwiched between two cubes of cheese, simply to give her hands something more to do. Lately, she seemed to lose her mind around Wade, not to mention her control. She hoped he hadn't noticed.

Smiling as he approached, Tess swiveled the toothpick between thumb and forefinger. "What's the matter, cattleman? You look like you've seen the second coming of Slim Pickens."

He cocked his head and grinned. "Ain't nothin' slim about these pickins, darlin'."

She gave him a mock look of reprimand.

"I'm talking about the food," he said. "What'd you think I meant?"

"Uh-huh. Whatever you say." Then she slid the cheese cube off the toothpick, using her teeth and tongue in a way that had Wade squirming. She widened her eyes in innocence as he watched her chew and swallow.

"As a matter of fact, though," he said, helping himself to a black olive with ham, "you clean up real nice, Tess."

"Hey, it's not every day a girl turns twenty-one." She wriggled her eyebrows. "Speaking of cleaning up, have you seen your daughter?"

"Not since she left the house on horseback on a

mission." A pained look crossed his face, so comical she had to smother a laugh.

"It's not that bad, Wade. Just a little makeup. You did know she wanted to wear some to the party, right?"

"Uh, yeah. Right."

"Good, because I was hoping this wasn't another case of misunderstanding, like the one we had over Amber. Macy said it freaked you out when she brought up the makeup thing." Unable to resist teasing him, she added, "And I quote—'Dad acted like I'd asked him to help me shop for lace underwear.'"

Wade shifted from one foot to the other. "Well, it sort of took me by surprise." He lowered his voice to a mumble. "To say the least."

"You're okay with it, though?"

He shrugged. "Sure. I guess."

Tess laughed. "You don't sound sure, but at any rate, it's a little late now. Come on." She grabbed his hand, and immediately became acutely aware of how strong and warm it was. Finishing off her last bite of cheese more as a distraction than because she was hungry, she tugged Wade along behind her. "Don't worry. It's just a little mascara and lipstick." As she looked over her shoulder, she pointed the empty toothpick at him. "So don't make her feel self-conscious."

"I won't." He sounded indignant, as though he'd never dream of humiliating his daughter. Tess mentally rolled her eyes. Anyone who spouted corny comebacks was bound not to know enough to handle a girl's first makeup job with finesse.

Tess walked through the dining area to the kitchen, where Macy and Becky were working on a batch of homemade ice cream, taking turns at the old-fashioned crank-style ice-cream maker.

Macy grinned. "Hi, Dad! Me and Becky—I mean, Becky and I—are making strawberry-banana nut temptation. Tess thought it up."

"She did, huh?" Still holding Tess's hand, Wade reached out and tugged a lock of his daughter's hair. Then he cast Tess a look that reminded her of a naughty boy up to no good. "Hey, what's that on your lips, Macy? You must've gotten into those berries." He gestured at the containers of strawberries resting on the table on either side of a huge bunch of bananas.

Macy pressed her pale-pink lips together in reprimand. "Dad. You know what it is." Her blue eyes widened with excitement. "Tess helped me and Becky with our lipstick and mascara. What do you think?" She batted her lashes.

Wade hid a grin, and rubbed his chin in deep concentration. "Why, I think you ladies look lovely." He tipped his black hat. "How do, Miss Becky. I've heard a lot about you." He held out his hand and Becky giggled and gave it a shake.

"She's gonna join 4-H," Macy said, smiling at her new friend in a way that warmed Tess's heart. She understood Macy hadn't found it easy to make a new best friend after losing Sarah.

"Becky's my niece," Tess added. "Her mother and Zach got married a couple of months ago."

"So I heard."

"They took Becky with them on their honeymoon. To Walt Disney World!" Macy added. She gave Becky a good-natured poke in the ribs. "You lucky."

Immediately, the animated expression on Wade's face disappeared, and Tess couldn't help but wonder if he was pondering the cost of such a vacation. Her heart went out to him. She knew it wasn't easy raising two kids on his own. But he sure made it look that way—she'd give him that much.

"Hey, cattleman," she said, tugging on their still-clasped hands. "Wanna help me with something outside?"

"Sure."

He released her hand, as though only now aware he still held it, and Tess felt a bit foolish for not having been the one to let go after she'd tugged him toward the kitchen. But his palm had felt so good, gripping hers, that she hadn't really wanted to.

Wade bent and gave Macy a peck on the cheek. "You do look real nice, honey. You, too, Miss Becky." He tipped his hat again, sending the girls into a fresh fit of giggles.

"Keep cranking that ice cream," Tess said. "I'll be back to help in a minute."

"Okay." Macy picked up on her conversation with Becky, and Tess headed for the sliding glass doors that led outside from the kitchen.

On the porch, Lloyd sat with Seth, Zach and Donna—the only guests to arrive thus far outside of Wade and Macy. Tess's stomach churned with irritation as she watched her oldest brother. She hadn't yet had the opportunity to talk to him away from Donna.

Wade greeted her family, and Tess introduced him to her new sister-in-law. Then she spoke to her dad. "We'll be out in the barn for a minute. I want to show Wade what you brought home this afternoon."

"Okay, honey," Lloyd said.

"Stay out of the hayloft," Seth teased. "That's what got Zach where he is." He grinned at Donna, who laughed and turned bright red.

Tess shook a warning finger at her brother. "Get your thoughts out of the gutter. Your father's present."

"Don't mind me," Lloyd said. "I didn't fall off the turnip truck yesterday."

"I'd say you read enough of those romance novels to get your imagination going, anyway," Zach ribbed. "You oughta see the covers on some of them." He grinned at Wade. "Bright red. What d'ya call 'em, Dad? Blazing, flaming, something or other."

"You hush, boy," Lloyd said. But he let out a booming laugh.

Wade raised his eyebrows at Tess as they headed toward the barn. "Your dad reads romance novels?"

"Yep. Surprised?"

"A little," he acknowledged. "I would've taken him more for the Louis L'Amour type."

"He reads those, too." Tess smiled. "He got started on romance when he began to read them to Mom." Bittersweet memories filled her of the hours Lloyd had spent, first on the sunny back porch of their ranch house or next to a cozy fire in winter, and later at Rae's bedside in the County Care Facility. "He got hooked, and now he reads them by the truckload."

Wade chuckled. "That's great," he said. He sobered. "I like your dad, Tess. He's a good man."

"I know." She gave him a small smile, then walked through the open barn door. "Here's what he brought me today." She stepped up to a box stall and peered over the top. A tiny foal lay curled in the thick straw bedding, its coal-black nose tucked over one stockinged leg.

Wade leaned over to look, too. "Where's the mare?"

"She died of colic," Tess said. "One of Dad's customers came into the feed store this afternoon and asked him if I could take the filly. I'll be moving her to the sanctuary in the morning. She's only six weeks old."

"And you're telling me this because…?" A note of suspicion laced his voice.

She might have known he would never think she'd simply brought him to see the filly because it was cute. "She'll make a good 4-H project," Tess said. "She's on a bottle, and it'll be an experience to raise her. I thought Macy might want to help me."

"Why?"

It wasn't what she'd expected him to say. She'd figured he'd make some comment about coddling horses. "What do you mean, 'why?' I just told you. For 4-H. All Macy's group will be involved to some extent."

"That's exactly what I mean. Why single out Macy? To come over and help you more than the other kids in the West Slope Trail Blazers."

He made the idea sound like something devious. Tess glared at him. "Well, if you're wondering if it was to get close to you, cattleman, think again."

But her palms grew damp. Had she subconsciously

done so? *No way.* She didn't need a lame excuse to
get close to him. Not that she'd want to, anyway.
He'd almost kissed her the other night, and for a
brief moment, she'd wished he had. But then her
better judgment had taken over, and she'd told herself it was best he hadn't. "I figured Macy might
have fun with the foal, especially since she comes
to visit me now and then. Is that a crime?"

"She already has her hands full with Diego."

"I know that." She looked at the black filly as
the little horse struggled to her feet with a whicker
of greeting. Tess stuck her hand out, and the foal
latched on to her fingers and began to suckle. Tess's
heart went out to her. *No mother.* Poor little thing.
Her every instinct kicked into familiar gear. The foal
needed TLC, and that had always been her specialty.
She wanted to share the experience with Macy.

"And, yes, Diego will require a great deal of
Macy's time. Still, there's nothing like the feeling
of mothering something." It was what she'd clung
to growing up, first when her birth mother had abandoned her and she'd looked after her brothers, and
later, when Raelene had begun to falter in the grips
of her illness and Tess had tended her. Though
Macy's situation wasn't quite the same as her own,
she still felt it would be beneficial for her to experience the rewards of nurturing. It had helped Tess
so many times to be able to reach out and help rather
than need reaching out to. To this day, she got that
same feeling of fulfillment whenever she rescued a
horse. Wade himself had mentioned feeling such satisfaction just the other day when he'd help her save
Diego. So why was he being stubborn now?

"Where are you going with this?" he asked.

"Surely you've noticed Macy's loneliness." Tess pulled her fingers from the filly's mouth and looked up at him. Anger clouded his face, and she hurried to elaborate. "Don't get me wrong, Wade. You're a great father. Anyone can see that. But Macy told me all about her friendship with Bailey, and now she's starting to hang around me. I'd say she's lonely for some feminine company."

"She's got girlfriends, like Becky," he said. "If you've got a problem with her tagging on your heels, just say so."

Tess's temper flared. "Don't put words in my mouth. I love having her around. But I think she's aching for a mother figure."

"And a filly's gonna cure that?" Sarcasm laced his voice.

"Of course not." She took a breath, knowing she'd likely stepped over a boundary she had no business crossing. But she cared too much about Macy not to speak her mind. "Wade, motherhood and nurturing are something special." She gestured, groping for the right words. "It's a woman thing, you know? And if Macy's missing out on that—the same way I did by not having a mom part of my life—then it might benefit her to turn the tables and do a little mothering of her own."

Wade pressed his mouth into a line and hooked one hand near his belt. "Look, Tess. I'm sure you mean well, and I do appreciate you teaching Macy about makeup and helping her with Diego. But I told you once before. You're not her mother."

"I never—"

"And you're sure as hell in no position to cast judgment on what my kid does or doesn't need."

His face reddened. "Don't tell me how to parent. Okay?" For a minute it appeared as if he was going to lecture her further, then he shook his head. "Forget it. I'd better get back up to the house. I've got those bridles and belts in the truck for your dad." With that, he spun on his heel and walked off.

Tess stared after him, frustration and anger churning her gut. What the hell was wrong with him? Couldn't he see beyond his own stubborn pride? Maybe she'd stepped out of line, but why couldn't he understand she was only trying to help? Damn it! He went from flirting with her one minute, to pushing her away the next as though she had some sort of social disease or something.

Determined not to let Wade spoil her party, Tess stroked the filly's velvety nose, then headed toward the house. Damned if she'd let him spoil her mood, either.

She knew how to have fun, with or without Wade Darland.

CHAPTER SEVEN

FOR WADE'S ANGER to cool didn't take long. Tess's laughter had a way of getting to him, and tonight was no exception. He had been surprised to learn she'd be twenty-seven on her birthday, Tuesday. He supposed that her kidlike pigtails and way of dressing had made him think she was younger. But now, as he observed her entertaining her guests out on the back porch, he had to admit there was nothing at all childlike about Tess.

She'd blown his mind when he'd walked into the living room and seen her with her hair down, wearing just enough makeup to bring out the green in her eyes and the pink in her cheeks. Not to mention that she had curves in all the right places. She really ought to ditch those bulky overalls and dress up more often.

Wade licked his lips and told himself he should still be angry at her. She'd stuck her nose in his business—something he simply didn't tolerate from anyone. And yet, if he was totally honest with himself, he had to admit she'd meant well. He watched how she tilted her head back and laughed, completely carefree, the center of attention without even trying to be. The front of her blouse dipped in a V shape to expose just enough cleavage to make him crazy with longing. And her hair, long and thick, spilled across her shoulders and down her back.

A vision of Tess lying naked on cool crisp sheets, her hair draped across her creamy breasts, entered his mind and refused to leave. He knew better than to dwell on such a thought. It could lead nowhere, because he'd already made up his mind to raise his kids alone. How many times did he need to remind himself of this? Something about Tess kept making him forget lately what was best. She was driving him nuts, sending his emotions into a whirlpool of confusion that he seemed to have absolutely no control over.

If Tess was aware of the mixed feelings that ravaged him, she gave no indication. Her sole purpose at the moment was to have fun. She laughed and joked with her friends and family while opening her gifts. So many well-wishers had come. The porch and yard were crowded with people, and cars and pickup trucks lined the driveway on both sides all the way from the road to the house. The only one missing was Tess's mom, and as he watched Tess, Wade realized something.

She was right. She and Macy had a lot in common. Tess knew what it was like to have her mother taken from her, albeit not at the tender age Macy had experienced such a loss. Still, he supposed it was only natural for her, therefore, to sympathize with his daughter and try to reach out to her. Yet he couldn't help the irritation he felt deep down inside at the thought of her interference. He didn't want anyone trying to tell him how to raise his kids. He was a good dad. Even Tess had admitted as much.

So she could just keep her pretty little nose out of his business.

Feeling better, he moved away from the porch a short time later as Lloyd called out for everyone to "Come and get it." Wade helped himself to a plateful of food from the buffet table that stood near the barbecue pit while Lloyd piled hamburgers and hot dogs from the grill onto an oversize platter. There was enough to feed a Third World country, and Jason and some of the other boys his age appeared determined to do their part in chowing down a good portion of it. They heaped corn on the cob, potato salad and baked beans onto their plates, as well as hot dogs and hamburgers with all the fixins.

"You boys must have hollow legs," Wade said. He bit into his own burger and casually looked over to see where Tess had gone. She'd filled her plate with coleslaw, corn and the vegetable shish kababs Lloyd had grilled, and now sat at one of the picnic tables, next to Joy Isley. Macy slid in on the other side of her, across from Becky.

It figured. Even with her newfound friend, Macy continued to stick to Tess like dust to superglue. What on earth was he going to do with his daughter?

Telling himself he was being unreasonable, Wade turned away, determined to put Tess out of his mind and to simply enjoy the party. He didn't get out much, what with working the ranch and taking care of the kids. Plate in hand, he headed for a group of chairs where Lloyd Vega and some other cowboys sat. But he couldn't shake thoughts of Tess that lingered in his head.

By the time the party began to wind down, Wade realized he couldn't leave without making things right with her. He still felt she'd overstepped her boundaries, but for Macy's sake, he needed to keep things civil between them. After all, Tess was her 4-H leader. Scanning the area beneath the yard lights, he noticed some of the women cleaning up the picnic tables, but he saw no sign of Tess. Maybe she was in the house.

Wade walked over to the open front door and went inside. As he was making his way through the living room toward the adjoining dining area, the sound of Tess's angry voice, coming from the kitchen, halted him in his tracks.

"How can you say that? She's your mother, damn it!"

"She doesn't know that anymore. Hell, Tess, she doesn't even recognize us." Zach Vega's familiar drawl carried easily through the room, and Wade knew he should turn and leave.

But Tess's tear-choked words stopped him. "You can't be sure of that. Do you realize how much it would hurt Mom if she thought you'd stopped caring?"

"I *do* care. Damn it, you're not listening to me!"

Feeling like a heel, Wade forced himself to make his way back through the living room and out onto the front porch. Tess's crying had upset him more than he'd realized, and he stood, hands shaking, wondering what he could do to help. Probably nothing. From the bits of conversation he'd overheard, the family conflict was none of his business. Still, he couldn't help but be concerned.

Minutes later, Zach stormed outside and down the porch steps without so much as noting his presence. Wade hesitated, then retraced his steps through the living room. While the Vegases' family matters were none of his business, he couldn't very well leave Tess alone without at least being sure she was all right. Besides, he'd vowed to make amends with her before he took Macy and Jason home, and now was as good a time as any. Maybe he could take her mind off whatever was troubling her.

He reached the kitchen, only to find it empty. Through the open sliding doors, he heard the noise of a porch swing creaking and, beneath that, a barely muffled sound. Crying. His stomach turned to jelly.

Wade hurried to the doorway and looked out. Tess sat in the swing, elbows on her knees, hands covering her nose and mouth. Her eyes were closed, and even in the near darkness he could tell she was doing her best to fight the tears that squeezed from the corners of them. A part of him wanted to turn away and simply leave her to grieve privately. But another part drew him to her in a way he couldn't resist. His heart went out to her for what she must be going through, and quietly he slid the screen door open and stepped outside.

"Hey, spitfire." He reached out and placed his hand on her shoulder, giving it a gentle rub. "What's wrong? Did someone put meatballs in your spaghetti?"

Tess gave a half laugh, looking up at him as she wiped the tears from her cheeks with the palms of her hands. "Nothing so horrible as that." She bit her lip, embarrassed. "I thought you'd gone home."

"Not yet. I figured I'd better come find you first and tell you I didn't mean to bite your head off over the filly." He sat down beside her, his hand still on her shoulder. "You okay?"

She nodded. "Yeah. It's nothing, really. Just a family disagreement between me and Zach."

"Wanna talk about it?"

She hesitated. "I don't know." She remained quiet and Wade decided he'd pushed too far.

"Hey, I'm not trying to be nosy." He moved his hand and let it fall to his lap. "It's just that no one should have to cry on her birthday."

"Who said I was crying?" Tess sniffed, her tears gone. But not forgotten, he was certain.

"I guess you got a bug in your eye, then." Wade swiped at the air. "Gotta watch them little hummers. They're everywhere this time of year. Especially the zucchini-eating mamba-beetle." He reached up with every intention of giving her hair a playful tug, but instead found himself twining a lock around his thumb and finger. Slowly, he rubbed it back and forth, loving the texture, the smell of apple shampoo that he'd previously been aware of only in the back of his mind. "Why, they might even think this red hair of yours is a carrot. Or maybe a hunk of corn silk."

Indeed, her hair felt silky and soft beneath his touch, and was nowhere near the shade of a carrot. Light from the kitchen spilled on the deep, rich strands of red laced with gold. The shimmering color made him want to move his hand up beneath the curtain of hair and pull her toward him. Pull her into a kiss as hot as the one he'd imagined the other night.

He saw Tess staring at his hand. Surprise and something akin to desire filled her expression. Or was it only his wishful thinking? She met his gaze and Wade froze, his fingers still tangled in her hair, his breath caught somewhere in his chest.

"No bugs," she said. "Just one big, pesky cowboy who keeps getting under my skin."

"Yeah?" He let go of her hair and touched her cheek, wiping away the last trace of tears with his thumb. "You're pretty good at that yourself." He was a millisecond away from kissing her. A gnat's toenail from losing his resolve. He leaned forward and brushed his lips against hers, testing.

Tess seemed to hold her breath. She gave in to the featherlight touch of his mouth just enough to let him know she, too, was having difficulty containing her feelings. For what seemed endless seconds, their lips met in a kiss so sweet and gentle it did more for Wade than if he'd plunged his tongue into her mouth. Then suddenly Tess drew back and leaned against the corner of the swing. She let her hand wrap around the chain and gave the glider a push with one foot, setting it in motion. "Careful, cattleman. You're about to get us in trouble."

"Think so?" He ached to touch her once more, no matter what his more reasonable thoughts told him. To explore the kiss that had ended before it had barely begun.

"I know so, and I'm afraid what you're offering is a little too inviting right now." She looked at him from the corner of her eye. "I *was* crying."

Her abrupt admission took him by surprise, more so than if she'd admitted she wanted to kiss him, too. He said nothing, waiting for her to open up, if that was what she wanted to do.

"It's my mom." She gazed off into the distance,

her voice soft and low. "She's been sick a long time. I guess you know that."

He nodded. "I've heard. But like I said, I never really knew what caused her illness until you told me."

"It's gotten harder on the family as time passes, and Zach...he's not coping well. He and I had a fight over it." She pressed her mouth into a line. "My temper gets the best of me sometimes, and I hate when that happens."

"You don't say?" He wanted her to smile again. Her sorrow bothered him more than he would have imagined. "Red hair and all, huh?"

"Yeah. I suppose."

She grew silent, and Wade told himself to let things be. Talking them through was something women did. Lord knows he'd never been much good at it with Deidra. But for some reason, he wanted to draw Tess away from whatever was troubling her. Maybe he could at least lend an ear if she needed one.

Or a shoulder.

"So, what happened?"

Tess stopped pushing the swing. She stared down at her feet. "Zach hasn't been going to see Mom lately. I didn't know until today. Dad thought maybe her condition has gotten to be too much for Zach to cope with, so I confronted him."

"And?"

"Since Zach married Donna, he's realized the importance of putting the past behind him and moving forward." She waved her hand in the air. "He had a bad run with women before Donna, but that's neither here nor there. The point is, he wants to move on with his new life and forget about the negative.''

''What's wrong with that?''

She glared at him. ''Nothing. Except that he looks at Mom's illness as a bad thing he wants to move past, and that just isn't right. He thinks she doesn't recognize us anymore, and that there's no point in going to visit her.''

''That's a tough one,'' Wade said, genuinely at a loss for words. Seeing your mother in such a state of mind had to be hard. He had no idea how he'd react if he were in Zach's shoes, or Tess's. He didn't get along real well with his own mother. Still...

''Yes, it is.'' Tess leaned forward in the swing, gesturing emphatically. ''It's not easy for me, either, to see Mom like she is. But that's no reason to abandon her.''

''No, it's not. But maybe Zach just needs time to adjust to his new life with Donna and Becky. I bet he'll come around.''

''I certainly hope so.'' She looked at him, anger sparking her eyes. ''I'm just so mad at him right now. I felt like throwing something—or strangling my brother. One of the two.'' She shook her head. ''But instead, I came out here on the porch, and I guess I let off a little steam by crying, which I also hate.''

''Hey.'' Wade spoke softly, sliding close to her once more. He gave in to the urge to touch her, raking his fingers through the hair at her temples. He let the strands fall in a gentle cascade, then repeated the gesture. ''It's okay to cry, you know. It's not a crime.''

"No," Tess said. "But it doesn't do much good, either."

"You mean, it's a waste of energy?"

She nodded. "Yeah. I'd say so."

"Really?" Wade eased his hand around to clasp the back of her neck. "And you'd rather put your energy to better use?"

She laughed. "If that's a come-on, cattleman, you can forget it."

Wade froze just short of reaching to pull her into his arms. His face heated, and he felt ridiculous. She was right. His words rang like those of a teenager out to score in the back of his truck. *Damn, but he was out of practice with this sort of thing.*

"Sorry, Tess. I—"

"You can forget your sappy come-ons," she repeated, "and just shut up and kiss me."

Her pointed statement took a full ten seconds to register. Then his embarrassment turned to desire once more, and he slipped his arms around her. "I like a woman who doesn't mince words." And with that he did exactly what she'd said.

The touch of their lips made everything melt into the background. The sound of crickets, the surrounding darkness, the stars up above in a sky so clear it looked like black water. All of it faded away as Wade closed his mouth over Tess's and wrapped his tongue around hers. The gentle kiss they'd shared minutes before had been nice. This one rattled his brains.

She slid her hands around the back of his neck, tipping his hat out of place. He didn't care. He focused only on the fire of her mouth against his, kissing, seeking, again and again. He nibbled her neck, her ear. His heart began to pound and her breath came in gasps as he ran his hands up and down her shoulders, across her back, aching to feel her skin beneath the blouse that clung hotly to it. She seemed to burn beneath his touch, and it took a long moment for a sound to register. The sound of a voice, calling in the background.

"Dad! Dad, where are you?"

Jason.

Wade pulled back, his senses reeling, the swing tipping beneath him as his surroundings flew back into focus. He looked at Tess, and in the dim light he could see her eyes sparkling, her mouth moist and flushed. He wanted her more right then than he'd wanted anything in a very long time. His groin throbbed painfully and he shifted, grateful for the cover of near darkness.

From around the corner of the house, Jason appeared. "There you are. I couldn't find you."

Hastily, Wade righted his cowboy hat and scooted across the swing away from Tess, feeling as though they'd just been caught naked. He cleared his throat and noticed Tess smoothing her hair into place with one hand. Looking so much the guilty lover that he wanted to laugh with pure joy. She was sweet. Sweeter than he'd ever realized. He couldn't think, could barely breathe.

"What's up, son?" He hoped his voice sounded more normal to Jason than it did to his own ears.

Jason gave him an odd look, then a crooked grin. "I don't know, Dad. You tell me."

Wade felt his face color to the roots of his hair. "Nothing. Tess and I were just—talking."

"Uh-huh." Jason's grin widened. "I thought I'd

better tell you that Macy fell asleep on a hay bale. I figured you'd want to get her home.''

Wade stood up, tucking his shirt into his jeans. How had it come loose from his belt? ''She did, huh? In the barn?''

''Nah, on the roping dummy we were using earlier. I think she's had too much excitement for one day.''

And apparently, so had he, Wade thought as he glanced away from Tess. ''Probably so. I guess we'd better get her home, then.''

''I'll walk with you,'' Tess said, rising to her feet. She quirked her mouth and raised her eyebrows at him in a cute ''Oops—we've been caught'' gesture that had his heart racing all over again.

Together with Jason, they walked to the hay bale where Macy lay sleeping, mouth open, her ball cap tipped at an angle and her arms and legs sprawled in what appeared to be totally uncomfortable angles.

Tess's soft laughter sent Wade's toes curling.

''She looks so adorable,'' she said. ''Sleeping that easily…so innocent.'' She shook her head. ''I wish I could do that.''

Her comment took him by surprise. Did Tess have trouble sleeping? But before he could have time to ponder that, Macy stirred. Slowly, she blinked heavy eyelids, then sat up as though startled.

''Gosh, what happened? Where is everybody?''

Wade chuckled and offered her a hand. ''You fell asleep, twinkle toes. Guess we'd best get you home to bed.''

Macy covered a yawn with one hand. ''Guess so.'' She rubbed her eye, smearing the mascara Tess had applied earlier.

Jason burst into a fit of laughter. "Now you look like a raccoon. A coon with one eye."

"What?" Macy stared blankly at him, then down at her hand. "Oh, crud." She pursed her lips threateningly and sprang toward her brother. "I'm gonna get you for that one, Jace!"

With a howl of laughter, Jason sprinted away, Macy hot on his heels.

Tess laughed, too, shaking her head, then turned toward Wade. Her smile made him want to kiss her again. She wore her feelings openly, leaving it easy to see how fond she was of his kids. Easy to forget his vow to remain alone.

A warning voice inside his head whispered caution. He couldn't be certain of anything about her. He'd been down this road before and had nearly made the mistake of letting the wrong woman into his kids' lives. Two years after Deidra's death, he'd put aside the promise he'd made to focus only on taking care of Macy and Jason. He'd gone out with a woman he'd met who lived in Deer Creek, and had wasted three months with her before finally realizing she had no desire to be around his kids on a regular basis.

She'd put on a good front at first, tricking him with insincere words about Macy and Jason. He'd very nearly fallen for her act, and had sworn he'd never make the same mistake twice. Though Tess seemed sincere, he couldn't be sure. And he needed to remember that—no matter how good she kissed or how much fun she was to be around.

Shoving his hands in his pockets, Wade rocked back on his heels. "Thanks for inviting us tonight," he said. "I had a good time."

She stared at him, her expression suddenly serious. "So did I." He could see some doubt creep into her face. Was she sorry she'd kissed him, or could she simply read his thoughts by the way he looked at her? It seemed as though she wanted to say something more, but instead, she gestured over her shoulder. "Maybe I won't walk you to your truck after all. I need to go give the foal a bottle."

He nodded. The foal. It brought back the memory of their previous argument, reminding him all the more why he needed to tread carefully where Tess was concerned. They certainly had their differences. Besides, her statement sounded like an excuse. As though she thought he might kiss her again if she lingered.

Wade stiffened his resolve, glad to see she wasn't the only one trying to regain some sense and composure. "That's fine. We'll see you at 4-H on Thursday. And have a happy birthday this week."

"I will. Good night, Wade." She headed for the barn, her figure silhouetted in the shadows cast by the moon.

Wade turned away, trying to forget how it had felt to hold her and kiss her.

Wanting to forget that there were nights when he felt lonely.

CHAPTER EIGHT

TESS DROVE TO THE BANK on Tuesday in her newly repaired truck, an envelope of checks tucked into her pocket. A mighty thin envelope. She sighed, trying not to dwell on the fact that donations for Western Colorado Horse Rescue hadn't been rolling in on a very regular basis lately. But even though there often weren't enough funds to cover her many expenses, and a great deal of the money for the sanctuary came out of her own pocket, Tess wouldn't trade what she did for anything. The program meant a lot to her, and one day she hoped to expand it to the point of having both volunteers and paid assistants working with her to increase the number of animals WCHR could help.

The cool air from Colorado Western National's interior washed over her as she pushed the glass doors open and stepped inside the bank. To her surprise, Bailey stood in the lobby near her assistant's desk. She wore a lilac, floral-patterned skirt and short-sleeved blouse, and her once-long, light-brown hair was cut in a cute layered style that barely brushed the top of her shoulders.

"Bailey." Tess walked toward her. "What on earth are you doing back to work already?" She spoke to Jenny, Bailey's assistant. "I thought you were supposed to barricade the doors if necessary."

Bailey was a hard worker, devoted to both her family and her career. As president of Colorado Western National, she ran the bank in a way that kept her customers and employees happy.

"I couldn't keep her out," Jenny said. "But we're not letting her stay long," she added with mock sternness. "Until the twins are at least six weeks old, she's only allowed to check in on occasion."

Bailey chuckled. "Well, you know how we bankers are. Can't keep away from our job for long."

"I like your new haircut," Tess said. "It looks great." Almost unconsciously, she fingered one of her braids, unable to remember the last time she'd changed her hairstyle. No fuss, no muss.

"Thanks." Bailey rolled her eyes and her lips curved. "I thought Trent was going to pass out when he first saw how short it was. But it's a whole lot easier to care for."

"I'm sure so." Tess could imagine how much time it took to mother twin newborns.

Bailey folded her arms and leaned against Jenny's desk. "So, how are things going with you, Tess? And with your sanctuary?"

Tess wrinkled her nose. "Pretty good. Though funding could be better." She waved the envelope in her hand. "Seems I'm making more withdrawals than deposits lately."

"Really?" Bailey's forehead creased with genuine concern. "Macy told me about Diego, by the way. She sure is fired up over him."

"That she is." Tess's thoughts bounced immediately from Macy to Wade, and for the umpteenth time, she relived the kiss they'd shared three nights ago on the porch swing. The memory had been constant in her mind ever since, and she knew she had to do something to banish it. Quick. She'd dived into her work both at the feed store and her home office, and begun kicking around plans for a way to raise money for the sanctuary, as well. That ought to keep her busy. Busy enough to stop dwelling on Wade. Or so she'd thought.

"Are you free for lunch later?" Bailey asked.

Tess snapped her attention away from thoughts of Wade's hot, sweet lips. "Sure. What'd you have in mind?"

"I've got an idea that will help your situation with WCHR. We can talk about it over lunch. Are you up for seafood? There's a new place in Glenwood Springs I've been dying to try." Before Tess could answer, Bailey clapped a hand to her forehead. "What am I saying? You don't eat seafood. Never mind. Blond moment." She laughed good-naturedly and gave Jenny a wink.

"Hey." Jenny grinned, pressing a hand against her long, blond hair. "I highly resemble that remark."

"How about Rosarita's?" Tess suggested. The place served the best vegetarian tacos.

"Wonderful. I'm always game for Mexican food. One o'clock?"

"Meet you there or here?"

"There," Bailey said. "I'm headed home in a minute. I only dropped in to check on things, though I know I shouldn't worry with Jenny in charge."

"I keep trying to tell her," Jenny confided to Tess in a stage whisper, then smiled at her boss. "Actually, Bailey, we miss you like crazy. It'll be nice when the twins are old enough to put in the day care.'' One of the changes Bailey had made when she'd taken over as president of Colorado Western National was to add an employee day care center on the ground floor of the building that housed the bank.

"If I can pry them away from their father," Bailey said. "Trent's determined to be Daddy, horse breeder and husband in one swoop."

"Lucky you," Jenny said. "Are you sure he doesn't have a brother?"

"Nope. He's one of a kind." The love and pride in Bailey's voice was so apparent it did something strange to Tess's stomach.

Refusing to recognize the feelings of longing that pulled at her, she bade Jenny and Bailey so long and headed for the teller window. But her mind strayed once more to Wade. Engrossed in her thoughts, Tess barely managed to respond to the teller's greeting and small talk as she made her deposit, then exited the bank.

The short drive to the feed store did nothing to help her situation, either, especially since the first thing she heard when she walked through the door was Wade's name. A regular customer, Mallory Baldwin, stood near the register talking to Tess's dad. She held one of Wade's bridles, commenting on the craftsmanship and quality he'd put into making it.

"I tell you, I'm truly glad to see him starting up this new leather business," Mallory said. "I heard he was thinking of selling his cows, which would be a good thing. Lord knows those kids of his could use more quality parenting time, what with their mother being long gone.''

Immediately, Tess bristled. Wade was a good dad, and she had half a mind to tell Mallory exactly that. With five kids of her own, the woman seemed to think it her business to mind everyone else's when it came to anything that had to do with child rearing. In Mallory's eyes, being the mother of five qualified her as an expert. While Tess found nothing particularly wrong with that reasoning, she did take exception to the not-so-subtle put-down of Wade's parenting abilities.

Reminding herself that she, too, had thought pretty much the same thing about him until she'd learned better, Tess bit her tongue.

With her back to Tess, Mallory didn't notice her, and continued her conversation with Lloyd, who appeared pained by the subject matter. ''Of course, I'm sure a lot of the situation has to do with Deidra having been so much older than Wade. Why, she was practically a mother figure to him. He doesn't have the best of relationships with his own mother, you know.''

Lloyd sighed. ''Nine years' age difference isn't quite that much, Mallory.'' He cast a look over the woman's shoulder at Tess, widening his eyes in a plea for rescue.

''Mallory.'' Tess spoke from behind her, causing the woman to start and nearly drop the bridle. Reminding herself that two of the Baldwin kids were in her 4-H group, and that nosy or not Mallory was still a paying customer, Tess pasted a smile on her face. ''How are you?''

Mallory blushed as though realizing she'd said a

little too much in Tess's presence. Not that she could possibly have any idea of Tess's feelings for Wade. It was enough that Mallory knew that Tess, as 4-H leader, was friends with many of the parents in town.

"Fine, Tess, thank you. I was just telling your dad how much I admire Wade's leatherwork." She laid the bridle on the counter. "I'll take this, and see if you can get him to make a match for it, will you?" She smiled at Tess, still a bit red-faced. "They're for Shelly's and Kelly's graduations," she explained. "They'll have a fit over them." Again, she fingered the intricate tooling.

Tess sighed inwardly, aware that the eighteen-year-old twins had always been treated as one, right down to their identical haircuts, clothes and birthday presents. She admired Bailey's determination to see her boys as individuals, beginning with nonrhyming names.

Deciding that her own mood this morning had more to do with Wade than with Mallory, and that talking to the woman obviously wasn't helping her state of mind, Tess excused herself and went outside to the yard where fencing supplies and stock tanks were stored. A delivery truck was due to arrive shortly, and she grabbed her clipboard in preparation for taking count of the goods. Yet all the while she was deep in thought.

The kisses she and Wade shared had shaken her from the tips of her toes to the very ends of her hair. Being with him that way had been like nothing Tess had ever felt. Still, she was perfectly happy with her life the way it was. Why complicate things? But something had come over her the night of her party that had caused her to abandon all resolve.

At first she'd written it off as part of the highly emotional state she'd been in. Upset and frustrated by the situation involving her mother and Zach, angry beyond measure at her brother, she'd let her defenses down. Her good sense had fled, and she'd ended up acting like a flirt, kissing Wade, wanting him more than ever. He'd set her on fire with his yummy-smelling cologne and his thick, dark hair. And those hazel eyes, flecked with bits of green and gold, that put all sorts of crazy, romantic notions in her mind. She told herself her reaction was normal. Any healthy, red-blooded woman would have done the same.

But what she'd felt went beyond Wade's good looks and beyond her own emotional state. Wade wasn't just eye candy. He was funny, though at times annoying, and he was a great father. Tess had to admit that her fondness for Macy, and Jason, too, made it all the more easy to like Wade, in spite of their differences. But how to explain the strong attraction? Beyond the physical, that is. He so often drove her nuts with those differences. What was it about *that* that had her coming back to spar with him time and again? Apparently, she enjoyed it, or she'd avoid him, Macy or no.

But it did seem that the one thing she and Wade had most in common was their mutual concern for Macy's welfare. They disagreed on pretty much everything else. His way of thinking about animals. Her ideas about what Macy needed. Even though he'd supported his little girl's love for animals by rescuing Diego and letting her have the horse, there was still the fact that Wade raised cattle, at least for the time being. Mallory's comment had taken her by surprise. She'd had no idea Wade planned to sell his herd. Still, his leatherwork involved animal products.

Tess sighed. She was not a die-hard animal activist or vegan. She ate eggs and cheese and drank milk, and she rode a leather saddle. But the rest of her tack was made of nylon, and her ovo-lacto approach to food consumption contrasted sharply with Wade's meat-eating ways. Of course, her dad and brothers were like him in that respect. Meat-and-potato-loving cowboys who worked hard and liked a good hearty meal on the table each night—one that did not involve soy and tofu. Tess had learned to live with their choices. After all, her family had as much right to theirs as she did to hers.

She sighed again. None of this should really matter in regard to Wade. She reminded herself she was merely thinking about dating him, not marrying the guy.

Marriage. The thought made her laugh. Now, she was getting *way* too far ahead of herself in her musings. Who needed such a headache when so many marriages ended in divorce? But her thoughts kept coming full circle, and Mallory's words echoed in her mind: *I'm sure a lot of the situation has to do with Deidra having been so much older than Wade. Why, she was practically a mother figure to him.*

Tess's stomach whirled. Not because of the nine-year age difference. She hadn't realized Deidra had been older than Wade, nor did she care. The thing that had her belly in knots was that if what Mallory said was true—if Wade *had* married Deidra because he looked up to her as being a little older and wiser—then that would go a long way in explaining why he appeared to resent her own efforts in mentoring Macy.

Tess was pretty sure Wade was older than she was. Maybe that added to his opinion that she had no business trying to tell him what to do with his kids. Immediately, she rejected the idea. More likely, the simple reason behind his resentment was that Wade couldn't see anyone taking over Deidra's role, no matter what her age, viewpoint or shoe size.

Likely, no one would ever be able to fill Deidra's cowboy boots to Wade's satisfaction. Tess included.

The thought should have left her bitter, yet somehow Tess could relate to it. She'd seen women try to step in and take over when her mother had gone to live at the County Care Facility. And she'd resented the hell out of their sometimes-not-so-subtle attempts at wooing her father—a married man. They seemed to think that her mother's illness automatically put Lloyd up for grabs. He had quickly set them straight, but still, the situation had angered Tess beyond belief. And while Wade's situation wasn't the same, since he actually was a widower, she supposed she could still understand in part where he was coming from.

Which only made her all the more curious about what made him tick. Try as she might, she couldn't back away from him. She knew she was playing with the proverbial fire, but the temptation to get closer and see what would happen pulled strongly at her. If he'd wanted to be left alone, he would have said so. He didn't mince words any more than she did. Wade fascinated her, and she wanted to get to know him better, even if things went nowhere beyond the flirtatious, if at times tenuous, relationship they now shared.

Tess closed her eyes for a moment and let the memory of Wade's kisses wash over her once more.

Relationship. Or was it more like a friendship that had gotten a little out of hand? No. She didn't believe that at all. It went beyond that. Whether either one of them truly cared to admit it or not.

The question was, what on earth did they plan to do about it?

WADE GATHERED an armful of bridles and laid them carefully in a box. He still couldn't get over how well his leather business was doing, not just in Lloyd's feed store but on the Cowboy Up Web site, as well. He'd had more hits over the weekend than he ever could have imagined, and nearly a dozen orders to show for it. With all that, a person would think he'd have no room in his mind to think about anything else. Instead, his thoughts were full of Tess.

He wondered how far things might have gone had Jason not interrupted Tess and him the other night. Not that anything truly intimate would have happened out there in the open on her daddy's porch. Still, he had to admit he'd come damn close to giving in to the temptation to undo the buttons on Tess's blouse as their kisses had grown more and more heated. And then, thankfully, he'd heard Jason calling him. He knew it was just as well his son had done so, especially under the circumstances.

Wade had felt a lot of confusion lately when it came to Tess and the way she turned his emotions all topsy-turvy. For him to sort things out was going to take some time, and he figured the best way to do that was not to avoid Tess, as he'd originally considered doing, but to face her head-on. It was, after all, what his dad had raised him to do. Something he'd been taught his entire life. *Face your problems, son,* Tom Darland always said. *Don't let fear get in your way, or it'll overcome you and you won't be worth one spit in the dust.*

If Tess wasn't exactly a problem, she was the next closest thing. Sure, a lot of guys wouldn't see her that way at all, and would likely call Wade crazy for looking at Tess as such. But then, a lot of guys weren't in his shoes.

His mom and dad had never been the sort of partners he and Deidra had been. With their opposite ways of thinking, Ruthie Darland had never been truly happy as a rancher's wife. She was the one ultimately responsible for the recent subdividing of the family ranch, which had broken Wade's heart and accounted for much of the animosity between him and his mom. Deep down, he knew his mother's pressure to subdivide bothered his dad, as well. It wasn't the first time Tom and Ruthie had butted heads as a result of their opposing views, causing family strife when Wade was younger. Therefore he'd made sure when he married that it was to the sort of woman he had a lot in common with. The sort he could spend an entire lifetime with on an even keel.

Only, that lifetime had been cut short by a split decision and an oncoming train.

Shaking away the thought, Wade carried the box of bridles outside. He'd drop them off at Lloyd's, then come back to the ranch to see about sorting and gathering some of the cattle he planned to sell at auction on the upcoming weekend.

From around the corner of the house he heard the growls of his red heelers, Smokey and Bandit, followed by a volley of barking. Their signal that they'd found something worth chasing. Frowning, Wade set the box on the porch rail and started down the steps just in time to see what looked like an orange rat streak across the yard. It ran for the driveway, both dogs hot on its tail. Moving like a paper cup tossed on the wind, the scrawny cat bolted across dirt and gravel and dived underneath Wade's pickup truck.

With a sharp whistle, he called both dogs to heel. Reluctantly, they came to him, stubby tails wagging. Their red-and-white mottled coats were streaked with a stickiness that told him they'd been out in the sagebrush.

"What are you two troublemakers doing?" he asked. "Huh?" Frowning, he made his way across the driveway toward the pickup and knelt beside one front wheel. "Get back!" He waved an arm at Smokey and Bandit as the dogs hovered nearby, muscles tense, expressions alert. They backed off, though not far. Bracing one hand on the wheel well and the other on the ground, Wade peered underneath the Ford but didn't see a thing.

Then he heard it. Coming from the engine compartment. "Meow!"

"Ah, geez." Cats were not on his list of favorite animals. Macy had begged him for a kitten on more than one occasion, but he'd countered every one of her reasons for owning one with a reason not to.

Cats were good mousers.

Traps worked just as well and you didn't have to feed them.

Traps didn't purr, and you couldn't cuddle them.

No, but they also did not claw furniture or poop in the barnyard.

For some reason, Macy could not grasp the validity of that argument, considering that the cows and horses did their share of waste elimination and then some. Wade hadn't been able to find the exact words to explain. There was just something sneaky about the way a cat did what it did. Pooping in some obscure corner you'd never notice, then covering it up with dirt so you didn't realize until you were walking in the vicinity and it was too late.

"Come on, cat, I don't have time for this," Wade grumbled, rising to his feet. He banged on the Ford's fender. "Get out of there! Doggone it." He couldn't go anywhere until the critter decided to climb out. If he started the engine...well, there was no way he'd do that. He might not be fond of cats, but he certainly had no desire to see one hurt. Smokey and Bandit weren't helping matters any. They'd stepped closer once more, eager to give chase. "Go lie down," he commanded, pointing firmly toward the porch. Looking highly disappointed, the heelers trotted over to lie in the shade near the lilac shrubs.

Wade unlatched the Ford's hood, raised it and peered inside. At first he saw nothing. Then he spotted a scrawny, yellow-orange tail poking out from the midst of his engine. "Kitty, kitty," he called. "Hey, you. Come out of there." He leaned in and reached to touch the cat's tail. It gave a plaintive meow, then jerked its tail out of sight.

"Where'd you go?" Wade called, leaning to check once more under the truck. A tiny head with gremlin-size ears poked out from underneath the engine. Huge, green eyes blinked at him.

"Meee-ooow." For such a little mouth, the kitten had a big voice.

Its pitiful cry made him feel momentary guilt for disliking those of its species. But the next several minutes brought him nothing but frustration at his inability to coax the kitten from the truck's engine. He tried talking to it, rapping on the fenders, the bumper. He even honked the horn. But the little varmint refused to leave what it perceived as a haven.

Wade sank against the driver's seat. "Great! How the heck am I supposed to get to town now, cat? Huh?" And what in thunder was he doing talking to a cat, for heaven's sake? He'd obviously been hanging around Tess way too much. He thought about all the cats he'd seen at her place, hanging out on the porch, around the yard and in the house. He supposed he could call and ask her to come help him get the kitten out, but the prospect of doing so left him feeling like a complete idiot. He could imagine her reaction. He handled bulls that weighed two thousand pounds, but he couldn't manage to manipulate one itty-bitty kitten that probably weighed three pounds soaking wet?

The picture that came to mind of Tess having a good laugh at his expense turned his irritation to anger.

"Cat! Either you come out right now, or I'm going to let Smokey and Bandit finish what they started." Again, guilt plagued him as he spoke. He could never, ever follow through on his threat.

Wade sighed and climbed from the truck once more. "Kitty," he said in a softer tone. "Hey, I didn't mean it, okay? But I really need to get to town." Frustrated, he leaned against the fender and folded his arms. What did cats like? He thought about television commercials he'd seen, involving kittens and balls of yarn. He didn't have any yarn, but maybe the kitten wouldn't notice the difference between that and baling twine.

Wade headed for the barn and returned with a length of the bright-orange nylon string in his hand. "Hey, kitty, look here." He dragged it across the ground beneath the truck's bumper. "Come on out of there and get the string, you dad-gummed pain-in-the-butt cat." He drew the twine across the dirt, then moved around behind the Ford's front wheels and repeated the motion.

Suddenly, the kitten's yellow-orange face poked out from on top of the Ford's drive shaft, followed quickly by the ratlike body as the kitten pounced. Wade pulled the string away from the truck, then snagged the critter with one hand as it darted after the bait. "Aha! Gotcha, you rascal." He tucked it in the crook of his arm. The kitten meowed and squirmed, then stared at him with those big green eyes and blinked.

Green eyes.

Like Tess.

Oh, brother. His brain had to be totally addled now, thinking like that.

"You sure caused a lot of trouble for something so tiny," he said. Forget three pounds. He doubted it even weighed that. It looked as though it hadn't seen a decent meal in ages. Wade's heart gave that strange little hitch it had earlier, when he'd stopped the dogs from chasing the kitten. He couldn't stand seeing any living creature suffer, even though he wasn't an animal nut like Tess. He sighed. "You want a bowl of milk, kitty? I guess we've got time for that, but then I'm taking you straight to Tess. She can put you in her yard with all those other critters she harbors."

The kitten hooked its claws into his skin and purred.

"Ow!" Wade pried the animal loose and headed for the porch, casting a wary gaze toward his dogs. They rose to their feet and sniffed eagerly, necks stretched in an attempt to investigate at closer range. The cat dug its claws in once more and scrambled onto Wade's shoulder. He let out a colorful expletive and managed to stop the kitten just short of hooking itself around his neck. "Damn, but you're a quick little bugger. Get back, Smokey. Bandit."

He made his way into the kitchen and found a cereal bowl. Silent witnesses to his betrayal of sensibility, the red heelers watched through the screen as Wade poured milk over some dog kibble and let the starving kitten go at it. The animal ate so fast its breath came in gasps.

"Slow down, pardner. You're gonna choke." He reached to stroke it with one finger, fascinated by its ability to wolf down the dog food so quickly when its mouth was no bigger than a minute. His ministrations were rewarded with a warning growl that rumbled up from deep within the kitten's chest. Wade laughed. "Feisty little thing, aren't you? Yep, you and Tess will get along just fine."

TESS SIGHED and ran her hands underneath the water in the feed store's bathroom sink. She planned on taking a long lunch so she could meet with Bailey and stop by the County Care Facility, as well. She'd make the time up to her dad by coming back and working until closing so he could go home early.

She had an hour before she was supposed to meet Bailey. From the freezer in the back room, Tess took the small container of ice cream she'd saved from her party. After stuffing the ice cream into a paper bag with an ice pack to keep it cold, Tess added a plastic spoon, then headed outside to her truck. Today just wouldn't seem like her birthday without her seeing her mom.

For once, spring had actually come with a vengeance this year in late April, and now with May nearing an end, the temperature had already risen into the high seventies. The noon sun seemed to burn her shadow into the blacktop as Tess walked across the parking lot and climbed into her pickup. Minutes later, she pulled up in front of the County Care Facility and made her way inside. Raelene sat in her usual place in the chair near the window, staring outside, her expression blank.

"Hi, Mama. How are you feeling today?" Tess walked over to kneel beside the chair.

Raelene said nothing for a moment. Then she turned to look at Tess and frowned. "Where's Charlie?"

Tess had never met the man who would have been her uncle, and didn't care to from the things Rae had told her of him long ago. Older than Raelene by four years, he'd taken great pleasure in tormenting her when they were kids, pulling cruel pranks such as letting Rae's goats out into the road just before dark. Making her frantic. Tess wondered why Rae's mind would lead her to think of him now.

"He's not here, Mama. Don't worry." Tess folded her hand over her mother's. "I brought you some ice cream. It's homemade."

"No." Rae shook her head. "My goats can't sleep."

Tess took a deep breath. "The goats are fine. I promise." She rubbed her mother's hand in a soothing gesture, then removed the ice cream from the paper sack. "Look here. This is so good. You're going to love it."

"No!" Rae jerked away, her features screwed up in a petulant scowl. She moved her mouth as though groping for words that wouldn't come. "That shed has goat hair now." She emphasized the words by shaking one fist. Her eyes locked on Tess's, and Tess knew that whatever her mother was trying to say made perfect sense to her, and that she was now frustrated because Tess didn't get it. Rae stared at Tess as though she were the one with the mental block. As though to say, *What is wrong with you? Why won't you listen to me?*

It broke her heart. The alternative world her mother lived in was so far removed from the here and now. At times like this, she felt helpless to do anything to calm and comfort, to make her mom feel better.

She reached for a second chair that stood near the bed and scooted it over to sit in front of Rae. "Come on now, Mama. Everything's okay. Just relax. Here, try a little ice cream." After opening the lid on the

plastic container, she spooned a small portion from
it and held it out in offering.

Rae appeared not to see it at all. She let out a
frustrated sound and reached out to grip Tess by one
braid. Wincing, Tess lowered the spoon and took
hold of her braid above Rae's grasp. "Mama, let go.
It's okay."

Rae's lips curled in a snarl, and spittle dribbled
down her chin. Tess dropped the ice cream and
spoon into the paper sack and used both hands to
try to disengage her hair from Rae's hand. As she
did so, she turned slightly. And from her peripheral
vision caught sight of Wade. Standing in the doorway.

Her heart jumped and her breath lodged in her
throat. How had he known she was here? Better still,
what was *he* doing here? She didn't want him to see
her mother this way. "Wade." She gasped his name
in a combination of pain and surprise as Raelene
yanked so hard on Tess's hair it made her eyes water.

In three long strides, Wade was in the room, be-
side her chair. "Let me help." He spoke softly.
"Raelene," he said. "Can you take my hand, hon?
Come on." He held it out in offering.

Rae stopped struggling and looked at him. Her
expression full of suspicion.

"Come on," he repeated. "You don't want to
pull Tess's hair that way, now, do you?"

"She doesn't know what you're saying." Anger
welled inside Tess. He had no right. No business
being here.

But he ignored her. "Rae, take my hand."

Her mom let go of her hair so abruptly that Tess

nearly tumbled out of the chair. At the same time, Raelene bolted upright, shoulders hunched in a defensive posture.

"Not this dance day!" She reached for a serving tray that rested on the bedside table beneath a plastic pitcher of water.

Before Tess could so much as rise from the chair, Rae lifted the tray, sending the pitcher flying. Water spewed everywhere as Rae flung the tray with more strength than Tess would have believed possible. Straight at Wade.

Taken by surprise, he ducked, too late. The tray struck him in the face, hitting his forehead and the bridge of his nose. With a grunt, he stumbled backward, up against the bed rail. He shot out his hand to catch his balance and banged into the rail, rattling the entire bed.

Molly entered the room as Rae went into a screaming frenzy. Swearwords flew from Raelene's mouth with enough force to make a grown man blush. Before her illness, she had never in her life uttered a cuss. Another unexplained affliction of her disease.

"What on earth?" Molly's eyes darted from Tess to Wade and finally settled on Rae as a second nurse entered the room. "Raelene, calm down, dear." Molly spoke, moving toward Tess's mom. "You're okay."

Tess stood, hand clamped over her mouth, watching the scene before her unfold. Feeling as though she wasn't even a part of it. How had this happened?

Before Molly could reach her, Rae snatched up the pillow from her bed and threw it at Wade. It hit his cowboy hat, knocking it askew as he backed away from the bed, hands raised to fend off her wild-eyed attack.

Rae continued to scream a mixture of nonsensical and swearwords, and the stench of urine filled the air as her bladder released into the adult diapers she wore.

Sick—not with embarrassment, not with shame, but with sorrow—Tess turned and fled.

CHAPTER NINE

FEELING LIKE A TRAITOR, but unable to stop herself, Tess ran down the hallway to the exit. Outside, she leaned against her truck, head lowered, and let the dizziness claim her. With her hands braced on the hood, she sucked in air, her breath coming in rapid gasps. What the hell had just happened?

Behind her, she heard the sound of cowboy boots on concrete. Then Wade's arms were around her, pulling her against him. "Tess," he soothed. "My God, I am so sorry. I didn't mean to upset your mom." He squeezed her tight, his body snugged next to hers, his chin resting on top of her head. Her cap was gone. How she'd lost it she had no idea.

Tess shook as though someone had thrown her into a deep freeze. The sun burned down on her bare arms, and still she shook. She tried to speak, but the words wouldn't come. Nothing. Not one coherent thought.

"Let it out," Wade whispered against her hair. "Just let it out, Tess."

"No," she choked. She would not cry. She hated crying, had done so much of it in the past.

"Yes." He spun her around, hands on her shoulders, and looked deep into her eyes. "You don't have to be embarrassed. Not to cry, and not of your mother's behavior."

Tess shook her head. "You don't get it." She coughed over the lump in her throat, fighting to keep her voice steady. "I'm not embarrassed *by* her. I'm embarrassed *for* her." Her throat burned. On fire. Like her eyes. "If you could only know what she used to be like. What she used to...used to—" She broke off.

Wade wrapped her in his embrace once more, pulling her against his chest. "Let go," he insisted. "I'll hold you." He rubbed her back. "I'll hold you, Tess, for as long as you want."

Sobs racked her body and suddenly the tears came, spilling down her cheeks to dampen the front of Wade's shirt. Knowing people on the street must be staring, but powerless to care and unable to stop, Tess cried. And cried. Until she could cry no more. Until she felt that her very soul was dry and empty. Void of emotion, void of everything.

Her sobs tapered into hiccups, and she took a deep breath. Mortified beyond belief, she still somehow experienced a form of relief as she looked into Wade's eyes. What she saw there, though, left her shaky all over again. Normally, he watched her with either irritation or desire or sometimes a distance she couldn't quite comprehend. But now he watched her with genuine compassion, and something else. Something she'd often seen in her dad's eyes when he looked at her mother.

Certain her release of emotion had left her half out of her mind, Tess tried to draw away from him, but Wade held on to her, his arms looped gently around her waist.

"That feels better, doesn't it?" he asked. He

reached up to wipe her tear-dampened cheeks with one thumb. "Letting it all out."

In a way, he was right. Still, a deep-down sadness that no amount of tears could erase would not leave her. "It's just so unfair," she grumbled. "For something so horrible to afflict such a wonderful person. Yet you'd think I'd be used to it by now."

Wade chewed his bottom lip, hesitating as though seeking the right words. "How could you ever be expected to 'get used to' your mom's condition? Tess, sometimes black things eat us up inside. Dark, horrible things that we can't seem to get rid of. It's good to let them out whatever way you can." His voice grew soft, almost a whisper. "I know. I've been there."

Tess shivered. She could tell he was remembering Deidra and the awful way she'd died—trying to beat a train across the railroad tracks. An error in judgment and timing that had cost her her life. The town had been abuzz over the tragedy for weeks, speculating.

"Yes, you sure have," Tess said. "Want to talk about it?"

He raised his eyebrows. "I thought maybe you'd like to talk about what just happened in there." He gave a half nod over his shoulder toward the building.

She sighed. "Not particularly." She pressed her fingers against her temples, and felt the familiar throb that so often became a headache. The crying had provided only so much release. Something still churned deep inside her. Black, dark, hopeless, just as Wade said. Something that told her Rae's condition would only grow worse from here on out.

How could it not? No matter how much she wanted to deny the fact, there it was.

And for a split second she understood why Zach had chosen not to come visit any longer. But as soon as the thought was there, Tess pushed it away. *No.* She would never, ever stop coming. Never abandon Rae, no matter how bad she got.

"All right," Wade said. "We'll talk about anything you want. Let me buy you a cup of coffee."

"I'm supposed to meet Bailey in a while for lunch." Tess glanced at her watch. "But I guess I have a little time yet." She hesitated. She couldn't leave without making sure that her mother was all right. "Just give me a minute or two, okay?"

Wade nodded, and Tess went back into the County Care Facility, still trembling. In her mother's room, she found Molly sitting at Raelene's bedside. Rae lay on her back, staring up at the ceiling. Looking at nothing.

Molly gestured for Tess to come nearer. "Are you all right, dear?" she asked. The concern in her eyes left Tess feeling like a heel for having run out the way she had.

She nodded. "I'm okay. I had to make sure Mom was, too."

"She'll be fine. We gave her something to calm her. Judy will be back in just a minute and we'll get her cleaned up."

Tess swallowed over the lump in her throat. She longed to touch her mother, to caress her arm and reassure her, but was afraid to upset her all over again. "I'm going to leave for a while," she said. "But I'll be back later."

"That's fine," Molly said. "You go on, and don't worry now. We'll take good care of her."

"I know you will." Tess patted Molly's arm for lack of being able to hug her mother. "Thanks, Molly."

She left the room and strode quickly down the hall, feeling at more of a loss than she had in a long time. Her mother's vacant stare haunted her as she stepped outside and made her way to where Wade stood waiting.

"Everything okay?" he asked. She nodded, and he slipped his arm around her shoulder and steered her toward his truck. "Maybe you'd like something stronger than coffee."

"I don't drink anything stronger than Coors Light," she said, "and it's too early in the day for that."

He shrugged. "That's not what I had in mind, anyway."

"Oh?"

"Uh-uh. I was thinking you probably had some mean, nasty carrot juice or something in your refrigerator."

Tess wished she could smile. Wanted to.

"Come on," he said. "I see the corners of your mouth moving." He traced them lightly with one fingertip, making her shiver inside. "That's a smile I see trying to fight its way out. I know it."

She glared at him. "Wade, I'm not a little kid."

"No, but you look like one, with those cute pigtails." He winked at her. "I kind of liked the way you wore your hair the other night." He waggled his fingers in the air, as though demonstrating. "Down, all long and silky."

He couldn't have surprised her more if he'd suddenly announced that he'd decided to become a vegetarian. Wade Darland, cattleman and macho-cowboy deluxe. Paying her a compliment on her hair. But he'd also said she looked like a kid. Was that the way he really saw her? Smugness filled her: not if the kisses he'd given her the other night were any indication.

"Carrot juice, huh?" Tess retorted. "Think you could stand some?"

He pursed his mouth in deep thought. "Straight up, or with a chaser?"

"A chaser. Pineapple guava."

"Ack." He clutched his hands to his heart. "That stuff'll kill you, you know."

She huffed out a half laugh. "You think so?"

"I know so." He opened the truck door for her. "Just ask this little guy. I bet he'll tell you his drink of choice is milk."

Tess's jaw dropped. A tiny orange tabby kitten scrambled out of a box of bridles centered on the seat of the truck. Belatedly, Tess realized the Ford was parked under the cool sanctuary of a shade tree, with both side windows as well as the back sliding one cracked open for air. The kitten's plaintive meow pulled at Tess's heartstrings as it raced over to her. It sank its tiny claws into the front of her overalls and scrambled to her shoulder.

"Poor baby," Tess cooed. "You're so skinny. Wade, where in the world…what on earth are you doing with a kitten?"

"I see my reputation precedes me," Wade said. "And the rumors are true. I don't like cats." He frowned at the box of bridles, then reached over and pulled out a leather rein. The end was damp and chewed, marked by the kitten's sharp teeth. "And it's no wonder." He glared at the yellow-orange tabby.

"Then what is this one doing in your truck?"

"Smokey and Bandit chased it up into my engine compartment."

"Smokey and Bandit?"

"My red heelers."

Tess felt a smile curve her lips. And here he'd teased her about Duke and John Wayne. But of course, she'd started it.

"You have dogs named Smokey and Bandit?"

Wade's scowl disappeared and his face reddened. "Well. Yeah. I've always been a Jerry Reed/Burt Reynolds fan."

"So, your dogs chased the kitten. But I still don't see why you have it in your truck." Oh, this was fun. Making him squirm. Mister I-Can't-Stand-Cats. Who appeared to have rescued one.

"It's a long story," he said. "Wanna hear it over a guava-carrot-coffee?"

She laughed. "You're crazy."

"Uh-huh." Wade nodded and shut the pickup's door behind her after she climbed onto the seat. Then he spoke to her through the crack of the open window. "And the nuttiest thing about it is, I'm beginning to get a little crazy over you, cowgirl."

With that, he strode around to the driver's side, climbed in and fired up the engine.

As they pulled away, Tess sat clutching the kitten to her chest. Feeling as though she'd been bowled down with a power mower. One driven by a hazel-eyed cowboy who never ceased to amaze her.

UPON TESS'S INSISTENCE, Wade drove to the burger joint at the edge of town. Though he'd teased her about her carrot juice, he'd actually wanted to take her someplace for something to drink, to spend a little quiet time with her. He'd hoped she'd open up to him and talk about what had happened back at the nursing home. He also had something he wanted to give to her. Something he'd purchased yesterday on a whim, and had hidden in his glove compartment.

But Tess was worried the kitten would get too hot waiting in the truck and had instead suggested they get something cold at the drive-up window. Once they had two large to-go cups of iced tea with lemon, they headed for Tess's place. She'd said she had enough time to take the kitten home before meeting Bailey for lunch. Hiding his disappointment at not being able to spend more time with her, Wade sipped his tea.

"How did you come to stop by the County Care Facility, anyway?" Tess asked abruptly.

Wade thought he detected a note of defensiveness in her tone, though her expression remained neutral. He wished she would have stuck to joking around with him. He shrugged. "It wasn't planned. I was actually on my way to the feed store to bring you the kitten and your dad those bridles." He nodded toward the box on the seat between them. "I saw your truck in the nursing-home parking lot and decided to stop." Silently, he denied that his primary reason for doing so had been to see Tess. He could have just as easily left the kitten with Lloyd at the store.

But he'd had another reason for stopping, as well.

A natural curiosity to see Tess's mom. He couldn't help but wonder what she was like, and what challenges Tess faced in helping look after her. Now he knew.

"I also wanted to meet your mom," he said.

Immediately, Tess's expression grew completely sober. "Why?" she challenged. "Was it morbid curiosity?"

"No." He glared at her, irritated both by her accusing tone of voice and his own inner one that said her words were half true. "I just wanted to see her, Tess. I know your dad pretty well, but I'd never met Raelene." He softened his tone. "Look, I'm sorry I stopped by uninvited. I never gave it much thought. I didn't mean to scare her."

Tess sipped from her straw, then twirled her cup between her palms. The kitten did gymnastics on her lap, twisting and turning in an attempt to investigate the straw's origin. It tapped the cup's plastic cover with its paws, and Tess reached absentmindedly to stroke the tabby's fur.

"I know you didn't," she said. She looked as though she was struggling for the words to explain her thoughts and feelings. There was no need. He'd believed her when she'd told him she wasn't ashamed of her mother. Though he didn't quite grasp her reasoning in not wanting him to see Raelene, he supposed he could understand if Tess wanted to keep family matters private.

He never should have intruded. It was one more reminder that his life and Tess's were separate entities.

Minutes later Wade pulled up the driveway to her house and parked near the porch.

"I'll just be a minute," Tess said, climbing from the truck with the kitten in one hand and her tea in the other. Her dogs circled her, happily wagging their tails. The yellow tabby hissed and spat at them, puffing up its fur, clinging to the front of Tess's overalls. It tried to hide beneath her braids. Tess gently scolded the dogs, telling them to get back. Duke responded by turning his attention away from the kitten to bark at Wade through the open window of the Ford.

"Yeah, I love you too, buddy," Wade mumbled to the black-and-tan shepherd. He watched Tess climb the porch steps and go inside the house without bothering to unlock the door, which meant she'd left it open.

For some reason, that bothered him. Ferguson and its surrounding farm and ranch lands was a relatively safe place to live; still, you never knew. Macy had been the victim of a carjacking last year at the hands of a local resident, Lester Godfrey, and to this day Wade knew the incident had left him overcautious. He kept his doors locked. For the safety of his kids. Tess ought to lock hers, too. He eyeballed Duke, who sat staring him down, growling at him.

Then again, she did have her dogs. Wade watched the three of them, and chuckled at the antics of the miniature pinscher, who'd raised a ruckus upon their arrival. The pint-size dog now strutted across the yard marking territory, scratching grass with his hind feet as though making a statement. *I own every acre in sight, and buddy, don't you forget it.*

Tess and her critters. It seemed that she had a need to mother everything, including his kids. He still wasn't sure he'd ever be ready for that. So, what would he do if the two of them got seriously involved? If, say, he decided to forgo his resolve to be alone and give a relationship with Tess a shot? He pictured living among such an array of furry creatures and shook his head. Macy would be in paradise. Jason wouldn't have a problem with it. But the only part of it that would feel like paradise to him would be the part involving Tess.

Wade focused on her once more as she came back outside, wearing another ball cap to replace the one she'd lost during the struggle in her mother's room. He should have stopped to pick it up off the floor before he'd dashed outside after Tess, but he'd been far more worried about her than her hat. Now, as she climbed into the truck, he regretted once more that she had a lunch date with Bailey. He wanted to keep her all to himself.

"You sure you need to have lunch with Bailey?" The words came out almost of their own accord.

Tess creased her forehead. "Yes. Why do you ask?" The suspicion on her face very nearly made him laugh. She should be suspicious, all right. Because the thoughts he was thinking were surely dangerous.

"No real reason, I guess. It's just that it's so nice outside, I was hoping we could drop the bridles off at the feed store, then take a little drive."

Her suspicious expression turned to one that he couldn't quite read. Surprise? Apprehension?

He wasn't even completely sure what had made him throw out the invitation. Something about Tess led him to be spontaneous, which he normally wasn't. At least, not very often. But the prospect of a drive in the country with her had his emotions going places they shouldn't.

"Nice?" Tess said. "I'd say it's downright hot out." She quirked her mouth in that playful grin he was getting attached to. "Better than freezing cold, though, that's for sure. I'm not much on winter."

"So, do you want to go for a drive or not?" Wade asked. He didn't mean to sound abrupt, but he did. Something about Tess also made him nervous at times.

She raised one eyebrow. "Well, since you asked so sweetly..." Sarcasm laced her words.

He let out a huff of air. "Sorry. I didn't mean to sound like that."

She shrugged. "No problem. But I'm afraid I can't break my lunch date with Bailey. It's too important. And after that, I have to get back to work. I'm closing the store tonight."

"Oh." Surprised at how deeply disappointed he was, even though he knew he had plenty of work waiting for him back at the Circle D, Wade fought the urge to ask her what was so all-fired important about lunch with Bailey. "How about a rain check?"

"On the drive?" She looked as though she was considering the invitation for a moment. Then she gave him a quick smile. "Sure. That sounds nice, Wade. Call me when you're ready."

Ready, hell. He was more than ready to spend time with her right here and now. He couldn't shake the picture of her running from the nursing home, then collapsing. She still seemed vulnerable at this very moment, her eyes puffy from crying, and the overwhelming urge to do something to put her mind in a happier place wouldn't leave him. But what could he say? Tess was a grown woman, used to handling matters herself. He supposed he'd just have to wait.

Minutes later she climbed from the truck as he pulled up in the feed store's parking lot. She lifted the box of bridles off the seat. "I can take these in for you if you'd like. Save you some time."

He started to protest. To make yet another excuse to linger. Then decided he'd already acted lovesick enough for one day. "That's fine. Thanks. And tell your dad thanks, too."

"No problem." She waved. "See you at 4-H Thursday."

"Yeah. See ya." Then he remembered the gift. Maybe she wouldn't like it. Maybe he'd been out of line in even buying it. "Hey, Tess."

She hesitated with her hand on the truck door, ready to swing it shut.

Before he could lose his nerve, Wade leaned across the seat and popped open the glove compartment. "Happy birthday," he said, handing her the wrapped package. He and the kids had given her a gift certificate to the huge pet warehouse in Glenwood Springs at her party the other night, but he'd later wished he'd gotten her something a little more personal. Especially after the kisses they'd shared. Hence the impulse buy.

The pleased expression on her face—at his knowing that he'd remembered what today was—gave Wade an equally pleased feeling deep down in his chest when she took the package from him.

"Thanks," she said. "But you didn't need to do that. The gift certificate was wonderful."

"I wanted to," he said. Unable to drum up enough nerve now that he'd actually handed her the present to stay and watch her open it, Wade shot Tess a lighthearted wink. "See you later, cowgirl." His gift wasn't a diamond ring, but it was more personal than a pet-supply certificate.

Tess shut the door and waved. "Sure."

He watched her enter the store, but couldn't bring himself to drive away. She came back out, minus the box of bridles, and climbed into her truck, clutching the gift box. She looked over at him as though surprised to see him still sitting there in the parking lot. Wade shook the mental fog from his mind.

You'd think he'd be too old to let a woman tie him all up in knots. Apparently not.

After putting the pickup in reverse, he backed out of the parking space. His thoughts led to what had happened at the nursing home. Though he'd been in Rae's room only briefly, he'd seen that Tess didn't resemble her in any way; she looked more like Lloyd. He'd also seen Tess coping with her mother's condition, and had realized she must have gone through that kind of thing a very long time.

He thought of Deidra's accident. So foolish. So unnecessary.

But at least she had gone quickly. There was death, and then there was lingering pain that felt like death. He could only imagine how much of that Tess had suffered.

Feeling bad for having ever thought her silly and immature, Wade headed for home—knowing the new light he saw her in still didn't change anything as far as their differences went. Knowing that his thoughts were about to lead him straight into a fool's zone. But nonetheless unwilling to change his mind about getting romantically involved with Tess.

TESS RESISTED opening the gift box until she'd pulled into the parking lot of Rosarita's. What on earth had possessed Wade to give her a second present? She'd been speechless when he'd handed it to her out of the clear blue. Now, heart pounding, she pulled the shiny bow from the silver paper and lifted the lid off the small box. Earrings. They couldn't have been more perfect if she'd picked them out herself. Sterling-silver horse heads centered in a pair of horseshoes.

Tess closed the box. The earrings looked expensive. She couldn't possibly accept them. She'd give them back the very next time she saw him.

Then she opened the box again and looked at the earrings once more. When had he noticed she had pierced ears? She rarely wore earrings, but when she did, she loved Western and animal-themed jewelry. She'd had on a pair of cat-shaped earrings the night of her birthday party.

Tess's face heated as she recalled the way Wade had kissed and nibbled her earlobe on the porch swing. Oh, yeah, he'd most definitely been in a position to notice then. She sighed and fingered the earrings. They were beautiful, and the thoughtfulness of his gift took her more by surprise than she supposed it should have. Surely he didn't mean anything intimate by giving them to her. But then again...

Torn between returning them and keeping them, Tess placed them in her glove compartment and went inside the restaurant. Bailey showed up minutes later, and her idea turned out to be better than anything Tess had hoped for. She explained how the bank could bestow a certain number of grants on nonprofit organizations each year, and offered one to Tess to help fund Western Colorado Horse Rescue. All Tess had to do was come into the bank and fill out the paperwork. The grant would give her enough money to keep the horse sanctuary going for a little while.

In addition, Bailey suggested holding a fundraiser of some sort, and volunteered to help out as much as she could. Tess admitted she'd been thinking of doing just that, and thanked Bailey both for the grant and for her offer of help. On the way back from Rosarita's, Tess stopped by the County Care Facility to check on her mom once more. She still felt horrible for having run out on her earlier.

"She's resting comfortably," Molly assured her as Tess walked beside the nurse, down the hallway toward Raelene's room. "It's hard to say what sets them off sometimes." She shook her head sadly. "Alzheimer's is such a difficult condition to cope with. As I've said so many times, I admire your dedication to your mother." She gave Tess's arm a sympathetic pat. "I see a lot of things in my line of work. And a lot of variations in the same disease."

"I imagine so," Tess murmured.

"At any rate," Molly said, "I believe Rae's asleep, but you can go in if you want."

Tess shook her head. "I think we've all had enough excitement for one day. I'll just look in on her real quick, then go."

"All right— Oh, your ball cap is up at the nurses' station. We found it on the floor after you left."

"Thanks."

Molly strode off, and Tess made her way to Rae-lene's room and peered inside. Her mother lay in bed with the covers pulled up around her shoulders, her head lolling to one side of the pillow. Tess fought the urge to step deeper into the room and smooth the hair back from Rae's forehead. She hated what had happened earlier, what Wade had witnessed, and again irritation bubbled up inside her.

Why *had* he wanted to see her mom? He'd acted casual about it, made it seem like nothing. Yet she couldn't help but wonder. He'd said he'd been passing by and had stopped on the spur of the moment. But somehow, she didn't believe that. And suddenly she could understand how Wade had felt when she'd pressured him on personal matters regarding Macy.

She turned and walked back down the hall to the nurses' station to retrieve her favorite cap. Then she headed for the feed store, glad to lose herself in the everyday routine of work.

WADE HAD JUST FINISHED replacing the hinges on the paddock gate next to the barn when the school bus pulled into the yard. Jason bounded down the bus steps, Macy right on his heels, and for a moment, Wade was overcome by the sight of his two children racing toward him in the afternoon sun. When had they gotten so tall? Jason seemed to gain an inch every time Wade turned around, yet he hadn't really noticed until now that Macy wasn't far behind her brother. And her cheekbones had become more pronounced lately, as her face lost its baby fat and molded into the lines of the young woman she'd soon be.

Shaking off the melancholy thoughts, Wade let the kids' laughter flow over him like a pleasant breeze. "Hey, you two. How was school?"

"Great!" Macy said, clutching her backpack as it slipped off her shoulder. "Can I go riding with Becky? Her mom can drop her off here at four-thirty, and Jason said it's okay with him if she rides Spur."

"That's nice of you, son."

Jason shrugged. "I don't mind." Then he grinned. "Macy offered to take my dish night in trade."

Wade shook his head. "Scratch my compliment on that one, then." He feigned a punch to Jason's shoulder, then turned to Macy. "Have you got homework?"

"Nope. Dad, there're only three days of school left."

"True. But I figured that gives your teachers a little more time to be mean to you." He reached down to rumple her hair, stilling his hand just in time. Lately, she'd started taking offense at the gesture. "What about you, Jason?" he asked, glancing at the boy.

Jason shook his head. "No homework, either." He looked at the tools lying on the ground beneath the gate. "Do you need any help, Dad?"

Having no idea why such a rush of mixed feelings came over him, Wade studied his son. He was so grown-up. And in spite of the way he sometimes taunted his sister, Jason was always willing to help out. Both kids had been his partners for a long while now, particularly since their mother's death. They'd had to grow up too quickly. Forgo childhood pleasures to a degree. Wade was gripped by an urge to slow the clock, to savor his kids before they did indeed grow up. When was the last time he'd done something fun with his son, one-on-one?

Wade cocked his hip and rested his hand on his waist. "You know what, Jason? I do need some help, but not with the gate."

"Yeah?" Jason squinted up at him against the glare of the sun.

"I was thinking about putting a line in the water. It's been a while. You wanna join me?"

Jason's eyes lit up. "Fishing? You bet!"

"Do you mind, Macy?" Wade asked. "You can come, too, but it's also okay if you ride with Becky. Just as long as you let me know where you'll be and you don't go too far. She's not had as much riding experience as you have."

"I know," Macy said. "I'd rather ride with her if you don't mind, Dad."

"That's fine." Wade bent to pick up his tools. "You two go change your clothes, then, and grab a snack. I'll be in shortly."

"Race ya!" Jason shouted, turning on his heel.

Macy sped after him toward the back door, and Wade's heart gave a happy little jump. He was a lucky man. And just as fast as that realization came, his thoughts strayed to Tess. To the way he'd held her while she cried, and how good she'd felt in his arms. He'd hated seeing her sorrow, but being there for her had felt right.

After putting the tools away, Wade found his fishing tackle in the back of the barn and readied the poles. By the time he returned to the house, Jason was already outside. Macy came out on the porch as Donna Vega's truck pulled up in the driveway. Donna let Becky out, spoke briefly to Wade, then drove away. Wade made sure the girls were safely saddled and that their destination for their two-hour trail ride was clearly mapped out before Jason and he headed for his pickup to load the fishing gear.

A short time later, they were on their way to the stream that ran down the hillside three miles up the road. Ever since the kids were old enough to hold a pole, Wade had been bringing them here. The water pooled in a quiet spot beneath the overhang of some rocks, and several boulders on the embankment made for a good place to sit and dangle a line in the water. Sighing with pleasure, Wade sank onto the rock beside his son.

"Man, this feels great," Jason said. "Why haven't we done this lately, Dad?"

Why, indeed?

It was just one more example of how the ranch work had gotten a stranglehold on him. "I don't know, son. Just lost track of time, I guess." He shot Jason a smile. "But we can change that."

"Sounds good to me." Jason threaded a neon-orange salmon egg onto his hook and cast his line out over the water. The satisfying *plop* the sinker made as it hit the surface relaxed Wade. He cast his own line a few feet away and leaned back against the rock, letting the bobber float downstream a bit. Not caring if he caught so much as one fish. Relaxing out here in the fresh air with Jason was what appealed to him more than anything.

Wade's thoughts drifted like his line in the water.

He wondered if Tess liked the earrings he'd given her. He'd find out soon enough. Tomorrow was Thursday—4-H. The prospect of seeing her again sent a pleasant warmth curling through his middle. He knew he shouldn't be thinking such things. He ought to just resign himself to accepting Tess as Macy's 4-H leader and stop dwelling on how much he enjoyed being around her. After all, he'd gone over and over this in his mind and he realized he was treading in dangerous territory.

But the desire to be near her wouldn't leave him. He watched Jason reel in his line to check the bait, then cast it out again, his movements easy, carefree. The kids meant everything to him. Why on earth should he go and upset the balance by bringing a woman into the picture? But Tess wasn't just any woman. Somehow he was sure of that. And as far as balance went— A cold hard fact hit him.

Things really weren't so balanced. He loved Jason *and* Macy. But the father-son bond he shared with Jason was different from that of father and daughter. Something was missing for Macy. The bond she should have had with her mother. Jason had him, man to man, but Macy had no woman to relate to. Wade had already known that, but somehow now the thought drove home harder than ever. Both his kids had been cheated out of their mom, but Macy most of all.

Maybe he was wrong to think that raising her and Jason by himself was enough. And maybe the sun reflecting off the water was doing crazy things to his brain, luring him with excuses to keep seeing Tess.

Jason's pole suddenly bent at the tip, and he gave it a jerk, setting the hook. "I've got one, Dad!" His eyes lit up, and he grinned as Wade quickly reeled in his own line and set down his pole.

He hurried to his son's side. "Reel him in easy. Don't let him get away."

"I won't—don't worry." Jason cranked the handle on the reel, making it spin rapidly as he pulled in the rainbow trout—a pan-size one of about twelve inches. "Wow, he's a nice fish, isn't he, Dad?"

"He sure is. Let me give you a hand." Wade grasped Jason's pole to steady it for him, allowing his son the honor of unhooking his own catch.

Jason held the fish aloft, admiring the shine of its silvery scales, marked with the metallic-like colors that gave the fish its name. Then he frowned. "Geez, I'll bet Tess wouldn't like what we're doing one bit."

Wade's jaw went slack. "What on earth made you think of that?" he asked, guilt settling in his stomach. Not at the fact that fresh trout for dinner sounded good to him, but at realizing that Tess had been on his mind most of the day, right up until a couple of minutes ago.

Jason pursed his mouth and gave him a teasing grin. "I don't know. I guess it's kind of easy to see how much you like her. And I was just thinking about 4-H. I suppose it made me think of Tess. She's a vegetarian. I heard her talking about it with some people at the barbecue."

Wade shook his head and smiled. "I guess she's entitled to her opinion. But I was looking forward to trout for supper tonight."

Jason looked at the fish. "Me, too." He walked over to his tackle box, pulled out an aluminum stringer and slipped the trout onto it. After making sure the stringer was well anchored to the bank with a pile of rocks so the fish wouldn't float away, he lowered the fish into the water.

Wade pushed away another jolt of guilt as he watched the fish swim but get nowhere. He refused to bend to Tess's way of thinking. Let her enjoy her vegetables. That was fine by him. He liked them, as well, and right now fried potatoes and onions sounded mighty tasty.

And they'd sure go good with a mess of trout.

"Guess I better get my pole back in the water," Wade said as Jason put another salmon egg on his hook. "Can't let you skunk me." He gave his son a grin, and Jason grinned back.

"We'll see about that, Dad." He cast his line into the water once more.

They'd always done this when they'd gone fishing. Competed in a friendly way to see who could get the most fish. And if one of them happened to be the only one lucky enough to make a catch or two, then the other one was "skunked" and the teasing on the ride home was merciless.

But not as merciless as the thoughts that kept coming back to haunt Wade once he settled down to fishing again.

I'll bet Tess wouldn't like what we're doing....

Damn it! When was he going to come to his senses and stop thinking of her all the time?

Wade kept an eye on his red-and-white bobber, trying to rid his mind of a picture of a plate with nothing on it but onions and potatoes.

CHAPTER TEN

DURING THE NEXT TWO DAYS, Tess kept busy not just with work but with mulling over various options in her mind for a possible WCHR fund-raiser, glad for myriad things to help distract her from the mixed feelings she had in regard to Wade.

He'd upset her showing up at the County Care Facility. Raelene's illness was private, and Tess had never taken anyone outside of family to visit her mother. But the more she thought about it, the more she wondered if Wade's intentions hadn't been totally honest and good. She just couldn't picture him harboring some morbid desire to see what it was like to have a family member with Alzheimer's.

She recalled the way he'd looked at her mom just before Rae had exploded. Not with cold curiosity but with genuine warmth and concern. He'd spoken so sweetly to her mother, and Tess knew he'd only been trying to help. He simply didn't understand the extent of Rae's illness.

Tess thought about his invitation to take her, Tess, on a drive. Excitement filled her at the thought of their being alone together. It sounded romantic and wonderful and exactly like something she ought to forget about. But she couldn't.

Would he really call her? Maybe he'd forgotten about his offer of a rain check. Tess blew a puff of air through her cheeks. She couldn't believe how much Wade was on her mind lately. This was not good! She kept telling herself that she really didn't need a man in her life. That she didn't have time. But that didn't stop her from feeling lonely at night.

A strange longing she'd never before been aware of haunted her. Frightened her. What was the matter? Had she lost her mind over a few stolen kisses? Reminding herself that there was no reason to make changes in her life, Tess focused on her normal routine.

Thursday's 4-H meeting was a book meeting—one where the kids worked on their record books and gave an oral report on how their individual projects were coming along. These meetings were held at Tess's house rather than the arena. Knowing Wade would be here in a matter of hours left her stomach in knots as she worked on her dad's accounts, then did some data processing in her home office.

The knots turned to butterflies when she heard a truck pulling into the driveway. Calling herself silly for being so nervous, Tess hurried to the open front door.

And felt her heart do a cha-cha at the sight of his black Ford.

"Hey, Tess," Macy called as she skipped toward the porch. "How's the foal?"

"Hi, Macy. She's fine. We're going to do something fun later on in the meeting that involves her."

"Oh, good," Macy said. "That'll be way better than working on our record books." She shot Tess an apologetic grin and Tess laughed.

"Too much like homework, huh?" She gave Macy a mock thump on the head.

Macy grimaced, but Tess didn't even hear her reply as she looked up into Wade's eyes. He stood at the foot of the steps, dressed in faded jeans, a dark-blue Western shirt and his battered old hat. That, dressed up or not, he could still make her heart do such crazy things was not fair. What had happened to her resolve?

"I wanted to come say hi," he said. "But I can't stay for the meeting. Jason's schedule got switched around this week, and I've got to drive him to his meeting, too."

Belatedly, Tess saw that Jason was waiting in the pickup. She waved at him and he waved back. "Oh." She tried not to sound disappointed. "Do you need me to give Macy a ride home later? Or keep her here until you're finished with Jason's meeting?"

He nodded. "Keep her here, if you like. The kids both have plans later, since tomorrow's only a half day of school, and the last one at that." He shifted from one foot to the other and slid his hands into his back pockets. "I, uh, wondered if you'd like to go on that drive we talked about. The moon's full, and I know a spot by the lake where the elk bed down at night. I thought you might like to see them."

His suggestion took her by surprise. "Elk? You want to go watch elk?"

He shrugged. "Well, if you think it's boring, we could—"

She cut him off, hiding a chuckle. "No, I don't

think it's boring at all. I'm just surprised that you'd find them interesting. I mean, they *are* animals.''

"He did rescue the kitten," Macy reminded her.

Tess had nearly forgotten the little girl was standing there. "That's right—he did," she said, enjoying the way Wade squirmed. "You don't suppose he's starting to go all soft on us, do you?"

Macy eyed her dad, hesitating as though she meant to choose her answer carefully. "Maybe I'd better take the Fifth on that one," she said.

Tess broke into laughter. "Yeah, okay."

"Hey," Wade growled. He pretended to scowl darkly at the two of them. Then his frown disappeared. "My dad and I used to hunt elk when I was a kid," he said. "But I always enjoyed watching them more than—well—you know."

Tess's smile vanished. "Hunting, huh? One more thing we disagree on, I see."

"Oh, he doesn't hunt anymore," Macy spoke up. "Do you, Dad?"

Tess wondered at the tone of Macy's comment. It was as though she was trying to make Wade look good in Tess's eyes, which took her somewhat by surprise since she'd never before seen any attempt on Macy's part to play matchmaker. Was she carrying her longing for a mother figure a step further? Or was Tess letting her imagination run away?

"No," Wade said, interrupting her musings. "I don't." But he offered no explanation to the reason behind his answer. Instead, he locked his eyes on hers. "So, do we have a date?"

"Oooh, a date," Macy teased. "I'd better go inside and leave you two alone." With a giggle, she pushed the screen open and stepped into the house.

Tess held Wade's gaze. He was unlike anyone she'd ever met, and she still wasn't sure about some of his ways. But overall, she had to admit that Wade Darland was not a bad guy to be around. Not bad at all. And suddenly, she was glad to have Macy in her corner.

Her heart skipped in her chest. *A date.*

"I reckon we do, cattleman," Tess said, affecting a cowboy drawl. One that hid the nervous hitch in her voice.

With that, she turned on her heel and headed after Macy, before she could have a chance to come to her senses and change her mind.

TESS USED the familiar routine of the 4-H meeting to keep her sanity after Wade left. With enthusiasm, she dived into the task at hand. The kids reacted with even more enthusiasm near the end of the meeting when work on their record books was complete and Tess announced a fun project: naming the orphaned filly.

She had them break into groups of three. Each group decided on a name choice, wrote the suggestion on a slip of paper and placed it in Tess's cap. When she drew the winner, Macy seemed a bit bummed that it wasn't her group's pick. But later, she admitted she really did like the one Becky's group had come up with. Chantilly.

Macy was in the barn with Tess and Becky, bottle-feeding the foal, when Wade and Jason returned. "I'm going to drop off the kids," he said, "and then I'll be back."

Tess's heart moved into double time. Macy had

told her of her overnight plans with Becky. Jason had the same with a friend of his....

It was after Wade drove away with the kids and Tess had gone back inside the house that she caught a glimpse of her reflection in the mirror over the dining-room table. Wrinkling her nose, she twisted the end of one of her braids around her finger.

I like the way your hair looked the other night.... Wade's words echoed in her mind. On sudden impulse, Tess hurried to the bathroom and grabbed her brush from the vanity. She removed the bands, then raked out the tangles. But now her hair fell in kinky waves over her shoulders—a result of the confining twists of the braids. That wouldn't do. Should she wash it? If she did, what would Wade think? Would he know she'd gone to all that trouble just for him?

Good Lord, what on earth was she doing? Behaving like a fool, that was what. If she washed and styled her hair, she might as well change her clothes, and therefore she also might as well make an announcement: *I like you, Wade. I went to all this trouble just for you. I normally don't give a fig how casual I look.*

Tess laughed and the little male kitten Wade had given her, which had curled on the vanity near the edge of the sink, looked at her as though she'd lost her mind. *Meow?* he queried.

"Exactly," Tess harrumphed. She stroked his tangerine-colored coat, and immediately thought of a cute name for him. Tangie. "Hey, Tangie, what do you think? Do I go all out, or act like I don't care?"

The kitten rolled over, grasped Tess's hand in his paws and proceeded to do battle with his back feet in a mock manner that left his claws mostly sheathed. His needle-sharp teeth, however, were another story. Tess gave him a playful scolding and set him down on the carpet. "What the hey, cat. You only live once."

Forty-five minutes later, she was dressed in a nice pair of turquoise Rockies jeans with a cream short-sleeved blouse and cowboy boots. She'd washed and blow-dried her hair, added a little makeup to finish off her appearance—along with the horseshoe earrings, which she'd decided to keep—and had just settled onto the couch with palms damp when Wade pulled into the driveway.

Deciding that playing silly games like making him come up to the door and knock wasn't her style, she rose from the couch and headed outside. A pleasant warmth curled through her when she opened the door of the Ford. He, too, had gone to more than a little trouble to clean up, and was now dressed in a blue Western shirt, crisp jeans and his best boots and black hat. The only thing marring his appearance was the small cut across the bridge of his nose, where her mom had hit him with the serving tray.

"Hey, cattleman," Tess said, climbing into the pickup. *Mercy,* he smelled even better than he looked. Mentally gritting her teeth, trying not to inhale too deeply, Tess put on a casual air and reached for her seat belt. Wade stilled her movement with a touch of his hand on her wrist, and Tess froze, looking up into his hazel eyes.

"No you don't," he said softly. "This is an official date, remember?" With that, he patted the seat near his thigh, his lips curving in a flirtatious manner that had her heart racing.

"What do you think I am?" she quipped. "A lapdog? Come here. Sit?"

He laughed, low and deep, and the sound made her skin tingle. "Not hardly, Tess." The way he said her name left her mouth dry. "You look like…mmm." He made an appreciative noise. "A vision. How'd you know I dreamed about seeing you in a pair of Rockies?"

Tess banished the voice inside her head that said she'd been foolish to dress nice for him. To dress in a way that she'd hoped—had somehow known—he'd find attractive. "What, these old things?" she teased, borrowing his line from the night he'd driven her to 4-H.

He chuckled and shook his head, then simply waited. Staring at her. His gaze warmed her as he waited. With a half sigh, half groan, Tess unbuckled her seat belt and slid over next to him, avoiding the gearshift somewhat awkwardly. She sat with her left hip near Wade's, her legs thrown over to the right of the stick shift.

"That's better." He gave her a little wink. "Don't forget to buckle up again." With that, he put the truck in reverse, causing her to have to squirm to avoid being in his way, and backed out of his parking space.

Darkness had yet to completely claim the sky as they drove down the road, but the fading light had Tess wondering if she'd made the right choice in going out to the lake with him. After all, she was sure a lot of men would automatically assume that meant sex. The problem was, she wasn't completely sure what she wanted to give him or what Wade wanted from her.

She had no doubt he was as attracted to her as she was to him, yet he wasn't the sort of man who would simply try to jump her bones the minute they were in a secluded spot in the mountains. At least, she hoped he wasn't. She'd been wrong before, but somehow, she began to relax and feel perfectly safe with Wade.

The drive to the lake took about forty-five minutes, and when he parked beside the water, with moonlight from the near-full moon reflecting off the surface, Tess's breath caught in her throat. Something stirred inside her once more as she fully realized how close she sat to Wade and how much he'd been on her mind lately. She'd even entertained the idea of making love with him. But that would be stupid. She didn't know him that well, and she'd learned long ago that staying away from men guarded more than just her body. Her heart hadn't had one single opportunity to be broken of late, and she'd do well to keep it that way.

Yet, looking at Wade, Tess was pretty sure it was far too late for that. "So," she said, desperate to rid her mind of the thoughts that whirled inside it, "where are the elk?" Her heart thudded as she unbuckled her seat belt and made a show of gazing out the passenger window, using the excuse to inch away from him.

"Mighty impatient, aren't you?" He gave her a curious look as he unbuckled his own seat belt. "Don't worry—I won't bite." He leaned his elbow on the open window. "Listen to that." Visibly relaxing, he turned to focus on the sounds around him, and Tess did the same.

Crickets. A tree frog. The splash of water as a

fish jumped somewhere out on the lake. "I love the sound," Wade said.

"Which one?" Tess asked.

"All of them. The sound of nature." He gestured, the motion all-encompassing.

Tess scooted over a little more, just enough to take herself comfortably away from the gearshift. Enough to stifle her urge to put her hand on Wade's thigh. "Me, too. But I wouldn't have thought you'd notice things like that."

"Why?" he challenged, watching her in a way that told her he was aware she'd scooted over.

She lifted a shoulder, feeling her face warm beneath his stare. "I know you like the outdoors," she said, "but I figured you'd take things like the sound of Mother Nature for granted. Part of your working-ranch landscape or something."

"No way." He shook his head. "Remember how Macy told you I don't hunt anymore?"

She nodded.

"Well, it's because I discovered that I got far more satisfaction observing the elk than stalking them. As a matter of fact, the first time I hunted with my father and he bagged a bull, I didn't much like it."

"Really?" Tess couldn't stop the challenge that rose to her lips. "How on earth is that any different from shipping your cattle off to market?"

He scowled at her. "Hey, I didn't mean for this to turn into a debate. I brought you out here to enjoy my company." His voice held a teasing note.

For once his humorous arrogance didn't annoy her. Instead, it totally defused the irritation she'd felt a heartbeat ago. She was beginning to realize that

Wade was more talk than action. The cocky front he put on was a cover-up for the softer side of him. One she was beginning to see more and more of. It was almost enough to make her entirely forget their differences.

"All right, I'll let you off the hook for now," Tess said. They sat quietly for a few minutes, staring out over the water. Tess was about to suggest that maybe the elk were a no-show, when Wade quietly raised his hand and pointed.

"There." He spoke softly. "Look."

From the thick brush surrounding the water, two cow elk emerged and walked with ears and tails flicking, toward the lake. They moved cautiously, alert for any sign of potential danger. From their vantage point across the water, they eyeballed the truck, then lowered their regal heads to drink. Minutes later, a bull joined them, his massive six-point rack catching the moonlight as he moved up beside the cows.

"He's awesome," Tess whispered. "Takes your breath away, doesn't he?" But when she glanced at Wade, he was no longer focused on the elk but on her. Tess squirmed. "What?"

He reached out and ran his hand across a strand of her hair. "He's awesome, all right. But I didn't bring you out here just to see the elk, Tess."

"No?" Her throat grew dry. God, had she misjudged him? Did he expect her to peel off her clothes and have wild sex with him? Ignoring the way that thought made her blood run cold, then hot, Tess swallowed.

"No, and I'm not talking about what you're thinking, either."

She glared at him. "What's that supposed to mean?"

He grinned, cocky again. "You know what. Don't deny it." Then he sobered. "Look, Tess, I brought you out here so we could relax and I could talk to you without interruptions." He held her gaze, his expression suddenly serious. "How's your mom, by the way? I keep thinking about what happened the other day."

Tess sighed. "She's okay. Do we have to rehash all that?"

"Not if you don't want to." He paused as though searching for exactly the right thing to say. "Actually, I wasn't trying to do that. It's just that I can't help but feel bad about upsetting your mother. I mean, I realize she was already riled before I came into the room, but I think I made things worse when all I meant to do was help. And I didn't mean to upset you, either."

Tess once again noticed the cut on his nose and instantly felt guilty. "I know that. You don't need to worry about it." She folded her hands on her knee. "I'm not going to lie to you. Having you see her that way did upset me at first. Like I said, though, it was for Mom's sake, not mine. She may not even be aware of who's watching her or who is in the room, but it still bothers me."

He held up his hand. "I understand that now, and I apologize. I should've known better than to intrude when I'm not family or anything."

Tess's pulse fluttered. "You are something," she said. "You're a good friend." *And more.* Her body warmed as she pushed away the silent admission.

"Yeah?" Wade's boyish grin was back, charming her all over again.

"Yes." Tess tried to focus on the seriousness of their conversation and not on what his smile was doing to her. "There are times when I wish I had someone other than my family to talk to about my mom's condition. And then there are times when I don't want to talk about it at all. It tears me up to see her that way."

"I understand." He reached out and rubbed her shoulder. "And whenever you want to talk, I'm here. But I promise not to intrude again."

Tess reached up and covered his hand with hers. "Thanks." Then she let go, aware that touching him could easily lead to so much more. He, too, moved his hand, and she was somewhat sorry she'd broken their connection. Trying to stay focused, she smiled. "You should've seen what Mom used to be like." The memories welled up inside her, bringing both pain and pleasure. Pain for what Rae's illness had robbed Tess and her family of, and pleasure at knowing she'd always have those memories to treasure. "She was quite the horsewoman, and totally into any sports my brothers and I participated in. Soccer, rodeo, swim team, whatever. She even talked my dad into an outdoor wedding. They rode to the park, where the ceremony was held, in a horse-drawn carriage."

Wade's lips curved. "I guess you've looked at their wedding photos quite often, huh? "

"Sure. Being a part of it was pretty special." Tess smiled. "I was her flower girl."

He seemed surprised. "Flower girl? You mean your parents had you before they got married?" He shook his head. "But that can't be. You're the youngest, so that would mean that your brothers—"

Tess cut him off with a chuckle. "No, nothing like that. Rae's our adoptive mother. She married Dad when I was six."

"Really?" His smile grew. "Well, I'll be. I never knew she wasn't your real mom."

"She is my real mom," Tess said. "In every way that counts."

"Of course she is. I just meant…well, what happened to your birth mother, if you don't mind my asking?"

"She took off when I was five." Tess could barely remember the woman, and the pain she'd left in Tess's heart had rapidly faded under the loving blanket of Rae's mothering and her father's deep devotion to his family. "I'm not sure why. Dad always told us that she wanted more from life than he could give her and that she wasn't cut out to be a mother after all. That Rae was a whole lot more suited for the job and that she was his true soul mate." Sadness pulled deep inside her. "That's the one thing that makes Mom's illness most tragic of all. My dad misses her so very, very much."

"I can sure understand that." Wade spoke softly.

Tess's heart ached. Wade must be thinking of Deidra and how much he missed her. Yet there was something in his eyes that almost led her to believe he was focused on Tess herself. Was he beginning to feel the same way about her that she was about him? Telling herself to stop reaching for things that could hurt her, Tess pushed the thought away and listened to what Wade was saying.

"I'm so sorry your mom's ill. It's got to be hard

on your entire family. And I'm sure your dad misses her something fierce.''

Without fully meaning to, Tess said what she'd been thinking. "I'm sure you miss Deidra, too.''

"I do," Wade said. "She was a good wife and a good mother. But life goes on.''

"Yes, I suppose so." Tess didn't want to think about it. Though she knew that being jealous of a dead woman was silly and childish, she couldn't help the niggling voice in her that whispered it might be nice to be a part of Wade's life, and didn't she wish she could step into Deidra's place the way Rae had stepped into her birth mother's?

Wade's reply echoed her thoughts as though he could read her mind. "At least now I can better understand where you're coming from in wanting to mother Macy.''

"How so?" she asked nervously. Surely he didn't know what she'd been thinking.

"I didn't realize you'd lost not one mother, but two.''

Relief filled her. He hadn't been able to read her mind after all. He was only comparing her childhood situation with Macy's.

Still, his comment had startled her. She'd never really thought of it that way. Had mostly thought of losing only Raelene. Her birth mother was a stranger to her. Her father hadn't even kept any photos of her, and had spoken her name only once—when he'd done his best to explain why Jackie Vega had abandoned her family. After that, he talked about her no more.

"I suppose I did," Tess said. "But really, Wade, losing my real mom—Rae—is the reason I know how lonely Macy feels at times.'' She sighed. ''I guess we've had this conversation before, haven't we?''

He nodded. ''Yep.'' They sat silently for a moment. Then he spoke as though thinking aloud. ''I guess you have something else in common with Macy.''

''What's that?''

''You lost your mom to something that is hard to understand, and so did she.''

She waited, wondering where he was headed with this conversation.

Wade's expression grew sullen. ''Even though some folks speculated that Deidra simply didn't hear the train coming until it was too late, that's not what happened. According to the police report, witnesses said she tried to beat the train across the tracks.'' He gazed off into the distance. ''I'll just never understand why. What on earth made her risk losing her life that way?'' The sorrow on his face tugged at Tess's heart. ''Deidra lost it all in one foolish, split-second decision. Our life together, the kids…'' He let the words trail away.

''Wade, I'm so sorry.'' Tess laid her hand on his knee. She'd never thought about Deidra's accident in that way. The extra burden it placed on Wade made her ache for him all the more. ''Losing a loved one is painful, no matter if it's to death, illness or abandonment. My mother isn't dead, but her mind pretty much is. Some days seeing her so ill is like watching her die over and over again.''

Wade covered her hand with his, and the sorrow in his eyes faded, replaced by something that left Tess's heart racing anew. ''I'm glad we had this talk,'' he said. ''I think it helps us both understand each other a little better.''

Tess nodded. ''I'm glad, too.''

He held her gaze. ''Actually, I've been thinking a lot about you lately, Tess.''

Her mouth went dry, and she barely kept from admitting the same. ''You have?'' The words felt thick on her tongue.

Abruptly, he moved his hand away from hers and began to pick at a loose thread on the seat of the truck. ''Yeah, and quite frankly, I don't know what to do about it.'' He gestured as though seeking the right words. ''We don't have a whole lot in common, but...'' He took a deep breath. ''Oh, hell, I might as well come right out and say it. Tess, I'm more than a little attracted to you.''

Her head swam, and she felt floaty, as if she might wake up at any moment and find herself in her bed. Dreaming. But this was all too real. ''You are?''

''Yeah, and it bothers me.''

The dreamy sensation fled. Leave it to Wade to spoil her perfect fantasy. ''Why is that?''

He gave her a helpless shrug. ''I don't really know how to act around you, Tess. One minute, you're driving me crazy with your wild ideas, and the next, I'm kissing you.'' Before she could react, he went on. ''The thing is, I've dated hardly anyone since Deidra died.''

Tess noticed the qualifying ''hardly'' and couldn't help but wonder just how many women *had* been in his life. Macy had given her the impression that Wade was a loner. Again, a feeling of jealousy—one she didn't like—overtook her.

''I can't say as I've had a wild social life myself,''

she said, determined not to let him see that his words had any effect on her one way or the other.

"I went out with a woman a few years ago," Wade said. "But she wasn't very nice to Macy and Jason." His tone said it all.

"I guess some people don't like children," Tess said. She smiled. "I put them in the same category with those who don't like animals." She pursed her lips, glad to be back to sparring with him. She enjoyed the way he shot her a teasing look.

"Hey, watch it there, cowgirl. You're accusing me wrongly. I like animals, I just value them differently than you do." He sobered. "My point is, I'm not about to let anyone hurt my kids. And since I'm sure you'd never do that, well, it sort of scares me."

"In what way?" Tess narrowed her eyes.

Wade ran his tongue across his bottom lip, and she tried not to think about the way it had felt wrapped around hers when he'd kissed her. "Knowing how much you like Macy and Jason, and how much they like you doesn't give me much of an excuse to avoid seeing you."

"Are you looking for one?" she asked, already aware of the answer. He wouldn't have brought her here to the lake just to tell her he didn't want to see her anymore. Her palms grew moist. Her body burned in anticipation. She wanted his mouth on hers. And she wanted it now.

"Not hardly," he said. He reached out quickly, his movements in sync with her thoughts, and tugged her up against him. "And that is what scares me most of all." He pressed his mouth to hers, satisfying her craving, and Tess moaned and melted into his embrace.

Their lips sought hungrily, their hands and arms reaching to pull each other even closer...stroking, petting until Tess felt her control slipping over the line. With effort, she drew back. "Slow down, cattleman. I need to catch my breath." Shaking, she scooted away once more, and Wade stared at her with a mixture of longing and frustration.

Then he took a deep breath. "You're right. We need to take it easy." He looked her up and down. "But damned if I want to. Tess, you're driving me nuts. And I really don't know what to do about it. I've never met anyone like you in my life."

"Yeah?" The one-word reply was all she could manage. Because if she let herself say anything further, she would rush into admitting something she didn't want to. Tell Wade that she, too, felt something for him that she'd never experienced before.

"Yeah. And I do enjoy being around you." As though unable to resist touching her, he traced a circle across her cheek with his thumb. "You make me want to get to know you a whole, whole lot better, if you catch my drift. But I'm not so sure that's smart."

Tess suppressed the pleasant shiver that raced up her spine. "I can relate to that." She'd guarded her heart for a long while. Now was not the time to be rash. "Just for the record, I don't feel that my life is lacking in any way." Somehow, with her sitting here next to Wade, her lips still warm and wet from his kisses, the declaration didn't ring as true as it once had.

"Neither do I," he said. "At least, I didn't. Until lately."

His admission took her by surprise. She knew he was attracted to her, but Tess wasn't sure she was ready for where this conversation was headed.

She waited silently. Unable to say anything to him because his thoughts paralleled hers so closely it left her shaken. *What was the problem?* her inner voice demanded. *Why not just go for it? Caution be damned.*

But she knew the answer. It was because she cared more for Wade than she'd ever intended that she needed to hold back. She'd given her heart too quickly, which wasn't wise. He was right. They didn't have a whole lot in common other than their physical attraction, and she wasn't so certain he wasn't simply reaching out for a mother figure for his kids. Maybe all the things she'd said to him about Macy had finally sunk in.

Or maybe she was so confused she was grasping at straws.

"I'd like to keep seeing you, Tess." Both his tone and his expression were serious, causing her mind to race. "But I can't promise where it will lead. I don't know what I'm feeling for sure, and I'm not positive this is the wisest thing to do." He moved close to her once more, and this time his kiss was soft, gentle. "I hope you'll say yes. I need to be with you, to give us some time to see what happens. Because I'm really beginning to hate it when you're not around."

"Me, too," Tess murmured. Still, her stubborn inner self continued to fight the urge to give in to him. Why was she reluctant?

Her head swam. Her sensible side told her to say no. Tell him this was it. That after tonight, they had to remain strictly friends.

"So, will you keep seeing me?" Wade asked. The expression on his face reminded her of a boy asking her out on a date.

But there was nothing boyish about the man sitting next to her, and Tess kicked her sensible side to the curb. Closing her eyes briefly, she considered the consequences of her answer before giving it. She could be opening up her heart to something she really wasn't ready for.

"Yes," she said. "I'd like that."

"Good." He stroked the hair away from her temple, and tucked a strand behind her ear. His touch felt heavenly. Tess wanted to close her eyes and lean into it. Instead, she looked at him as he studied the earring in her lobe. "You're wearing them!" he said.

"Yes. I really love them, Wade. Thank you."

"You're welcome." He admired the pair, cupping her nape to turn her head from side to side. His fingers massaged her neck, her scalp. "They look good on you." He licked his lips, then moved his hand away.

"But you really shouldn't have bought them. I almost gave them back," she confessed.

He frowned. "Why? I thought you said you liked them."

She did. Too much. And she liked him too much, as well. "No, I said I loved them." Her heart skipped a beat as her thoughts wove together. Like, love… Did she mean the earrings or Wade? Tess gave herself a mental shake. "Never mind. I just didn't want you to get the wrong idea, that's all."

"And what idea is that?"

"What we just talked about—not taking things too fast."

He nodded. "I suppose so. And on that note, why don't we head back to town before I end up doing something neither of us is ready for yet." He brushed his lips across hers once more, then put the truck in gear and pulled toward the road.

With regret humming deep inside her, Tess leaned forward and turned up the radio. Her heart hammered and her soul seemed to cry out in rhythm with the words to the Patsy Cline song that bled through the speakers.

"Crazy."

CHAPTER ELEVEN

ON THE LAST WEDNESDAY in May, Tess drove to the County Care Facility, her foot light on the gas pedal. To travel well below the speed limit on a day like today, with summer just around the corner and wildflowers blooming everywhere, was easy. Nothing beat spring on Colorado's western slope, and Tess would never tire of looking at her surroundings. In the distance, the mountains glowed with subtle color, the various greens of scrub oak, sagebrush and piñon juniper flowing down to meet grassy slopes dotted with wild daisies and Indian paintbrush.

The picturesque scenery reminded her of her night at the lake with Wade a few days ago, which had given Tess an idea. It had been a while since her mother had seen anything outside the walls or the yard of the nursing home. Strange surroundings tended to confuse and frighten her, so of late, Tess and her family had made it a practice not to drive Raelene anywhere. Tess recalled the days when she and her dad used to take Rae on a picnic. It was usually just to the park or sometimes to a little clearing by a stream on the edge of town. But at least it got her out in the fresh air, away from the sterile and sometimes depressing atmosphere of the CCF.

Though Tess appreciated the attentive care her

mother received from Molly and the other nurses, she still hated to see her spend all her time in the nursing home. Lately, Tess had felt even more sad and overwhelmed by her mother's condition. That, coupled with her mixed feelings about Wade, left her wanting to reach out to Raelene. To do something special with her for a change. Maybe a small outing would do both of them some good.

She'd visited her mother several times since the incident with Wade just over a week ago, and Raelene seemed no worse for wear because of what had happened. It was Tess who couldn't forget.

Once she'd parked her truck in the CCF parking lot, Tess headed inside. Molly greeted her, a potted plant in one hand. "Tess. How are you?" She held up the plant. "Look what Dr. Jeffries gave us. Wasn't that sweet?" An abundance of leafy green foliage and tiny pink flowers spilled over the edges of the ceramic pot.

"It's beautiful," Tess said. "I love springtime."

"Me, too." Molly smiled. "Your mother's having a pretty good day. I showed her the plant, and it really caught her attention. Sally just finished washing Rae's hair." She gestured with her free hand toward Rae's room. "She's blow-drying as we speak. You can go right in."

"I'm glad to hear that about Mom," Tess said. "I'd like to take her home with me for a little picnic in my backyard. Say, for about an hour?" She turned her hands in a palms-up gesture. "The weather's so nice I feel like getting her out to enjoy it." The temperature was in the low seventies today, the sun soothingly warm. "I thought I could sit with her on a blanket beneath my shade trees and feed her some soft food.''

A brief look of concern passed over Molly's face. "Well, that does sound nice.'' She hesitated, then waved her fears away. "I'm a worrywart. If you think you can handle it, then I trust your judgment.'' She held up her finger in a motherly gesture of warning. "But no more than an hour. You don't want to tire her. It's been a while since she's been anywhere but the sitting area out back.''

"I know. And I promise I'll be careful and on time." Tess smiled and Molly did, too.

"Do you need help getting her to the car?''

"That might be a good idea,'' Tess said.

"Let me put this plant away, then I'll meet you in her room.''

"Okay.'' Tess headed down the hall, appreciating the fact that Molly could just as easily have gotten one of the orderlies to assist with her mother. Molly's caring enough to do it herself meant a lot to Tess. Again, she was thankful for Molly and the other nurses. If Raelene couldn't live at home, at least she had good people to tend to her.

Sally had almost finished blow-drying and brushing Raelene's hair when Tess entered the room. Tess greeted her, then faced Raelene. "Hi, Mama.'' She took her mother's hand and bent to place a kiss on her forehead. "How are you? Would you like to go for a little drive?''

"Yes.'' Rae smiled, her gaze darting to Tess before flickering to the window.

Molly came through the door. "Tess is taking you on a picnic, Rae. Won't that be nice?''

"No.'' But Raelene turned to Tess and smiled.

She reached for Tess's hand and gave it a squeeze, and Tess held on.

"Let me help you up, Mom. Then Molly will walk with us outside, okay?"

Rae muttered a few nonsensical words, but stood willingly and ambled between Tess and Molly as they led her toward the doorway and out into the hall.

"Some liver and wind today," Raelene muttered as they moved toward the exit.

Tess draped one arm around her and rubbed a gentle circle against her mother's shoulder with her thumb. "It's fine, Mama. You'll enjoy the fresh air."

"Give her a minute to stand here," Molly said as they stepped outside.

They paused momentarily, then continued walking the short distance across the parking lot to where Tess had left her pickup. Rae hesitated at the truck's door, a frown of confusion creasing her forehead. But then she smiled at Tess and climbed inside without any fuss. Tess buckled the seat belt and turned to Molly. "I think she'll be fine with this, but I'll call you if I have any problems." Belatedly, she wondered if she should have gotten her dad or Seth to come with her on their lunch break. However, Wednesdays were usually busy, with deliveries and such. Her dad and whoever else worked that day most often ate a sandwich behind the counter rather than take an actual meal break.

"I'm sure she will be, too," Molly said. "We're here if you need us, though." She closed the passenger door, then waved as Tess climbed behind the wheel and pulled out of the parking lot.

Tess looked over at her mother. Raelene was fiddling with the buckle on her seat belt. Tess reached across and stilled her hand with a gentle touch. "It's okay, Mama. Leave that there, all right?"

"Yes." But Rae picked at the strap as she stared straight ahead through the windshield.

Tess drove slowly through town, then down the county road to her house. She'd already locked the dogs up in the barn so they wouldn't startle Rae by barking. Tess parked her truck near the front steps and got out. After opening the passenger door, she unbuckled Rae's seat belt and took her by the hand. "Come on, Mama. I've already got our picnic basket packed and ready for the backyard." She helped Rae walk toward the front door. "That's right. You're doing fine."

Looking all around, Rae hesitantly followed Tess into the house. Again her forehead creased. "Not my dresser today."

Tess studied the expression on her mother's face, hoping she hadn't been wrong in bringing her here. But Raelene seemed okay with the situation so far. "Through here, Mama." Tess led her to the kitchen, where she took a small, plastic picnic hamper from the refrigerator. Inside were containers of gelatin, tapioca pudding and juices, along with napkins and plastic spoons and straws. Tess carried the basket in one hand and led Rae with the other.

She paused to snatch up the picnic blanket she'd left draped over a kitchen chair, then headed for the back door. Raelene seemed delighted with Tangie and Inky as they laced themselves around her ankles, then followed her and Tess outside. Rae made cooing noises at the cats and wriggled her fingers in a gesture of wanting.

Tess lifted Tangie into her arms and guided Rae's hand to stroke the kitten's fur. "Isn't he soft?" she asked.

"Yes," Rae said. She smiled, and her gaze appeared alert and aware. There were moments when Rae almost looked normal. But the moments never lasted, and Tess had to face reality once more.

Determined to focus only on enjoying her mother's company, Tess smiled back at Rae, then set Tangie on the ground. The kitten scampered off in pursuit of a butterfly. "We'll sit close to the porch, Mama. How's that?" Tess led Rae carefully down the three steps, then spread the blanket on the grass. "There you go." She helped her mother sit on the blanket, then laid a napkin in her lap. As an afterthought, Tess hurried back up the steps and reached inside the door to grab the cordless phone from its cradle. She set it on the porch railing...just in case.

As she rejoined her mother, Rae took hold of the paper napkin and pulled it from her lap. Her fingers worked along the edges and she began to shred one corner. "No, Mama." Tess spoke gently. "Let's leave that in your lap, okay? Here. Look what we've got." She opened the picnic container and arranged the food on the blanket before them. After peeling the top from a container of strawberry gelatin, Tess dipped a spoon into it and offered her mother a taste.

Rae opened her mouth like a little bird, taking the gelatin. But her eyes darted around the yard, not focused on any one thing in particular. Tess watched her, wishing there were some way she could seize

the web of confusion in her mother's mind and re-
move it. For the life of her, she'd never stop wondering what caused such a tragic disease and why it
had to affect someone as dear and sweet as Raelene.

Shrugging off thoughts about something she had
no power to change, Tess concentrated on feeding
her mother. "That's good, isn't it?" she asked, dab-
bing at one corner of Rae's mouth where a tiny bit
of the strawberry gelatin clung.

Rae didn't answer. Instead, she reached for a box
of juice. Tess opened it and inserted a straw, but
Raelene made no move to drink from it. Instead, she
squeezed it, causing the juice to ooze out from the
straw and spill down the side of the box.

"Here, let me help you," Tess said. She reached
for the juice container, but Raelene clung stubbornly
to it. "Mama, it's sticky. Let me wipe your hands
and give you a new one. All right?"

"Not mine," Rae said. She held the box away
from Tess.

"All right," Tess said. "You can keep it. We'll
worry about cleaning you up later."

She steadied Rae with a gentle touch to her arm
and Rae finally took a sip of the grape juice. A little
of it dribbled down her chin, and Tess wiped it away
with a clean napkin.

She glanced at her watch. Already precious
minutes had ticked by, marking off her hour with
her mother. Each task was so tedious where Raelene
was concerned. Tess remembered how her mother
had always joked about time passing quickly when
you were having fun. It had always felt that way
when they'd gone horseback riding, with two or
three hours flying by in what seemed like minutes

as they rode the familiar trails surrounding the ranch.

Tess wished Rae were capable of riding still. How she longed to sweep her mother up onto Angel's back and ride like the wind with her. To simply run and run until they outdistanced the disease that held Raelene in its grip. If Tess could be sure her mom wouldn't be afraid, she'd put her on the mare and lead her around. But that would be pushing things too far. As it was, she'd taken a risk in driving her out here alone. Her father would be worried if he found out. Deep down, Tess realized it was the real reason she'd chosen not to call and invite him to join her. He most likely would have talked her out of the picnic.

Yet the expression on her mother's face as she breathed in the fresh air told Tess it was worth it to have taken a chance. No matter how much she reminded herself that Raelene was in good hands at the CCF, Tess still hated the walls that closed her mother in 24/7. They were every bit as constrictive as the disease that imprisoned Rae's mind. If all she and Rae could have together outdoors was a moment like this one, then she intended to make the most of it.

"Would you like to listen to some music, Mama?" Tess had found that a nature tape or classical music often soothed Rae.

"Yes," Raelene said, though her answer seemed meaningless as she looked around the yard. She was staring at the lilac hedge, where Tangie now lazed in the shade of the deep-green foliage.

The portable cassette player Tess often took to the barn now sat on the kitchen counter. She glanced at the screen door. It was a short distance away, not much more than she'd gone to retrieve the cordless phone. "You sit right here, Mama, and I'll be back." Tess patted Rae's hand, hoping that by the time she returned, her mother would be willing to relinquish the sticky juice box.

Tess hurried up the steps and into the kitchen. She spotted the cassette player and, at the same time noticed Champ crouched on the opposite end of the countertop. Chewing on the leaves of a potted plant. "Champ, no!" Tess clapped her hands. "Get down from there. You know better."

The cat shot her a guilty look and scrambled off the counter, knocking the plant over in the process. It rolled off the counter and crashed onto the floor. Pottery shattered, scattering dirt everywhere. "Damn!" Tess glanced toward the screen door, then back to the broken pot. It would have to wait. But as she turned to go, Champ slunk back into the room, his curiosity overriding his sense of caution. He made his way across the tiled floor to explore the shards of pottery, treading through the spilled soil. "Get out of there, Champ," Tess scolded. "You'll cut your paws."

She made a shooing motion with her hands, then glanced around the kitchen. No way could she leave her mother long enough to clean up the broken pot. Improvising, she snatched up a dish towel and threw it over the shattered pottery, then anchored the towel with the leg of a chair. Hopefully, that would keep Champ safe until she could clean the whole mess up.

Tess retrieved the cassette player from the

counter, checked it briefly to be sure a tape was inside it, then headed for the back door.

Her heart leaped to her throat as she pushed the screen open.

A bright-purple stain spread across the picnic blanket where Raelene had dropped the sticky juice box.

And her mother was nowhere in sight.

WADE SADDLED DAKOTA, grumbling. He couldn't believe that after he'd checked the fence just days ago and found it intact, some idiot had run a truck through it, letting half a dozen steers escape and wander off to God knows where. It was a miracle the entire herd hadn't gotten out. They likely would have if not for the fact that the majority of the animals had been content to lie in the cool, shallow water and insect-repelling mud of the pond located near the barn.

"Don't worry, Dad. They couldn't have gotten that far," Jason said. "I know the wire wasn't down this morning when Macy and I left on our ride." The kids had discovered the break in the fence line only after returning from their outing.

"I can't believe whoever did it drove away without saying anything." Macy rolled her eyes. "How rude."

"Those tire marks are pretty wide," Jason added. "I bet it was someone with four-wheel drive."

"More than likely," Wade said, flipping his stirrup into place after tightening his cinch. "A lot of folks don't realize a gravel road can be just as slick as one covered with ice and snow." And most of the teenagers in the area thought themselves invincible and unstoppable in their four-wheel-drive vehicles.

"We'll find the steers, Dad," Macy said, nudging Amber into a trot as the three of them rode down the driveway toward the road. Smokey and Bandit followed.

"They might've wandered toward Trent and Bailey's place," Wade said. *Or Tess's.* The thought cheered him up a little. If his steers had gone missing, then the least they could do was end up wandering over to Tess's place. Of course, she might be at work, so even if the animals were there, he couldn't count on seeing her.

Wade sighed. This was getting ridiculous. Tess was on his mind far more now, since their drive to the lake, than ever before. For all their talk of taking things slow, he was having a difficult time putting his words into action. All he wanted lately was to pick up the phone and call her, or make excuses to drive to her house. Maybe it was a phase he was going through, some sort of weird spring fever or something. He could only hope it would pass.

Urging Dakota to pick up the pace, Wade headed down the road, Smokey and Bandit trotting ahead. Tracks from the break in the fence suggested that not all the steers had headed in the same direction, which was odd. "Maybe we ought to split up," he said. "You kids could ride that way—" he pointed in the direction opposite Tess's place "—and I'll check Trent and Bailey's and Tess's. If you don't see anything by the time you reach the Andersons' ranch, then turn around and meet me back this way and we'll figure something else out."

"Okay." Macy swung Amber around and trotted off with Jason.

Wade rode along the shoulder of the road, looking for more tracks. He wondered if whoever had been in the pickup hadn't possibly made a game of chasing the steers with it once they'd gotten out on the road. That would explain why the animals had split in two separate directions. Anger churned in Wade's gut as he continued on his way.

He'd just about reached the foot of Tess's driveway when he spotted four of his steers up ahead, grazing in the bar ditch. But before he could breathe a sigh of relief, something else caught his eye. He had to blink and do a double take in order for the sight in front of him to fully register.

Raelene Vega wandered down the driveway toward him, holding what looked like an oversize baby bottle in her hands. On her heels trotted Tess's miniature pinscher, Bruiser, with her Australian shepherd bringing up the rear. Duke was nowhere in sight. Wade turned Dakota into the driveway and proceeded at a walk. "Rae?" he called. "Is that you?" Of course it was. It was just that never in a million years would he have expected to see her out here. What on earth was going on? And where was Tess?

Rae looked up at him as he drew near, her expression full of worry. Maybe she was afraid of the horse. Pulling the gelding to a halt several feet from her, Wade swung from the saddle. "It's all right, Raelene. Do you remember me?" Again, he mentally chastised himself. She wouldn't, of course, but he somehow felt it important to talk to her, even if his words didn't register. He held out his hand. "You're okay. This big ol' horse is harmless."

"Goats," Rae said. She clutched the bottle to her chest and Wade recognized it as the one Tess had used to feed Chantilly, her orphaned foal. He'd seen it—or one like it—sitting in the barn the night Tess had first shown him the foal.

"Well, no," Wade said, not sure how to handle the situation. "No goats out here, ma'am, just a few loose steers and this old horse of mine." He looked around once more, seeking Tess. What in thunder was Rae doing here? He held his hand out to her. "Want to walk with me? Come on, Raelene. Let's go back up to the house, okay?"

"No." Rae shook her head. She held up the bottle and frowned at him. "Goats this time."

Wade thought about how Raelene had pitched the serving tray at him at the County Care Facility, and decided caution was in order. Not that he was afraid of the poor woman; he just didn't want to upset her. "All right, then. You show me where the goats are and we'll take care of 'em."

But she only stared at him blankly. Her right armed drooped to her side, the foal's bottle hanging upside down. Empty. Rae lifted her free hand and gestured, her mouth pursed as she scowled and tried to form words that seemed to elude her.

Wade looked toward the house, the barn. He hated to startle Raelene by raising his voice, but he had to do something. "Tess," he called out, keeping his voice as low as possible. Then louder, when no response came. "Tess!" Surely she was nearby. She wouldn't leave her mother alone. "Hey, Tess!"

"No!" Rae dropped the bottle and clamped her

hands over her ears. "No, no, no." She began shaking her head violently.

Uh-oh. Wade took a step toward her, still grasping Dakota's reins. "Easy, there, hon. It's okay. Raelene, please don't get upset." Knowing his words were useless, he continued to soothe, to try to coax her to be calm.

But it was no use. Hands still clasped to her ears, Raelene crouched in the driveway and tucked her knees beneath her chin. She began to keen, her voice sharp, piercing…heartbreaking.

TESS HURRIED ACROSS the backyard, her heart seeming to stand still. "Mama! Mama, where are you?" Rae's childlike mind could have led her anywhere, but surely her mother hadn't gone far. She'd turned her back on Rae for only a moment. But then, she supposed it was the same as turning one's attention away from a toddler for a split second.

As Tess hastened toward the driveway, Duke trotted up to her, coming from the barn. Alarm filled her. That meant Rae had gone inside and let the dogs out. Certainly they wouldn't have harmed her. Duke was a good watchdog, but he was more bark than anything else. And he didn't appear to be agitated. Actually, now that she looked at him more closely, Tess noticed the dog was behaving strangely.

Whining, he trotted toward her, his tail drooping. He halted, staring up into Tess's eyes. His gaze seemed to implore her to take heed of something. She wondered where Sasha and Bruiser were. Duke whined again, then headed down the driveway toward the road. Tess hesitated, wondering if she should check the barn first or follow the dog. Did he sense something, or was he simply wandering? Knowing he normally didn't leave the property, Tess decided the dog wasn't merely roaming.

Palms damp, she hollered for Rae once more. It was then that she heard Wade calling her own name. Followed by a shout. Her mother. Tess ran. Duke bounded before her as though playing the role of Lassie. He must indeed have sensed something amiss. Tess spotted Wade holding on to Dakota's reins, Raelene huddled in the driveway in front of him.

Duke barked a warning, then, to Tess's surprise, thrust his massive body between Wade and Rae. The dog leaned into her, and Rae immediately flung her arms around the shepherd's neck, burrowing her face into his fur. The keening that came from her throat began to die down.

Tess hurried forward. "Mama. Thank God." She looked up at Wade. "How did you happen by?" Feeling foolish, she knelt beside her mother. "I turned my back for a minute and she was gone." She wrapped her arms around Rae's shoulders and pulled her into a hug. "There now, Mama, it's okay. I'm here. You're fine."

But Rae clung stubbornly to Duke, who accepted the weight of her arms around his neck without a fuss. He eyeballed Wade and growled. "Duke," Tess said. "It's okay. Be nice."

"What in the world is your mother doing here?" Wade asked. "I saw her as I rode past and I thought my eyes were playing a trick on me."

Tess felt her face warm. It was a trick all right— a stupid one on her part. She never should have tried to take her mother on an outing alone. She sighed, full of guilt as Rae sobbed quietly. "Mama, I'm so sorry." Tess looked up at Wade. "I brought her here for a little picnic. I thought the fresh air and change of scenery would be nice. But I guess it was a bad idea."

Wade led Dakota over to the edge of the driveway and looped his reins around a tree branch, then returned. Cautiously, so as not to startle her mother, he crouched beside Tess and laid his hand on her shoulder. "It was a nice thought," he said. "You couldn't have known."

She shook her head. "I should have. Dad and I used to take her out quite a bit, and sometimes my brothers did, too. But it's been a while." She noticed Chantilly's bottle, lying a Raelene's feet. "What is she doing with this?" Tess picked it up, and Rae reached out for it with one hand, still clinging to Duke with the other. Tess gave the bottle to her, then stroked the hair away from Rae's face. "Shh, Mama. It's okay." She glanced at Wade. "She must've gotten this out of the barn. She used to take care of her mother's goats when she was little. Sometimes she obsesses over the past that way."

Wade nodded. "She said something about goats. I think she was looking for them."

"I should've known better," Tess repeated as she continued to soothe her mother. "It's my fault, sweetie, all my fault for bringing you here. Come on. Let me help you." She encircled her mother's waist and with gentle pressure coaxed her into letting go of Duke and standing.

"I can help you get her back to the CCF," Wade said. "Just give me a minute to do something with my horse."

Tess fought the urge to refuse him. She hated taking the risk of upsetting Rae all the more by letting Wade come along, but then, she supposed she'd already done enough harm there that it really didn't matter. Besides, it probably wasn't Wade himself who'd upset her mom but simply the situation, just as it had been the day Wade walked into Rae's room and caught her pulling Tess's hair. Tess had to admit she could use his help right now. But before either of them could move, a dark-green Chevy truck pulled into the driveway.

Tess grimaced at the sight of Zach and Becky. "Great," she muttered. This was all she needed. She and Zach hadn't spoken since their blowup at her birthday party, and if her brother said or did anything right now to further upset their mother, Tess didn't think her temper would hold, and Raelene definitely did not need more tension.

Zach turned off the ignition and spoke briefly to Becky before climbing from the truck. "What the hell is going on here?" he demanded as he strode toward Tess. Though his words were harsh, at least he had enough sense to keep his voice low. Shouting would definitely frighten Raelene.

Tess opened her mouth to answer, but to her surprise Wade stepped between her and Zachary. "Just take it easy, Zach. Your mother's already upset. Let's not do anything to complicate the matter, all right?" Firmly, he held Zach's gaze.

Zach scowled at him, then looked at Tess. "What is Mom doing here?"

"Never mind," Tess said. "You and I can talk about this later. I need to get her back to the nursing home."

Zach let his breath out in a huff, his hands hovering at his waist as though he was about to punch someone. "I guess you do." Sarcasm laced his reply. He pursed his lips and stared at Tess, obviously finding it difficult to hold back.

"What are you doing here, anyway?" Tess asked her brother, rubbing Rae's shoulders. Her mother had grown quiet, and now stared blankly at a point beyond Zach's shoulder.

"I was on my way to Wade's place. Becky wanted to see if Macy could go with us to look at some horses." He glared at Wade. "Did you have something to do with this?"

Before Wade could answer, Tess held up her hand. "Zach. I said later. Okay?"

Suddenly, the irritation disappeared from Zach as he watched Raelene. His expression filled with sadness. "Yeah, okay. Can I help you with Mom?"

Tess shook her head. "Wade's already offered. You have Becky to think of."

"Macy's riding," Wade added. "I've got steers loose on the road. The kids went that way—" he pointed "—looking for some of them. I spotted four of them right up there." He gestured, indicating an area down the road, where Tess could see the creamy-white steers grazing in the ditch.

Zach nodded. "I saw them. I was going to tell you." He looked at Tess once more. "Wade can't leave his steers in the road."

"It's all right," Wade said. "I'll worry about them later."

"No," Tess said. "He's right. And you can't just take off and let the kids wonder where you went, either."

"I realize that," Wade said. He gave her a scowl that said he wasn't stupid. But it wasn't a sarcastic one. His tone of voice told her he wanted only to lend a hand. "I was thinking I'd help you get your mom in the truck, then you can follow me to my place while I round up the kids."

"Thanks, Wade, but Mom needs to go back to her room right away. I've put her through enough already." She glanced from him to Zach. "Why don't you two get the steers home and the kids gathered and I'll take Mom back. I can manage. She's calm now."

Wade hesitated. "Are you sure?"

She nodded. "I'll follow you in my truck," Zach said. "Becky can wait a bit to catch up with Macy while Wade gets his steers in." He looked at Wade. "Unless you'd like me to help herd them with the truck."

"No." Wade waved his hand. "I'll be fine. Smokey and Bandit are all the help I need." He indicated the dogs, who were circling the ditch, keeping the four steers from wandering farther.

Tess met her brother's gaze, knowing that he didn't intend to follow her simply to make sure she got her mother back to the CCF safely.

His expression said their confrontation from days earlier wasn't over, and that he had a lot on his mind. Which was fine with her. She had a few things she wanted to settle with him, as well.

"Thanks for stopping, Wade," she said.

"Come by the house on your way back home if you can." He gave her arm a squeeze, his eyes full of concern. "At least let me walk you and your mom to the truck."

Tess nodded, then guided her mother toward the Dodge. Wade helped her inside, and Tess buckled the seat belt into place. Her keys still dangled from the ignition. She slid into the driver's seat and started the engine.

Wade came around to her side and leaned on the open window. He laid his hand on her arm. "Tess, don't let your brother upset you. I'm sure he means well."

She nodded, not totally sure what Zach thought or felt anymore. "I suppose. I'll see you later." She turned the truck around and watched Wade retrieve his horse and swing into the saddle. His concern for her and her mother touched her—and at the same time made her wary. Not of him, but of her feelings toward him. If she wasn't careful, she'd end up giving in to her desire to have more than a casual relationship with him.

With a wave of his hand, Wade rode past Zach's pickup. Zach backed out of the driveway and halted in the middle of the road, waiting to follow Tess to town. Sighing, she put the Dodge in gear and pulled forward, glancing over at her mother. Again, Rae was staring blankly ahead. Looking so lost it broke Tess's heart.

She'd only meant to show her mother a good time. To brighten her day. And instead she'd ruined it. With a sigh, Tess headed for town, her every protective instinct kicking into high gear.

What was done was done. She wouldn't dwell on a mistake she'd made with good intentions. And she wasn't about to let Zach walk all over her, either.

CHAPTER TWELVE

TESS PARKED as close to the back entrance of the nursing home as she could. Zach found a spot a short distance away. Ignoring him, Tess concentrated on getting Rae out of the seat belt. She still clutched the foal's bottle, and gently, Tess extracted it from her grasp. "Let me take that for you, Mama," she said. "That's right."

"What is she doing with that?" Zach spoke from behind her. Tess glanced over her shoulder and saw him glare at her. "She's obsessing about the past again, isn't she?"

Her patience nearly gone, Tess whirled around to face him. "Zach, just help me get her inside, will you? We can talk about this once she's in her room."

"Fine." Without another word, he helped her assist Raelene from the truck seat and walk to the back door.

Once inside the care facility, Tess found Molly.

"How'd it go?" The nurse smiled at her, then frowned with worry at the purple juice stain on Rae's blouse and the faraway look in her eyes. "Did we have a bit of trouble?" She laid her hand on Raelene's shoulder.

"I'm afraid so," Tess said. "Mom's a little shook up, and I feel just awful about it."

"Well, there, there," Molly soothed, slipping her arm around Rae's waist. "Are you okay, Raelene, honey? Let Molly help you." She walked with Tess to Rae's room, Zach lagging behind in the hallway.

Determined to ignore her brother for the moment, Tess focused on getting her mom situated. While Molly found a washcloth and wet it in the sink, Tess explained what had happened. Molly wiped the rag soothingly over Rae's face and hands, then helped her out of her stained blouse. Tess got a clean one from the closet and dressed her mother in it.

"Don't be too hard on yourself, kiddo," Molly said. "You meant well, and that's all that matters. I'm sure the fresh air did Raelene some good, and as for her little escapade, she'll be all right. She's already moved past it. Look." Molly indicated the way Rae had relaxed in the chair next to the window. She stared out at her familiar surroundings, mumbling, but otherwise calm.

"I hope so," Tess said, still wondering what went on in her mother's mind. "I didn't mean to cause her stress."

"Of course you didn't. Now, why don't you just go on and get yourself home to a nice cup of tea. Relax. I'll take care of your mom."

Tess nodded. "Maybe that's best. If I leave her to settle down, I mean. I'll come back a little later."

"That's fine. We'll be here." Molly smiled and Tess waved at her, then kissed her mother's cheek before heading back out into the hallway. She looked around, but Zach was nowhere in sight. Surely he hadn't skipped out on her.

Outside, Tess found Zach leaning against her

truck. His own pickup was now parked beside it, empty. Tess frowned. "Where's Becky?"

"I drove her to the feed store. Told her to pick out a new halter for the horse I'm going to buy her." He glared at Tess as though she'd purposely set out to spoil his outing to shop for a horse with his step-daughter. "Is Mom okay?"

Tess glared back at him. "Yes. Not that you seem to bother checking anymore." She knew he'd gotten Becky away so the little girl wouldn't witness the two of them arguing. Might as well jump right into things, then.

"Tess, what were you thinking?" Zach asked. "Taking her home like that. You should've known it wouldn't work out."

"Yes, I guess I should have," Tess said, opening the door of her truck and sliding onto the seat. She sat sideways, facing Zach. "But it was such a nice day I just wanted to get her out of here for a while." She gestured toward the care facility.

To her surprise, Zach said, "Yeah. I guess I can relate to that." For a moment, he was quiet. Then he laid his hand on Tess's shoulder. "Look, sis, I'm sorry I got mad at you. And I'm sorry you're dis-appointed in me for not visiting Mom in a while."

Tess leveled her eyes at him. "Yes, I am disap-pointed, Zach. I'm not going to sit here and sugar-coat that." She gestured, frustrated. "What would it hurt you to come see her? Was it so painful to help me out with her a little just now?"

Zach actually hung his head before answering. "I can't explain it, Tess. It's hard for me to see her this way. Not knowing who we are. Living in some time warp, back in the past with her goats or whatever."

"And how do you suppose she feels?" Tess studied her brother's face. "Answer that, Zachary."

"I don't know."

"That's right. You don't, and neither do I. But I'm sure having Alzheimer's is no day at the fair." Tess put her hand on Zach's arm. "She's still our mother. And she needs us to be there for her. Period. I wish you'd reconsider the way you feel and start visiting her again."

Zach let out his breath. "I'm going to have to give it some thought, Tess." He moved back a step. "I'd better go pick Becky up. We're late as it is."

Disappointed, Tess let her hand fall to her side. "All right, then. I'll see you later."

"You might want to stop by the store," Zach added. "Dad was upset when he heard what happened."

Tess graced him with a frown. "You told him?"

"I had to. He wondered why I was dropping Becky off."

Closing her eyes, Tess sighed. She hated to upset her father. "All right. I'll go talk to him." She swung her legs around beneath the steering wheel, then closed the door.

Why was it that her good intentions often went awry? Well, at least she'd tried to give her mother a pleasant day. Which was more than she could say for Zach.

Still irritated with her brother, Tess pulled out of the parking lot and drove to the feed store.

WADE FOUND IT HARD to believe his baby girl would turn eleven in just ten days. Where had the time gone? Working extra hard to keep up with his orders for tack and belts, he used his nights when the kids were in bed to work on Macy's birthday present. A saddle for Diego. Macy would love it. Her old one had seen a lot of miles, and with Diego coming along in his training, a new saddle seemed like a good idea.

He'd also been busy organizing things at the Circle D. He'd shipped a load of cattle off to market two weeks ago, and was contemplating just how many he might ship again this month. He'd decided not to do anything rash until he was certain Cowboy Up was indeed going to be a success and his sales numbers were not just a temporary run of good luck that would fizzle, leaving his family in a bind.

Meanwhile, the ranch work had to be kept up with. He'd yet to find out who had run through his fence last week, and the incident had made him wary. He'd keep a close eye on his steers to make sure no more got out. He was doing just that on the second Saturday of June, riding fence in his lower pasture, when he ran into Tess.

At first sight of her, he could feel his heart trip in his chest like a horse stumbling over a log. For the life of him, he couldn't figure out what had happened to his good sense and judgment of late. He'd enjoyed kissing Tess on the night of her birthday party. But it was the night they'd shared at the lake that had really done him in. And not just the kissing part. The way she'd opened up and talked to him from her heart was what had truly gotten to him. He couldn't remember the last time he'd shared his thoughts and feelings in such a way with anyone.

And ever since that night, he looked forward more than ever to seeing her at 4-H meetings, at the feed store, the café…anywhere he could contrive to run into her. He wanted to ask her out and planned to soon. He felt like a kid in love, and told himself that was ridiculous. Whatever it was that had taken hold of him would surely pass.

On the more serious side of things, he also continued to dwell on Raelene's illness. He wished he could help Tess somehow, but she'd made it clear he wasn't welcome in that area of her life. At least she'd accepted his help the day Raelene had wandered off. Wade had felt bad for Tess when that had happened, knowing she'd had the best of intentions where her mother was concerned. He hated to see her be so hard on herself. After watching Tess with Raelene that day, he now had a better picture of Tess's mothering needs. Clearly, the two women's roles had been reversed a long time ago.

Though Tess's proud strength broke his heart, Wade knew the entire situation regarding Tess's mother wasn't any of his business. Still, he wished he could find out if Zachary had changed his mind about not seeing Raelene. Tess had said little about their obvious confrontation that day. Wade also wondered how much support Seth and Lloyd were to Tess. Lloyd sounded like a devoted father and husband, so Wade knew he really shouldn't worry about her. But that didn't stop him from doing what he was doing at this very moment—wanting to wrap her in his protective grip.

She rode toward him on a sorrel-and-white tobiano paint. She wore her usual ball cap, but this time her pretty red hair was plaited in a single braid that exposed the earrings she wore. The ones he'd given her. He liked the fact that she donned them often.

Her jeans gloved her hips, and Wade moaned inwardly.

Tearing his eyes away from where they didn't belong, he gave her a smile. "Hey, cowgirl," he said when she pulled the paint to a stop on the other side of the fence. "Long time, no see," he teased, having just seen her two days ago at 4-H. But it felt like forever.

The expression on her face made him wonder if she didn't feel the same. "Riding fence?" she asked.

He nodded. "Somebody's got to do it."

"Where're your little helpers?"

"Up at the barn. Macy's helping Jason work on a rabbit cage."

Tess's eyebrows shot up. "Oh?" Suspicion laced the single word.

"Don't get alarmed. I'm not aiming to raise any bunnies for supper."

She glared at him. "I should hope not. But Macy told me you wouldn't let her and Jason have cats or bunnies for pets."

He sighed. And felt his face warm. She made it sound as though he was an ogre. Had he been that bad? "I never was crazy about the idea. But Jason's thinking of giving up showing steers and doing poultry and rabbits, instead. Apparently one of Bailey's rabbits had babies, and before I knew it, she and the kids had me talked into letting them have a couple."

"Ooo, look out," Tess joked. "The cattleman is going soft."

Wade put on a mock scowl. "Hey, I could hardly

refuse when Bailey offered the bunnies as early birthday presents for the kids.''

Tess chuckled. "I like her strategy. I know Macy's birthday is this month, but when is Jason's?''

"July 3.''

She nodded and shortened her reins as the paint mare fidgeted beneath her. "You have anything special planned besides a bunny?''

"Yep. I'm making Macy a saddle, and I've been working on one for Jason's birthday, too. Their old ones have seen better days.''

Tess's eyes lit up, and Wade reprimanded himself for noticing something so crazy as her looking far better with her natural eyelashes and sun-kissed cheeks than with the makeup she'd put on for her birthday party.

"That is so sweet,'' she said. "I'm sure Macy will love it, and Jason, also. But how on earth do you find time to make two saddles and still supply your customers' needs?''

Her words turned his smile to a frown. There she went again. Whenever he started thinking he liked her—a lot—then she had to go and poke her nose in his business. "Don't worry, I can handle it,'' he said. "My kids are worth every minute of the time it takes.'' He didn't tell her he'd stayed up late and gotten up early every morning this week to put the finishing touches on Macy's saddle so it would be ready for her birthday.

"Hey, no need to get defensive,'' Tess said. "I was just curious, and you've already got me convinced you deserve the Father of the Year award.''

"I wouldn't go that far,'' he mumbled, feeling his

face heat once more. Was she being serious or sarcastic? Her genuine expression told him she was serious, and the good feeling her compliment gave him did funny things to his heart. "So, what are you doing out this early?" he asked, more to change the subject than anything else. Obviously, she was going for a ride. It was just that he had never cottoned much to the idea of riding for pleasure. He did so with the kids on occasion, but to him, early mornings were for work.

"I'm taking tap dancing lessons," Tess said, then laughed. "I'm going for a ride, silly. Is that so hard for you to comprehend, Mr. All-Work-and-No-Play-Cattleman?"

That she read him so easily didn't sit well with Wade at all. He let out a sigh of irritation. "If you ask me, horses *are* for working, not playing."

"Really? What about the kids' 4-H activities?"

"That's different. Fun is for kids."

Tess licked her lips and shifted in the saddle, as though she was settling in for a good argument...and enjoying every minute of it. "Is that so? Then you mean you didn't have fun with me the other night at the lake?"

Wade fought a smile. "'Course I did. What do you think I am, dead or stupid?"

She laughed. "I'll bet you'd find that riding can be fun, too, if you'd quit being so all-fired stuffy and try to see your horse in a new light."

"What's that supposed to mean?"

She gestured, palm up. "Go ahead. Look at him. He's gorgeous. Blue roan, all muscle, silky mane and tail."

Wade frowned down at Dakota. "I see the roan and the muscle, but the silky escapes me."

Tess rolled her eyes. "Now, why does that not surprise me? Does he have a name?"

"Of course." She raised her eyebrows, waiting, and he answered. "Dakota."

"Ah. Now I see where Macy probably came up with Diego. It has a similar ring, and she looks up to her daddy, you know."

It was Wade's turn to raise his eyebrows. He'd never given the matter much thought. "You figure?"

"Sure. Why should that surprise you?"

"I guess it doesn't." He shrugged. "They're supposed to look up to me. I'm their dad." Nevertheless, pleasure skittered in his stomach.

"Yeah, and I'll bet you've gone riding with them before, right? I mean, they had to learn their skills somewhere. And I doubt they started by jumping into the saddle and pushing cows."

"True." He shrugged away memories of Deidra riding in the arena with Macy and Jason, and instead recalled the times he'd spent with them in the corrals and pastures when they were barely old enough to walk. Riding on the front of his saddle. Then graduating to ponies of their own.

It had been a while since he'd thought of those days. A long time since Deidra's death and the happy moments that had seemed to disappear with her.

"So you have to admit riding is fun, at least some of the time."

"What's your point?"

"My point is, you just might learn to enjoy it again if you'd give it a shot."

"How do you know I don't go riding with Macy and Jason?"

"Because I have eyes and ears," she countered. "Macy told me you ride when you work the ranch and that's it. Do you know that makes her sad?"

He glared at Tess. "We're not going to get into another discussion about what my daughter needs, are we? Because—"

She cut him off with a raised hand. "Wade, I'm simply trying to get you to come away from that fence and go for a ride with me. Is that okay?" Her voice softened, and her honest request, coupled with the look in her eyes, was enough to break down his defenses.

He let out a breath. "I suppose." He eyeballed the fence. He'd just about finished riding the perimeter and had found nothing wrong with the fence thus far. He supposed the rest could wait until later. Wade nodded toward the far end of the fence, which paralleled the road. "There's a gate in the corner down there. Why don't you come on in and we'll ride back to the barn and let the kids know where we'll be."

Tess smiled in triumph and Wade did his best to ignore the sparkle in her eyes. "All right." She kneed the paint mare into a lope.

He met her at the gate and swung down from the saddle to open it. "Where do you want to ride?" he asked as she passed through.

She shrugged. "Doesn't matter to me. I know a lot of good trails, or you can pick one."

He shook his head. He'd only ridden with the kids on the ranch or in an arena. "I'll let you decide."

"Okay." She waited while he remounted Dakota, then the two of them rode toward the barn, with Wade wondering how he'd ever explain this to his kids. They knew him well enough to understand that he considered horses working animals. So how did he make it sound logical that Tess had talked him into doing something so foolish as going for a pleasure ride in the middle of a work morning?

He simply wasn't prepared to fully admit he was beginning to feel far more for her than he'd ever believed possible. Not to himself, much less to his son and daughter.

MUCH TO TESS'S AMUSEMENT, Macy and Jason did a fair job of ribbing their dad about leaving his chores to go off on a ride with her. Tess started to ask the kids to join them, but then a selfish voice inside her head whispered what fun it might be to have Wade all to herself. After all, she could hardly believe she'd actually talked him into going for a trail ride. And she couldn't help but think about how good it had felt to be alone with him at the lake two weeks ago.

Wade was pretty much all that had been on her mind lately. No matter how hard she tried to focus on other things and put her relationship with him back into perspective—friendly, neighborly, Wade merely a customer of the feed store and the father of one of her 4-H kids—she could not manage to do so. Instead, she thought about all the things he'd said to her that night at the lake, and how good he made her feel, especially when he teased her. Or when he smiled at her in that cute way. The one that made his sexy lips do wild things to her heart. The smile that caused his hazel eyes to spark with mischief and her knees to turn to wet noodles.

Waving goodbye to the kids, Tess headed off down the driveway with Wade to the county road. It led to a break in the trees and a bridle path that wound through public Bureau of Land Management land. He didn't say a word for the first few minutes of their ride, and Tess began to worry that maybe she'd talked him into doing something he really hadn't wanted to do at all. But then she glanced over and saw the relaxed way he sat in the saddle and the expression in his eyes as he took in the natural beauty of Colorado.

Breathing a little easier, Tess settled deeper in her saddle and let the scents of aspen and pine engulf her. A blue jay swept across the path into the high branches of a tree, scolding them for invading its territory, and a chipmunk darted across the grass, in a hurry to get wherever it was going. For as far as the eye could see, tall mountain grass spread before them. The distant peaks of the Flat Top surrounded the meadows like the loving arms of a guardian angel, their sharp, clean outline giving the impression you could practically reach out and touch them.

Tess loved it here. So many of her classmates back in high school had been in such a rush to graduate and leave Ferguson, but not Tess. Not only had she been devoted to taking care of her mother, she'd also been devoted to her entire family, the feed store and the town itself. She found the familiarity comforting somehow. A nice, established routine she could live with.

"You sure are quiet." Wade's statement broke in on her thoughts.

"Just enjoying the view," she said.

"It is something," he admitted. "Guess we're pretty lucky to live here."

Once again, the way his words reflected exactly what she'd been thinking jolted Tess. She supposed she needed to stop judging Wade with preconceived notions, since he often had a way of surprising her with insightful comments.

"I think so, too," she said. Then she grinned. "Wanna take advantage of this cool breeze and let the horses stretch their legs a little?"

"Sure. I could go for a good gallop."

She shot him a challenging grin. "Not a gallop. A run. A race."

He grinned back, then tugged his hat low over his eyes. "You're on. Around the bend and across the meadow?"

"On three." She counted, then let her mare take off on the fly. Tess let out a shriek of pure joy as the wind whipped across her face, pulling her braid away from her neck. She grabbed at the bill of her cap with one hand as it nearly tumbled from her head and shoved it down tight, then bent low over Angel's neck and urged her on.

The horses ran, neck and neck, along the dirt shoulder of the road, then across the open meadow Tess had galloped through many times. She knew it was safe and level, with no tangled wire hidden in the grass. And because of that, it was a place where she could always give her horses free rein and let them run to their heart's content.

Wade shouted encouragement to Dakota, urging

the blue roan to move faster, and the gelding began to pull away from Angel. Tess spoke to Angel. "Come on, Angel, come on. Let 'er fly, girl!" The paint's ears flickered and she pinned them back, running, loving it as much as Tess did.

She and Angel were a nose ahead of Dakota when they sailed past the big blue spruce that marked the end of their race. Tess waved her fist in triumph over her head as she slowed Angel to a lope, then halted. Wade's smile matched her own as he pulled up beside her. "I let you win," he said.

"You did not." Tess laughed and swung down from her saddle. She loosened the cinch just enough to allow Angel to breathe more easily.

Wade followed suit with Dakota, holding on to the horse's reins as he plopped down on a fallen log. "'Course I did," he teased. His eyes sparked in that way Tess found so intriguing, and her heart picked up a beat.

She sat on the log beside him. "How do you figure?"

"Why, I let you get a head start."

"You did not."

"No?"

"No." She pursed her lips, looking at Wade's, wanting to kiss him.

"Well, if you won honestly, then I guess I have to be a graceful loser," he said. He draped his arm across her shoulders and his touch set her skin on fire. He drew her close. "Congratulations." Then he brushed a kiss across her lips, which started out playful and ended up anything but.

Tess closed her eyes and slipped her free hand behind his neck, still clutching Angel's reins with the other, nearly forgetting and letting go of the horse in the process. Wade deepened the kiss and Tess took his tongue into her mouth, loving the warmth of him, the taste of his lips on hers.

And wild, crazy questions rushed into her mind. How would it feel to spend every day of her life like this, with Wade? Tess let herself slide into the fantasy she knew could never come true. Riding, kissing, working as a team…helping him raise his kids. She imagined sharing a home with him, their days filled with working side by side on their ranch, followed by a relaxed, family conversation over a home-cooked meal.

Reality poked its ugly nose into her daydream. How could she share a home with a man who would never welcome her many pets? And where would she and he live? On his cattle ranch, where she couldn't bear the thought of participating in sending helpless animals off to a cruel death? Or on her rented sanctuary, where Wade would likely never understand what drove her to rescue horse after horse?

She ignored the voice that said he'd helped her rescue Diego, that he'd even acknowledged the rewarding feeling it gave her. That had been an isolated incident. Surely a man who viewed horses primarily as working animals wouldn't be able to see things that way for long. She could hardly expect Wade to lend her the emotional support her rescue work required. And she would never be able to lend him support in his lifestyle. How on earth could she ever give her heart to him under those circumstances?

Tess moved away from Wade's embrace, and a

cold sensation washed over her as his lips left hers. She hated putting a halt to what they'd begun, but it was for the best. She simply couldn't risk loving a man she could not have a future with. She'd been a fool to agree to keep seeing him.

Wade frowned, puzzled. "Something wrong?"

She shook her head, unwilling to get into the issue now. She'd think of a graceful way out later. Tugging on Angel's reins to pull the mare's attention from the grass that grew tall around the fallen log, Tess moved toward the horse's side. "No, nothing's wrong. I just thought we ought to get back to riding. Since that's what we came out here to do."

He scowled at her as though she'd lost her mind.

And she had. Over him.

Sighing inwardly, Tess swung onto her paint. "I know where there's a really nice trail that runs along the river," she said. "If you want to ride there."

"Sure." Wade slipped into the saddle, his easy movement making her stomach churn with longing to hold him in her arms and continue the kisses she'd put an end to.

His manner was reserved, and he didn't say much as they rode away. Tess wished she could find the exact words to explain to him why she'd stopped what was happening, in spite of how she felt about him. But she couldn't.

Because she didn't totally understand it herself.

MACY HAMMERED WIRE onto the rabbit hutch, lost in thought. She couldn't believe how good her dad and Tess had been getting along lately. They even seemed to be having fun together. These days her dad never rode horses just for the sake of riding, and

Macy knew that Tess must mean something special to him if he'd let her talk him into doing so. The thought left her all tingly inside.

Sometimes she wished her dad would get married again. She missed her mom, even though memories of her were few and vague. And the burden of guilt she carried, knowing her dad was alone because of something that had been her fault, added to her desire for a mother. Not just for herself and Jason, but to see her dad completely happy. Sure, he behaved as though everything in his life was okay, but Macy was old enough to recognize there were times when he felt lonely. And that made her sad beyond words.

When she'd first become friends with Bailey, she'd thought maybe her dad might end up liking her. That Bailey might one day become her step-mother. But right away she'd seen how much Bailey liked Trent. And then the two of them had gotten married shortly after Trent had rescued Macy from that horrible Lester Godfrey, who'd carjacked her in Bailey's truck.

Macy would never forget that day. Lester, who worked at the local gas station and drank too much beer. He'd sold Bailey his classic Chevy pickup truck, then wanted it back. When he'd had no money to pay for it, he'd decided to take it anyway. Macy had been sitting in the truck, which was parked at a local convenience store, when a drunken Lester climbed behind the wheel and drove away. She'd never been more scared in her life. And she knew the incident had frightened her dad way more than he'd cared to admit. She'd seen it in his eyes when he'd clung to her in the emergency room at the hospital, where the ambulance driver had taken her to treat the bump she'd gotten on her head during the carjacking. He'd told her that she and Jason were all he had in this world. And that he was very thankful she was safe.

Macy felt lucky to have a father who cared so much. Some kids she knew didn't. But still, she continued to wonder if her dad would ever find someone to be her mother. He'd once dated a woman from another town, but she hadn't been nice at all, and Macy was glad when her dad stopped seeing her.

Macy wanted him to like Tess.

She was so perfect, the way she loved animals and the way she treated Macy and Jason as though they were special to her. She'd make a great mom. Macy admired Tess at least as much as she did Bailey. Maybe more. She'd learned about role models in school, and she felt that both of them were good ones. She wouldn't mind growing up to be a sharp businesswoman like Bailey, but overall, she'd prefer to be just like Tess. She was smart, too, and she worked hard. Two jobs, plus 4-H, and her horse rescue... Now, *that* was something Macy would love to do.

The distant sound of a train whistle cut the stillness of the air, and Macy shivered. It was a sound that still bothered her, though she'd never told her dad. What could he do about it, with them living so close to the railroad tracks?

Pushing the thought away, Macy continued to hammer. And to daydream about having Tess for a mom.

CHAPTER THIRTEEN

THE NEXT FEW DAYS Tess focused her efforts on coming up with a plausible fund-raiser to benefit the Western Colorado Horse Rescue. After kicking around several ideas, she finally decided on holding a fun-event—an open gymkhana. While a normal gymkhana consisted of traditional speed events such as barrel racing and pole bending, this one would have things like the egg-and-spoon race and other silly made-up contests meant more for entertainment than competition. She arranged for the use of the arena at the fairgrounds, and as the weekend of the gymkhana drew near, she finalized the last of the details.

Macy, Jason and several other 4-H kids helped do up and distribute posters, and the local radio station agreed to make, at no charge, announcements of the event throughout the remainder of the week. Bailey insisted on paying for ads in the two local papers, and also took flyers to some of the larger nearby towns and handed them out. All in all, everything looked good, and Tess hoped for a great turnout.

She tumbled into bed on Thursday night after her 4-H meeting, exhausted but looking forward to the weekend. It wasn't often that she slept well. She worried constantly about her mother, and forever dreaded a fateful phone call in the night. The past few days she'd slept even more fitfully. Raelene had caught a bacterial infection a few days ago and had been unable to shake it. Tess had spent as much time at the County Care Facility as she could spare, and between that and getting things ready for the fund-raiser, she hadn't had much rest.

She awoke this night in the grip of a dream she couldn't remember. Disoriented, she looked at the clock. Nearly 1:00 a.m. She wondered how her mother was doing. Picking up the phone, she dialed the County Care Facility.

"Your mother's condition hasn't changed any," one of the night nurses told her. "Don't worry, honey. We're keeping a close eye on her. Try to get some sleep."

Tess put down the receiver and moved to the kitchen, Bruiser at her heels. There she filled a mug with water, stuck in a wooden stick for safety and placed the mug in the microwave. Maybe a cup of herbal tea would help her sleep. Tangie trotted into the room and twined round her ankles. Tess sat on the floor, cross-legged, and let the kitten comfort her. Her heart still raced.

And for once in her life, she wondered what it would be like to have another human being to reach out to in the night, or any other time when loneliness and sorrow seized her. She thought of Wade, and wished she could feel his arms around her right now.

Tess shook her head. What was wrong with her? She'd learned long ago to stand on her own, and had always found plenty of comfort in her four-legged friends. She stroked Tangie and listened to him purr. Animals didn't argue or expect a thing from you. They loved unconditionally and rarely abandoned you. People were another story.

She'd already decided she'd been a fool to agree to see Wade. Yet she hadn't found the time or energy to tell him so. She'd used the excuse of being busy with the upcoming gymkhana to avoid going out with him, and with her mom not feeling well, she'd had even more reason to spend time away from him. Not that he hadn't offered to come to the CCF with her, because he had. But she'd turned him down, telling him it wasn't necessary. And she'd seen the hurt in his eyes when she'd done so.

Could he sense she was pushing him away?

The bell on the microwave dinged, and Tess rose and took the cup of hot water from it. She removed the stick, added a bag of chamomile tea and walked into the living room, where she curled up on the couch with Tangie and Bruiser.

Scratching the dog's ears, she reminded herself that the decision she'd come to was for the best. She'd tell Wade the truth, after the gymkhana.

FOR THE LIFE OF HIM, Wade couldn't understand what had come over Tess of late. He tried to determine the exact time that she'd begun to act strangely toward him, and finally decided it was when he'd kissed her while they were out on their horseback ride days ago. What he couldn't pinpoint was what had caused her sudden turnaround in attitude. She'd seemed to have had no problem kissing him any other time, and she'd been the one who'd asked him to go out for a ride with her that day. He hadn't done anything overbearing or out of hand. So what the hell had gotten into her?

She'd been using every excuse in the book to avoid spending time with him. Sure, she was busy with the upcoming gymkhana, and it wasn't her fault Raelene had gotten sick and needed extra attention. But though Tess had let him help prepare for the fund-raiser, she still refused to let him accompany her to see her mother. Maybe that was it. Maybe she'd come to realize that he was good for some fun and kissing, but when it came to the serious things in her life, like family, she had no use for him.

The thought left him fuming. She'd let him get close enough to step past a casual friendship, past a platonic relationship, only to turn away from him. And just when he'd begun to fall in love with her.

There. He'd finally admitted it. He was quickly falling for Tess, and he hadn't a clue what to do about it. Especially since the feeling obviously was not mutual. He'd probably be smart to stay away from her as much as possible. To forget about the crazy ideas that were so often on his mind and go back to the way things had been when they'd first met.

But he couldn't. No matter how hard he tried. And as the weekend of the fund-raiser gymkhana drew near, Wade decided that he and Tess needed to have another heart-to-heart talk. He wanted to get her alone, but how to do so when she kept avoiding him? He supposed he'd just have to go to her house on a day she'd likely be home and confront her.

The perfect opportunity presented itself the very next day. Wade's mother had never been the grandmotherly type, preferring extensive travel over staying home with her family. His dad spent a great deal of time alone, so much so that Wade sometimes wondered why his parents even bothered to stay married. But the one time Ruthie Darland always made an effort to do something fun with her grand-kids was on or around their birthdays. With Macy's being this month and Jason's the next, Ruthie had called and offered to take the kids to Denver on an overnight trip.

The excursion would include shopping and a day at the Six Flags Elitch Gardens amusement park, followed by an overnight stay at a hotel because of the three-and-a-half-hour drive between Denver and Ferguson. Wade knew his mother would make sure the hotel was a luxury one. Something the kids would find a novelty. How could he refuse?

Ruthie pulled into his driveway promptly at 9:00 a.m. Her Lincoln Town Car glided to a stop near the back porch, looking totally out of place next to his pickup truck. Only his mother would insist on driving a luxury car in a small town where SUVs and trucks were far more practical.

He opened the car door for her and reached inside to give her his hand, knowing she expected it. "Hi, Mom."

"Wade. How are you, dear?" She unfolded her tall, thin body from the car. Her silver hair was cut in yet another new style, this one short, though somewhat less severe than her previous one. She wore a lemon-yellow pantsuit and too much per-fume. Leaning forward, she bussed his cheek quickly, then opened her arms to envelop Macy and Jason as they hurried outside to greet her.

For the life of him, Wade couldn't figure out why she'd never been a very good mother, but she still managed to fill the role of grandma to his kids' satisfaction. Taking control, as she so loved to do, Ruthie ordered the kids to go inside, get their suitcases and bring them to the car so they could get rolling, and not to forget jackets, in case of rain. Then she turned to Wade.

"I haven't seen you in a while," she said. "What with my traveling and your working." She glanced around, taking in the ranch in one fell swoop. "Your father says you're thinking of selling all the cattle."

"That's right." He didn't offer to elaborate.

Ruthie's eyes sparkled. "I think it's a splendid idea. You need to move past all this." She waved her hand at the ranch in general. "Take your kids someplace where they can live closer to town. Gain a little culture." She sniffed. "Ferguson hardly fills the bill on that. Now, I know you'd never consider Denver, and Aspen is beyond your budget, but maybe you'd consider Grand Junction, at least?"

Wade shook his head, unable to believe her gall. When would she ever learn that subdivisions, shopping malls and theaters didn't appeal to everyone, his father included. Again, he marveled at the fact that the man had put up with Ruthie's ways all these years.

"Who said anything about moving?" Wade asked, folding his arms in front of his chest. "I'm simply thinking of getting out of ranching. But the kids still have 4-H and their horses, and the Circle D will always be home for us."

Disappointment shadowed Ruthie's face. "Oh, Wade. I thought surely you'd come to your senses."

"What's wrong with being a rancher, Mother? You married one, you know."

Ruthie's laugh sprinkled the air. "Of course I did,

dear. Why, nothing's more romantic to a young woman than a cowboy. But we all get older and wiser, and I was hoping you'd done the same. You're too old to play games."

"This isn't a game for me." Wade shrugged. "It's my lifestyle. The one I prefer, the one Dad prefers. When are you going to understand that?" God, he hated the way she always managed to push him into an argument. "Look, Mom, let's not fight. I appreciate your taking the kids to Denver. They're really looking forward to it."

"I imagine," Ruthie said. "The city does have its benefits, you know."

"I'm not denying that," Wade said. "It's just not a place I'd care to live." Thank goodness, that was one thing he had in common with Tess. Eager to see her and sort out what it was that bothered her, he shifted impatiently from one foot to the other, silently willing the kids to hurry.

As though reading his mind, they burst from the house in tandem, suitcases and jackets in hand. "We're ready, Grandma," Macy called.

"Dear, don't run," Ruthie said. "You'll soon be a young lady. It's time you learned to slow down a bit. Maybe wear a dress now and then."

To Wade's amusement, Macy shot her grandmother a teasing grin. "A dress? No, thanks, Grandma." She slipped her arms around Ruthie's waist and gave her a squeeze. "There's nothing wrong with being a cowgirl."

Ruthie shot Wade an accusing glare, and he couldn't hide the chuckle that welled up in his chest. "She said it." He reached out to give his daughter a hug, then chucked Jason under the chin. "You two

behave yourselves, and stick close to your grandmother. I don't want to have to come down to that
big city with a search party if you wander off in a
crowd somewhere.''

"We will, Dad," Jason said, shoving his suitcase
into the trunk, which Ruthie had popped open.
"Shotgun!" he shouted, heading for the Lincoln's
front passenger door.

"No fair," Macy said, tugging on her brother's
arm. "You got to sit up front last time."

"You can take turns," Ruthie said, rolling her
eyes. Still, her face said plainly that she was looking
forward to this outing with her grandkids. And suddenly, Wade realized the reason. She could take
them someplace for a little fun, then bring them
back. It was exactly the way she'd mothered him as
a boy. Part-time, leaving serious matters to his father.

Wade wanted to hold it against her, but he
couldn't. She wasn't perfect, but she was his mom,
warts and all. And his dad obviously loved her or
he never would have put up with her. That much,
Wade was sure of.

Impulsively, he reached out and gave Ruthie a
hug, brushing a kiss across her cheek. He knew that
Tess would give anything for Raelene to be able to
make a trip to Denver. He should count himself
lucky that his mother had her health.

Ruthie drew back, eyebrows raised. "What was
that for?" she asked, suspicion lacing her voice.

Wade grinned. "Nothing. Just wanted to say
thanks again, Mom. Drive safe."

"I will." She slipped her arm around his waist
and returned his hug, then climbed into the car.

"Here we go. Everyone buckle up." She closed the door and waved at him, then drove away.

Macy faced him through the back window, smiling and waving, her fuss with Jason over the front seat already forgotten.

Again, Wade thanked his lucky stars. His kids were the best. No wonder Tess had grown attached to them. And no wonder he continued to be drawn to her. Now, if he could only find out what had been bothering her lately. With that in mind, he climbed into his truck and headed for Tess's place. No sense in putting things off. But a sudden case of the jitters washed over him as he parked and got out of the truck. So much so that he barely noticed Duke didn't bark at him until he was directly at the bottom of the porch steps.

"Slipping up, aren't you, dog?" He spoke to the shepherd as Tess came outside. Maybe the dog had begun to accept him that day he'd found Raelene roaming along the driveway.

"Hi, Wade. What are you doing here so bright and early?" Tess frowned. "Is something wrong?"

"I was hoping you'd tell me." He rested one foot on the steps and leaned his elbow on the railing. Trying to look casual. Not wanting her to know his pulse was racing like a runaway horse. He couldn't believe he was actually doing this. Maybe he ought to just forget the whole thing, turn around and go home.

"What do you mean?" Tess put on a perplexed expression, so convincing he nearly believed her. But her eyes flickered guiltily, and she reached down and made a concentrated effort of patting Duke's head.

"I think you know." He held her gaze as she looked up at him once more. "How's your mom feeling, by the way?"

"She's holding her own. No better really, but no worse, either, thank goodness."

"Well, I hope she gets over her infection really soon. And I know you've been busy watching out for her and working, and getting ready for the gymkhana. But I have a feeling all that's made a handy excuse to avoid seeing me."

"Don't be silly."

"So, you haven't been avoiding me?"

"Of course not." She tucked her hands in her back pockets. "I've just been busy, like you said. That's all."

"Then you won't mind if I come in?"

She lifted a shoulder. "No. Be my guest." She opened the screen and he followed her inside. "Everything okay with the kids?" she asked, glancing at him over her shoulder.

"They're fine. Keeping busy. Getting excited for the gymkhana."

"Me, too." Tess kept up the casual conversation as she moved toward the refrigerator and offered him something cold to drink. She whirled around in surprise when he stepped quietly up behind her, nearly slamming into his chest.

Wade put his arms out to steady her, then removed the cans of pop from her grasp and set them on the counter. Tess looked up at him, face flushed. "What are you doing?"

He braced his arms on either side of her, palms against the countertop, effectively cornering her. "Making up for lost time." He pressed his mouth firmly against hers. Tess stiffened, then gradually relaxed. Her mouth opened beneath his, hesitant at first, then more eagerly as her tongue sought his. Her hands found his shoulders, and he slid his arms around her waist and pulled her up against him.

When he drew back, he could see the pulse hammering at the base of her throat. It matched the rhythm of his own. "Now, was that so bad?" He kept his voice low, teasing. But in reality, he couldn't have been more serious.

"Of course not." She licked her lips. "What's gotten into you, Wade?"

"Not a thing. I like kissing you. And from the way you kissed me back, I'd say you like it, too. So what's the problem?"

She shrugged away from him and reached for the pop cans. "I don't have a problem. But obviously, you must. I'd wager you didn't come over here just to maul me in my kitchen."

"Maul you?" He raised his eyebrows and huffed out a laugh. So, she wanted to play it like that. Cool, defensive. "No, Tess, that's not what I'm here for. I came to let you know that I don't like the way you've been avoiding me. I thought we'd agreed to see each other. To take things a step at a time and see where it went."

Tess popped the tab on her can of pop and took a drink. "We did agree." She nodded. "But the more I think about it, the more I'm not so sure it's a good idea after all."

"Why is that?" Genuine annoyance washed over him. What the hell had suddenly changed? And if that was how Tess felt, then why hadn't she said something to him right away?

She looked straight at him, and he was sure he saw an expression of genuine regret in her eyes. "Think about it, Wade. I did." She picked at the pop tab, creating an annoying pinging sound. "We really don't have all that much in common. I guess I just don't see our relationship going anywhere."

Wade's pulse throbbed at his temples and his mouth went dry, and his confidence took a dive. What she said held some truth—about them not having a lot in common. But that didn't stop him from feeling the way he did about her. Surely he hadn't mistaken the signals she'd given him when he'd held her and kissed her.

"So, you don't want to see me anymore. Is that it?" Wade could have sworn he saw panic in her expression for one fleeting moment. It gave him hope.

"I don't know what I want. To be honest, I feel a little confused right now."

She wasn't the only one. He leaned forward and covered her hand with his, as much to touch her as to stop her from making that irritating sound with the pop tab. "What about the old saying? You know—opposites attract?" He moved closer, aching to kiss her once more. He'd hated being apart from her. And while the sensible side of him said Tess had a point, the idealistic side said they had enough common interests, as well as differences, to make things interesting.

Maybe that was what had kept his parents together all these years.

"I suppose that's often true," Tess admitted in response to his comment. She glanced down at his mouth, and his heart picked up tempo.

The look in her eyes told him she wanted to kiss him again, just as much as he wanted it. "Damn straight." Wade reached for her once more and covered her mouth with his. Moaning, Tess gave in and kissed him back. He pulled her nearer still. "I have an idea," he whispered. His tongue traced her earlobe.

She groaned and let out a little gasp. "Yeah?"

"Uh-huh. Maybe I was wrong the other night when I said we should take things slow. Maybe we ought to just dive in and see what happens." He nibbled kisses along her neck.

"You keep that up and you're liable to make a believer out of me." She braced her hands against his shoulders in a halfhearted effort to push him away.

"Are you saying you might be tempted to make love with me if I don't stop?"

"Wade..." She sighed and kissed him again.

He readily returned the favor. "I have to be honest with you, Tess." He spoke between kisses. "I'm already more than a little tempted. So if you want me to leave you alone, you'd better tell me now."

She fisted her hands in his shirtfront, mumbling curses at herself. "You're making it awfully hard to say no."

"That's my every intention." He sought her mouth once more and slid his hands along her shoulders to slip the straps of her bib overalls down. He sprinkled kisses on her sun-freckled skin and raked her gently with his teeth. "You know, maybe these things are sort of sexy after all." He unhooked the snaps on her bib. Telling himself this was crazy. But so much fun. "Oh, yeah, I could get into this." His fingers found the bottom of her tank top, and he moved his hands beneath it, caressing her bare skin.

Lord have mercy. Her stomach was flat and velvet soft, and she smelled so good. Good enough to eat. He needed to stop screwing around and leave. Now. He had no business pressuring her this way.

Abruptly, he pulled away. "Damn it. Tess, I'm sorry. I didn't mean to get so carried away.... Look, I don't want to push you into something you're not ready for." He raised one hand, palm out. "If you need me to back off...if you think there's really no hope for us, then I'll do it. But I'm not saying I'm going to like it." He braced his hand on his hip and held back the words that were in his heart. He couldn't tell her he loved her. Not yet. She obviously wasn't ready to hear it—and might never be.

But her body language told him what her words did not. That maybe there was hope for them yet. Disappointment dimmed the flicker of desire in her eyes as she fastened the straps on her overalls. She licked her lips and faced him. "Don't be sorry." Tess clenched her jaw muscles. "I'm going to tell you something. You've been honest with me, and I want to be honest with you."

He tensed. "Fire away."

"I'm really, really attracted to you, Wade. And I'm confused by what I'm feeling. I've never had time in my life for a relationship." She gave a dry laugh. "You don't bring boys home when your mother's got Alzheimer's."

Her words hit him in the pit of his stomach. He'd imagined difficulties in her life, coping with Rae-lene's illness from such an early age. But he'd never given it so much as a thought that she might not have had normal dates…a movie or a night at the prom.

If Tess harbored any resentment, it didn't show. "Don't get me wrong. I'm not complaining. When Mom grew sick, she became the most important person in my life, and she still is. My family means everything to me." She waved her hand in a circle that encompassed the room. "So does this ranch, the horse sanctuary, my 4-H work…it all means the world to me. I'm happy, Wade, and I'm not sure I want or need to fit anything else or anyone else into my life."

"Okay." He took a step backward, hurting deep inside. But willing to give her the space she needed. Yet the expression in her eyes shifted suddenly once more, making him believe her heart was telling her one thing, even while her head denied it. He held her gaze, studying the emotion behind it. "Tess?"

Sure enough, she didn't speak for a moment. Her silence and hesitation left him wondering if she wasn't having second thoughts. She seemed to doubt her decision to reject him. She stopped him from stepping away any farther by gripping his belt loops. "Hang on, cattleman." She gave him a sad smile. "I may not be sure I need anyone in my life, but I'm also not totally convinced that I don't. All I can say is I've missed you lately."

"You have?" Confusion of his own churned inside him.

"Oh, I know we've been seeing each other at 4-H and all that, but I've missed spending time alone together. Like when we were at the lake. Or on the porch swing at my birthday party…and on our horseback ride." She sighed, long and deep. "I thought I didn't want to see you anymore, and I was going to try to find a way to tell you that. I was wrong, though." She swallowed hard. "I can't make you any promises, but I can tell you this much. I'd like it an awful lot if you'd ask me out on a drive again. Or a ride, or whatever. I want to keep spending time with you, Wade."

Relief washed over him. "Then that's what we'll do." He reached for her once more, but she stopped him with a gentle touch of her finger against his lips.

"I'm afraid right now I'm wanting you a little too much. So unless you can deal with making love to me while your kids are home alone, then I think you'd better go."

"Ah, there's just one thing wrong with that line of reasoning." He gave her a wicked smile. "Macy and Jason left for Denver about a half hour ago with their grandmother. They won't be back until tomorrow."

Tess raised her brow, anticipation and suspicion mingling in her eyes. "Really? Did you plan it that way? Did you mean to seduce me all along?"

"No. Actually, I didn't—though it's a great thought. I drove here thinking we'd get into our usual argument when I told you what I had to say. I figured I might need some time to convince you to see things my way. So, yes, I guess I took advantage of the fact that the kids are gone."

"Is that right?"

"Yes, ma'am. The way I see it, we need to keep seeing each other. At least that way, we can say we gave it a chance." He swept a stray wisp of hair away from her temple. "Hell, Tess. I don't know what it is about you that makes me so crazy, but I came over here prepared to do whatever was necessary to convince you that we ought to give this thing a shot.''

''And you feel you've done that?''

''I don't know. Have I?''

Tess put on a look of mock uncertainty. She tapped her finger against her chin and glanced at the ceiling, then back at him. ''I'm not sure.'' She widened her eyes in innocence. ''Maybe I need further convincing.''

''Think so?''

''Oh, yeah.'' She leaned into him and dipped her tongue briefly into his mouth. Teasing. Taunting. Getting fully into the moment.

''And just how much convincing will you require?''

''Oh, I don't know.''

He flicked the tip of his tongue against the corner of her mouth and was rewarded with a moan.

''Maybe an hour,'' she whispered. ''Or two.''

Wade didn't need further invitation.

CHAPTER FOURTEEN

TESS'S HEART HAMMERED as she led Wade down the hall to her room. She must be out of her mind. How had things progressed so rapidly? One minute she'd been sure she was doing the right thing in keeping her distance from him, and the next she was leading him to her bed.

But she didn't want to stop and listen to the voice of reason. It no longer made sense, when she felt exactly the same way Wade did. No matter how hard she'd tried to distance herself from him, she'd missed him, and now saw that avoiding him was both cowardly and childish. So she was a little mixed up. So what? On one issue, she was completely clear. She felt more deeply for Wade than she'd ever felt for a man in her entire life, and she and he were both healthy, consenting adults. So what was wrong with making love?

Tess's body ached at the mere thought. It had been way too long since she'd shared her bed with a man. Looking at Wade as he sat on the edge of her bed and unsnapped his shirt did just as much for her mind and heart as it did for the physical ache deep inside her. He was fun and exciting and nice, not to mention sexy as all get out. What on earth would she do if things didn't work out between them? Truth be known, she really, really wanted this man to be a part of her life.

Refusing to think about anything except the moment at hand, Tess reached out to help Wade out of his shirt. Then his jeans. He returned the favor, slipping the straps of her bib from her shoulders once more. Trailing kisses across her skin. He made her shiver, then gasp as his caresses heated her body. He tugged off her clothes until she wore nothing more than the lacy panties that were her one feminine indulgence. Lying on top of the covers beside her, Wade raised his eyebrows.

"Lace under denim, huh?" He kissed her breasts, then began to undo the bands on her braided hair. Gently, he ran his fingers through the strands. "Who would've thunk it? You're just full of fantastic surprises."

"So are you," she said, letting her hands trace a line down his muscular stomach to the front of his briefs. "I'd taken you for a boxers kind of guy."

"Nope. Just the traditional, average…" He let the words trail away on a moan as she slipped her hand inside and caressed his hardened flesh.

"Nothing average about that," she whispered, giving his shoulder a nip. "Mmm, I just want to eat you up, cattleman."

"Who's stopping you?" He caressed her nipples, kissing his way down her stomach to her inner thighs. He stripped her of her skimpy panties, using his hands and his teeth, making her crazy with his tongue.

Tess melted beneath him, torn between wanting him to ease up and make the sensation last and letting him tumble her over the edge into oblivion. In the end, she chose to tumble. Then she went to work on him. Making good on her promise to devour every inch of him. He spoke words of endearment and tantalizing encouragement, inviting her to shed every last inhibition. To completely let go and thoroughly enjoy the erotic sensations they created together.

Wade left her body hot and moist with longing, and caused her heart to pound with anticipation and pleasure. She wanted this man, not just physically but emotionally. She wanted to love him and share his life with him. No matter what the consequences. Yet she knew reality would not allow her to do so, and that when he left her bed, be it an hour from now or a day from now, that would be it.

But that didn't stop her from loving Wade with more than her body. As he entered her and took her to heights she never wanted to come down from, she loved him with her heart and soul, as well.

THEY MADE LOVE for the better part of the morning, then crawled from bed and strolled to her kitchen hand in hand. He, clad only in faded jeans; she, in her panties and favorite oversize T-shirt, the one she usually slept in. "If you're hungry, I can feed you," Tess said. "But I doubt I have much you'd approve of eating."

"Who needs food?" Wade murmured, nibbling her earlobe.

Laughter bubbled up inside her as she pushed him away. "We have to eat, cowboy. To regain our strength."

"Yeah? Why is that?" He feigned innocence with half-closed eyes.

Tess giggled, feeling silly and happy and very, very content. "Why, you might need it. I'm not so sure I'm letting you go back to the ranch just yet, since I'm working at home today and can pretty much set my own hours."

"Promise?" He smacked her bottom lightly, then poked his head into the refrigerator after she swung open the door. "Hmm. Cheese. Butter. Eggs. I can make us omelettes."

"You're going to cook for me?"

He shot her a grin. "Sure. Why not? I am capable, you know."

Enjoying herself immensely, Tess folded her arms and leaned against the countertop. "Okay." She gestured toward the fridge. "Be my guest."

With a wink, he set to work, whistling as he cracked eggs into a dish and added cheese, onion, even some mushrooms.

"Wow. I didn't think cowboys ate froufrou food."

"What's froufrou about mushrooms and onions?" Wade raised his eyebrows in genuine surprise. "I eat 'em on pizza all the time."

Tess chuckled. "You're too much."

"Mmm, and I can't get enough of you." He nibbled her neck while the skillet heated. "So I guess I have to cook you something with a little substance if you're not going to send me home right away."

Tess chuckled and slipped into his arms, taking his tongue into her mouth. Ignoring the nagging voice in the back of her mind.

If only things were so easy. The two of them making love...happily sharing a simple meal together. But she knew that what was happening between them was a fantasy, just for today. It couldn't possibly last, because sooner or later, he'd realize just how different they truly were and become bored with trying to fit into her world or fitting her into his. The only sure thing in life was that nothing lasted forever. And knowing that, Tess decided to take what she had with Wade right now and enjoy it. *What the heck.*

She'd simply pull a Scarlett O'Hara and worry about the rest tomorrow.

THE MORNING of the gymkhana found the temperature at a pleasant sixty-five degrees, though Wade knew it was bound to rise as the day wore on in spite of the light cloud cover and breeze. Enjoying the pleasant moment, he helped Macy and Jason load their horses into the trailer.

Amber went in easily, as usual, as did Jason's overo paint, Spur. But getting Diego into the trailer was another story. The gelding had been difficult to load when they'd brought him home the night they rescued him from Clem, and Wade had since spent a lot of time with Macy, working to coax the horse past his fears. Diego had shown some degree of improvement for their efforts. But today the horse chose to be stubborn.

"Come on, Diego," Macy coaxed. "Be a good boy and load up. Look, Amber's in there. And Spur. You don't have to be scared."

"I'm afraid we're going to have to use the butt rope on him," Wade said. The training aide was harmless and effective. It consisted of a soft, thick, cotton rope, which you attached to a ring on one side of the trailer entrance, then passed around behind the horse's hindquarters and looped through a ring on the other side of the trailer entrance, forming a pulleylike guide to ease the animal inside. Most horses didn't much care for it, painless or not, and chose to climb into the trailer in order.

"Aw, Dad, do we have to?" Macy asked. "I really hate to use a rope on him after what Clem did."

"You've got a point." Wade sighed. Because of the inhumane way Diego had been bound and tied, he was liable to react with fear to anything more than a lead rope. "All right, we'll give him a little more time. But if he won't load soon, then we'll just have to go without him."

Macy wasn't entering the chestnut in any events anyway. The horse needed a lot more work before he'd be ready for that. They'd simply decided to haul Diego to the fairgrounds as a measure of training. Exposing him to the noise and excitement of the crowded arena and surrounding area would be a good experience. It would teach the gelding not to fear such things, and to be calm when Macy eventually did enter him in 4-H events. So, for her sake, Wade hoped the horse would get in the trailer.

His hope was met a few minutes later, when at last Macy was able to coax Diego to load using the bucket of grain they'd been trying to tempt him with for the past twenty minutes. "There you go!" Macy said triumphantly. "I knew he'd do it, Dad." She beamed like a proud parent, and Wade chuckled.

"Good work, kiddo. Now, let's go, before we're late."

A short time later they pulled into the fairground entrance, and Wade's heart began to race in anticipation of his seeing Tess again. He couldn't stop thinking about the day they'd spent making love, and he'd found it more than a little difficult to act normal and casual in front of Macy when they'd attended their weekly 4-H meeting two days ago. He'd wanted nothing more than to take Tess into his arms and announce to the entire room of kids and parents that he loved the woman with a madness that went beyond reason. But instead, he'd kept their secret, exchanging an occasional stolen glance or discreet wink with her.

Now his visual search was rewarded as he spotted Tess standing next to her own horse trailer, brushing her paint mare. She wore jeans and a T-shirt, and her hair was plaited in a single braid. Today, she'd abandoned her ball cap, and had on a straw cowboy hat. He loved the way it made her look. Like a cute, saucy cowgirl.

She turned to smile at him, her freckled nose wrinkling in a way that had him on fire all over again, then waved her slender fingers in a flirty, come-on-over-here sort of gesture. Being around Tess was like being around a rainbow after a hard storm, and he reminded himself that he needed to tread lightly. She'd made no offer of anything beyond what they'd shared the other day, and he truly wasn't sure he could offer her anything more than that, either, if he was to be completely honest with himself.

Clamping down on what his heart felt, making every effort to listen to his head, Wade parked near Tess's vehicle and got out of the truck. "Hey," he called to her.

"Hi, Wade. Macy. Jason, that is one good-looking paint you've got there. I meant to tell you that the last time I saw you with him."

"Thanks." Jason glanced toward the horse trailer with pride, then grinned at Tess. And Wade noticed something that hadn't quite registered before. His son no longer gazed at Tess with the moony-eyed look he'd had in the past. As a matter of fact, Jason had been doing a lot of talking about her lately, in the same way Macy so often did. And from the sly glance his son now turned on him, Wade got the sudden feeling his kids were in cahoots, plotting to throw him and Tess together. Not that he'd mind, but it was another red flag, warning him to be careful. His own heart notwithstanding, he didn't want the kids to get hurt.

"I see you brought Diego," Tess said, walking around to the back of the trailer. "Did he give you any trouble loading?"

"Some," Macy said. "But I finally coaxed him in with some sweet grain." Her eyes sparkled with excitement. "I can't wait to ride him in the arena."

"Now, hold on there," Wade said. "I don't know about that. We'll just saddle him and see how he acts while we lead him around the fairgrounds first."

"Your dad's right," Tess said. "For now, Macy, you ought to just walk him around the fairgrounds. Maybe tie him to the trailer after a while and let him get used to the sights and sounds. But keep an eye on him if you do."

"Okay."

Wade should have been filled with annoyance that his daughter so readily listened to Tess, whereas she frequently fussed with him, but he wasn't. Tess was

Macy's 4-H leader, so he supposed taking instruction from her came naturally. But there was something else about Macy's easy relationship with Tess. Something that gave him a good feeling. He knew it had to do with what he'd shared with Tess the other day.

Watch it. The voice inside his head reminded him yet again that he'd taken a really big step in making love with her and that he'd be a fool to completely abandon caution now. But another voice told him it was too late to turn back now, and he'd be an even bigger fool not to relax and see where things led.

Wade nodded toward the parking lot. "Looks like you're going to have a pretty good turnout." Already, the area was quickly filling with trucks and horse trailers.

"Looks like," Tess said with a grin. "I'm sure happy about that. I need to do everything in my power to keep WCHR up and running strong."

Her statement left him with another sudden realization; that he really *had* gone soft when it came to Tess. While he'd always supported the kids' 4-H projects, he'd never dreamed he would see the day he'd be taking part in a fund-raiser to benefit a horse sanctuary.

Trying not to dwell on the many things Tess had caused him to do lately, Wade turned to Macy and Jason. "Let's get these horses unloaded, you two." But he couldn't resist giving Tess a long look over his shoulder. One that reminded her he hadn't forgotten their lovemaking, and that let her know he'd like to take her in his arms right now and kiss her senseless. If not for shocking his kids and Mallory Baldwin, the biggest gossip in the county, who'd just pulled into a nearby parking spot with her own five kids and huge gooseneck horse trailer, he would have done just that.

A short time later, with Amber and Spur saddled, Macy and Jason rode off to look for their friends. Wade saddled Diego and led him around by the lead rope attached to his halter.

From the back of her paint, Tess raised her eyebrows. "You're going to work with him?"

"Why not?" He returned the teasing look she gave him with one of his own.

"You mean you didn't bring Dakota?" She fought a smile. "I was sure you'd want to enter in the pop-and-boot race...or maybe the egg-and-spoon."

"Don't push it," he growled, loving the familiar routine of sparring with her. He had a feeling Tess enjoyed it just as much as he did. Unable to resist, he led Diego up beside her horse and leaned close to Tess's saddle. With one finger, he motioned her to bend down and allow him to whisper in her ear.

She did so, and he cupped his hand and spoke softly. "I don't need to ride in the gymkhana, because I can think of a much better, way more fun way to get hot and sweaty."

Tess turned a cute shade of pink and rapped the brim of his hat with her knuckles. "Behave yourself, cattleman. This is a family event."

"The other one could be, too," he muttered as she rode away from him toward the arena. If a baby were involved.

A baby. With Tess. *Oh, yeah.* That was gonna happen. Shaking his head at his wild thought, Wade walked Diego in the direction Tess had gone. He might as well take the horse right over to where the action was. It would give him something to do to take his mind off Tess.

The kids found him a short time later. They were clutching sign-up sheets for the fun events they wanted to enter. Wade signed the release forms, then dished out entry-fee money, pretending to grumble over the cost. Macy rolled her eyes at him and Jason grumbled right back. Wade smiled. *What the heck.* He grudgingly had to admit it was for a good cause. Watching Diego begin to recover and witnessing the happiness the liver chestnut had brought to Macy had given him a whole new outlook on Tess's rescue work, even though he couldn't see himself ever taking part in it on a regular basis. Still, he had to admire her for working hard at what she believed in.

Wade was actually surprised at the large turnout. Tess, Bailey and the kids had all put a great deal of time into publicizing the event, and apparently their efforts had paid off. The arena and the grandstands were clogged with spectators and participants. The official start time was 9:00 a.m., and Tess began the proceedings a few minutes prior by addressing the crowd over the loudspeaker.

"Good morning, everyone. I'd like to thank each and every one of you for coming here today, whether to participate or just to have fun watching. Your support is greatly appreciated. And if you'd like to see exactly where your dollar is going, please feel free to stop by our booth, located at the west end of the fairgrounds. I've got a photo display with before-and-after shots of some of my rescue cases. If you look around, you might even see one or two

of them here today, taking part in the gymkhana.
I've also got some horses that are available for adop-
tion in the porta-pens near the booth, and anyone
interested can see me during or after the gymkhana.
So have fun, ride safe and let's get started with our
Fun Day Fund-raiser.''

Cheers and whistles resounded in the air, and
lively country music poured over the loudspeakers.
The announcer took over the microphone and ran
down a list of the opening events. Wade leaned on
the fence, thoroughly enjoying the chance to watch
his kids ride. And Tess.

She'd entered most everything available that
morning, though only for fun. As the founder of
CWHR, she wasn't eligible to win prizes. But she
and her little paint mare made an impressive team
as they worked their way through some of the crazy
events such as the egg-and-spoon race and the bare-
back-dollar-bill contest. It was hard to believe the
mare had been a rescue animal. Then again, Diego
no longer looked like one, either. The welts on his
body had healed, and he'd filled out nicely under
Macy's loving care, his coat now slick and shiny.

The liver chestnut flicked his ears as he watched
the events unfold, not so much with fear as with
curiosity. He spooked a time or two when the riders
in the arena gained momentum and raced directly in
front of him at top speed. But overall, Wade was
impressed with the gelding's levelheaded reaction to
the sights and sounds of the gymkhana.

At one o'clock, a one-hour lunch break was announced, and Wade met Macy and Jason at the gate.
"Ready for a bite to eat?" he asked.

"I'm starving," Jason said from the back of his horse.

"Now, why doesn't that surprise me?" Wade clamped his hand on his son's knee. "You guys looked pretty good out there. Better save a few ribbons for somebody else."

"Dad." Macy rolled her eyes at him. "We haven't won that many."

"Well, as long as you're having fun." Leading Diego, he walked beside Amber, scanning the crowd for Tess. He'd lost track of her while cheering Macy and Becky on in the team barrel race.

There. He spotted Tess's paint, Tess walking at the mare's shoulder, headed in their direction. Happiness washed over him, and he wondered, not for the first time, how he'd gone so long without having someone like her around. How was it he'd never before seen just what sort of person she was? Funny, how you could be around a person for a long time without *really* knowing her.

"Hey, Tess," he said. "Good job on 'Rope Lucy.' I didn't realize you knew how to use a lariat." The contest event had involved a roping dummy, and Tess had proven her skills by throwing a loop in an impressive time during the demonstration run she'd given the audience.

"What—are you saying I might even make a fair ranch hand?" she teased. "For your information I've done my share of work on my dad's place."

He didn't know why that should surprise him. He'd realized Tess had grown up on her dad's sheep and cattle ranch. It was just that her opposition to raising animals for meat had given him the impression she would never have lifted a hand to help out in anything that involved shipping animals to market.

"Is that a fact?" Wade shook his head. "I had no idea. I figured you left that sort of thing up to your dad and brothers."

"These days I do," Tess said, confirming his assumption. "But when I was a kid Dad taught me how to work the ranch and how to rope. And knowing how can come in handy at times working with horses, too."

Her words reminded him that she'd changed from the working ranch cowgirl she had been growing up to one who simply rescued horses, which put Tess and him right back to square one. With polar views on ranch life.

Brushing the negative thought aside, telling himself he was nuts even to be toying with the idea of having a solid future with Tess, Wade slung his arm over her shoulder. He couldn't help it. The need to touch her overwhelmed him, even if it was just casually. "Hungry?" he asked. "I've got potato salad, chips and baked beans if you're interested." He hadn't gone to any special trouble with the picnic lunch—had done up fried chicken he and the kids favored for outdoor meals. Of course, he normally didn't bring as much potato salad and baked beans, but when he'd packed the meal this morning he'd had Tess on his mind—as usual.

"Now, that's an offer I can't refuse," she said, taking hold of his right hand, which rested on her shoulder. She caressed his wrist in a way that left his skin tingling and his body aching for more than a casual touch. They locked eyes for a long moment, but then she let go of him, and he reluctantly moved a few steps away, creating a space that was necessary if he didn't want to be tempted to sweep her into his arms and ravish her mouth.

After tending to the horses, the four of them sat beneath the shade of a huge cottonwood. Macy spread an old quilt over the ground to serve as a picnic blanket, while Tess distributed cans of pop from the cooler. "That breeze sure feels good," Jason commented as he helped himself to a drumstick and a huge scoop of potato salad.

"It does, but I hope that cloud cover doesn't turn into a storm," Tess said, frowning up at the sky. The distant horizon showed signs of charcoal gray and near-black.

"Me, too," Macy said. "The gymkhana's going great so far, Tess. I'll bet you're going to raise all sorts of money for your horse sanctuary."

"I'd say so." Tess smiled at her. "Hey, Macy. Why don't you let me ride Diego for you after lunch before things get started up again." She turned toward Wade. "That is, if it's okay with your dad."

Wade scooped a spoonful of potato salad onto his plate. "Sure, if you feel he's ready."

"He's handling the sights and sounds better than I expected he would," Tess said. "It will do him some good to get a little practice workout in the arena." She looked at Macy. "This time next year, you'll have him out there taking part in the events."

"I sure hope so." Macy sat down next to Tess, legs folded, and balanced her plate in her lap. "I'd like to get him started on walking the barrel pattern by the end of this summer."

"I think that's a reasonable goal," Tess said.

Wade half listened to their conversation, content

simply to absorb the mood of the moment. It felt good to sit under the shade tree with Tess and his kids, almost as though they were a family. Once again longing pulled at him. He hadn't realized just how much he'd missed feeling this way. Over the past few years, he'd told himself he and the kids were a solid unit...and they were. But something had been missing. Something he hadn't totally been aware of until now.

After lunch, the kids helped clean up the trash and put away the picnic supplies, then Macy hurried off to get Diego, eager to see how her new horse would do in the arena. She put his bridle on him and re-tightened the cinch on the saddle. Tess adjusted the stirrups. She'd ridden Diego several times at the Darlands' ranch, and Wade had helped Macy work Diego, as well. The chestnut was broke; he was just still a little green in the knowledge department. Wade figured time was all the gelding really needed to turn him into a good 4-H animal for Macy. He was glad now that he'd helped Tess rescue the horse and happy he'd bought him for his daughter. Over-all, the horse had come around.

Before the events started up once more, Tess put Diego through his paces in the arena. The gelding did well, his ears flicking as he listened to and obeyed the cues and commands Tess gave him. He held his head high and proud, checking out the sights and sounds of the arena while she loped him in circles and figure eights. Tess halted near the fence where Wade and the kids leaned against the pipe rails.

"I think I'll take him outside the arena," she said, "and ride him around through the crowd a bit. He needs to get used to that, as well.'' She patted Diego's neck. "He's doing fine, Macy. You've got a good horse here.''

"Thanks," Macy said. She looked up at Wade. "Can I ride him next, Dad?''

"We'll see," Wade said cautiously. "There's a lot going on here today. First let's watch how he does for Tess, 'kay?''

"Okay." Macy sighed.

Tess rode the gelding from the arena and wove her way through the crowd. Wade watched her, admiring the graceful way she sat in the saddle. A thousand thoughts ran through his mind, all of them involving what sort of future he might be able to make with Tess, if she'd let him. He couldn't seem to steer his mind off the one-way track it had put him on for the better part of the day, and was so deep in thought that it took a moment for what happened next to register.

As Tess circled the outside perimeter of the arena, two teenage boys rode past her. Talking and laughing, they seemed focused on the rope one held. The dark-haired boy, who carried the lariat, shouted something at his buddy and twirled the rope in the air. With a flick of his wrist, he threw the loop at his friend. It glanced off the kid's straw hat as he ducked, and bounced toward Diego.

When the loop brushed his pasterns, the chestnut snorted and leaped sideways. Before Tess could get him under control, Diego dropped his head and bucked. Tess made a nice recovery, sitting deep in the saddle. She pulled on the reins, struggling to bring Diego's head up and prevent him from pitching further. But he responded by bolting into a dead run. Tess sawed on the reins. However, the gelding strained against them and sped off, heading for the trail that wound through the trees behind the fairgrounds.

"Tess!" Macy shouted. "Omigosh. Dad." Frantic, she turned toward Wade.

"Give me your horse, son," Wade said.

Obediently, Jason handed Spur's reins over to Wade. With no time to adjust the stirrups, Wade sprang onto the paint's back and rode without them. Mindful of all the kids riding in the area, he kept Spur at a trot as he wove his way around to the far side of the arena.

But once he cleared the crowd he let the gelding have his head and set out in hot pursuit of Tess and Diego. They'd disappeared into the trees. Wade prayed Tess had managed to get the chestnut under control.

CHAPTER FIFTEEN

MACY KNEW that Tess was an excellent rider and that she could handle Diego. Still, her heart raced as she watched her horse take off with Tess. Sweat beaded her forehead as her dad swung up on Spur's back and headed after the runaway gelding.

"It'll be okay," Jason reassured her. "Dad will catch them." Pride lent confidence to his voice. "Spur's fast."

"Yeah, but so is Diego," Macy said. She shook her head in amazement. "Whew, is he ever." She hadn't had the opportunity to see just how fast her new horse could run until now. Together with Jason, she hurried across the arena, clambered through the rail and ran toward the trees. They halted on the edge of the bridle trail, just past where the trucks and horse trailers were parked behind the arena. Macy leaned against a tree trunk and waited.

Several people had witnessed the runaway. They hustled over to ask questions and see if they could help. Macy gave a hurried explanation and assured them everything was under control. She fully expected to see her dad and Tess ride back down the trail at any moment. Therefore, it was with shock that she saw Diego come galloping back a short time later...riderless.

"Oh, no." Macy felt the blood drain from her

face. Quickly, she moved away from the tree. "Whoa, Diego," she called, forcing her voice to sound calm. "Easy, boy. Whoa now."

Jason, too, rushed forward, and with the help of some fellow 4-H kids, they managed to corner the gelding and catch him. Diego's sides heaved as he breathed loudly through flared nostrils, and nervous sweat dampened his neck and flanks.

"What happened?" Sharon Jenkins, the nice lady who'd helped rescue Diego, rode toward them, looking down at Macy from the back of her pretty gray Appaloosa.

"Diego ran away with Tess." Fear choked Macy's voice. "Dad rode after her on Spur."

"Which way?"

Macy pointed, and Sharon loped off down the trail, a worried look on her face. Macy hesitated, then shoved Diego's reins into Jason's hands. "I'm going, too," she said.

"No, Macy. Stay here." Jason frowned. "Dad can handle it."

But she paid no attention. Her heart pounded as she ran for the horse trailer where Amber was tied. Hands shaking, she bridled the palomino and swung into the saddle. Amber eagerly gave her all as they galloped toward the trees and headed down the bridle path.

A lump lodged in Macy's chest and refused to leave. *Please, please, let her be all right.* Over and over, she chanted the words in her mind. Diego had to have done something pretty drastic to throw Tess. She was such a good rider. Hands clammy, Macy clutched Amber's reins as the little mare hurried along the trail. As they rounded the bend, the lump in Macy's chest turned to stone.

Both Spur and Sharon's Appaloosa were tethered to a tree branch at the edge of the path. A concerned look on her face, Sharon stood next to Wade, who had knelt on the ground beside Tess. She lay flat on her back, not moving.

Tears sprang to Macy's eyes. *Oh, God, please no.*

Neither her dad nor Sharon noticed her presence. "I'll get the paramedics," she heard Sharon say as she swung onto her Appy.

Macy choked on a sob, unable to tear her gaze from the sight of Tess's pale face and still body. And it all came back to her in a rush.

The distant sirens.

A policeman pounding on their door.

And her mother...dead. In an accident that had been all Macy's fault. Just as Tess's accident with Diego had been.

Her vision blurred with tears, Macy turned Amber around and, ignoring her father as at last he saw her and called her name, sped down the trail, back the way she'd come.

"I'M FINE," Tess insisted, clutching her head. She sat in the middle of the bridle path, her backside aching, her head throbbing where she'd made contact with the hard ground.

The fall from Diego had knocked the wind out of her, and the blow to her head had nearly caused her to black out. She'd lain still for what felt like an eternity, unable to move or breathe as she heard Wade and Sharon ride up and dismount. The lead weight in her chest would not budge, and she'd fought the panicked feeling that came with not being able to inhale or exhale. She'd been unable to do more than try to communicate to Wade with her eyes the fact that she wasn't really injured. At least, she didn't think she was.

The paramedics had managed to maneuver the ambulance down the dirt trail to where Tess had fallen. Feeling more embarrassed than hurt, Tess sat through their ministrations, wishing they would just let her get up and walk back to the arena.

"Hush up now, and let these people do their jobs," Wade scolded.

Tess shot him a glare but kept silent, figuring it the best and quickest way to get things over and done with.

"You've got a bit of a goose egg," the woman paramedic told her. "Why don't you let us drive you back to the arena."

Grumbling, Tess gave in and climbed into the back of the ambulance, feeling like a fool. How on earth she'd managed to fall from the saddle she still wasn't completely sure. Diego had been slow to respond to her side pull on one rein, which would have put the runaway horse under control, but gradually, he'd succumbed. Tess had been sure she had him well in hand, when he'd bolted all over again. He'd shied sideways, then spun in a one-eighty maneuver, and this is what must have put her on the ground. She remembered nothing between being in the saddle one moment and being flat on her back the next.

Minutes later, Tess exited the ambulance, barely paying attention to the instructions the paramedics gave her. Instead, she was focused on Wade, who'd ridden back on Jason's paint gelding. An odd, worried look had crept into his eyes as he glanced around the area surrounding the arena. Tess's stomach gave a lurch as she followed his gaze and spotted Jason but not Macy.

"Where'd your sister go?" she heard Wade ask. "I saw her ride back this way."

Mumbling a fast thank-you to the paramedics, Tess hurried toward him, her own injuries forgotten.

"She took off on Amber," Jason said. "She went after you and Tess, and then all of a sudden she came galloping back this way." He pointed. "She headed off in that direction. Dad, what's going on?" He turned toward Tess. "You okay, Tess?"

"I'm fine. Where do you think Macy went, Jason? Did she go searching for Diego?"

He shook his head. "No. Sharon and some other people helped us catch Diego and tie him up at the trailer. I don't know where Macy was going. She didn't even hear me when I hollered at her." Again, he pointed toward a dirt road that led away from the exit located at the back of the fairgrounds. "She galloped up the road, and Dad…I think she was crying." He frowned.

"Crying?" Wade exchanged a look of concern with Tess.

"She must've seen me lying on the ground," Tess said, feeling horrible for having given Macy such a fright. "It probably scared her."

"But why would she run off like that?" Wade shook his head. "It doesn't make any sense. I've got to go find her."

"Hang on. Let me get Angel."

"You're in no shape to ride."

"The heck I'm not. There's no way I'm going to

sit around and wait, when Macy might need us.''
She clenched her jaw, daring him to refuse.

"All right, but let's hurry. Here.'' He reached
down and held out his hand, moving his leg away
from Jason's shortened stirrup so Tess could swing
up behind him. "I'll ride you over to get your horse.
It'll be faster.''

Tess pulled herself onto Spur's backside, ignoring
the slight dizziness that claimed her as she slid behind the saddle and gripped Wade's waist. She
wished she could blame the dizziness on the way it
felt to touch him; however, she knew it came from
her injury. A headache oozed its way from the knot
on her head to her temples. But all she cared about
right now was finding Macy safe and sound. She'd
worry about her goose egg later.

Minutes later, she bridled Angel while Wade took
a moment to adjust Jason's stirrups, then the two of
them set off for the dirt road. Raindrops began to
spatter the ground as they rode, and by the time
they'd gone a short distance, the clouds had opened
up, spilling rain down on them in earnest. Thunder
rumbled in the distance and Tess's heart thudded in
her chest. Riding in a lightning storm was not a good
idea. But they had to find Macy.

"Macy!'' Wade shouted. "Where are you?''

Tess called her name, as well, looking down at
the ground as they trotted along the shoulder of the
road. Shod hoofprints appeared in the dirt, not yet
washed away by the sudden downpour. "I think
we're on her trail, Wade. See?'' She pointed at the
prints and he nodded, nudging Spur into a lope.

The road angled up a hill and turned sharply, now
running parallel with the railroad tracks that wove

along the edge of town and stretched for miles in either direction. As they topped the hill, Tess felt the hot surge of adrenaline as a bitter taste filled her mouth. Macy was on the ground near the railroad tracks. Amber stood near her side.

"Macy!" Wade shouted, and let Spur go in a rush to close the last several yards between Macy and him. He vaulted from the saddle even before he'd pulled the gelding to a complete halt.

Tess followed, belatedly realizing that Macy was sitting on the ground, not lying there. She had her knees tucked up against her chest, with her arms looped around them, her head down, face concealed by her cowboy hat. But Tess could clearly hear her sobs.

Wade knelt beside his daughter, mindless of the mud around them. "Macy, honey, what's wrong? Did you fall?"

Macy shook her head without looking up. Her muffled reply was indecipherable through her crying and the sound of rolling thunder.

Tess dismounted and crouched beside Wade. She touched Macy's arm. "Sweetie, what happened? Why did you run off that way?"

Instantly Macy snapped up her head, a look of stunned surprise on her face. Then her expression turned to one of relief mingled with joy. "Tess! Omigod." She clapped one hand over her mouth. "You're okay." She threw her arms around Tess's neck, and Tess hugged her close.

"Of course I am, honey. But what happened to you?"

Once more, tears coursed down Macy's face, mingling with the raindrops that found their way past her hat brim. "Oh, God. I thought you were hurt bad...or...or even dead. I rode after dad when Diego took off with you, and I saw you lying there on the ground. I...I—" She broke into fresh sobs, her words once more becoming incomprehensible. But Tess thought she heard Macy say "my fault" and "again."

Wade pulled Macy into his embrace. "Macy, slow down, sweetie. I can't understand a word you're saying." He wiped her damp hair away from her face where it had escaped one of her pigtails.

Macy exhaled on a sigh. "I said I thought it was my fault that Tess got hurt." She pursed her lips in a thin line, as though afraid to speak her mind. Then she let the words burst forth. "Just like when Mommy had her wreck and died."

Genuine shock pulled Wade's features into the most troubled expression Tess had ever witnessed. "Your fault?" He stared at Macy. "Honey, you're not making any sense." He held her at arm's length, searching for injuries. "Did you hit your head?"

"No." Macy impatiently waved her hand. "I didn't fall off Amber. I just came here because..." Her eyes darted toward the railroad tracks, then back to her dad. Her voice trembled. "I can't remember her face anymore." She bit her lip. "I look at Mom's picture and I see it just the same as I've seen it a thousand times, but I don't remember her for real, Dad." She clutched Wade's arms, crying so hard it broke Tess's heart. "I can't remember the way she sounded or the way she looked when she laughed or anything. And it's all my fault!"

Sudden realization dawned in Wade's eyes, and a chill raced down Tess's back. The railroad crossing was located just yards away from where they now sat. The one where Deidra had been killed.

"Oh, Macy." Wade's voice thickened, and he gently squeezed his daughter's shoulders. "You're not to blame for what happened. How can you say such a thing?" He ran his hands up and down her arms. "Never mind. We'll talk about it back at the fairgrounds. We've got to get you out of this storm. Come on." Taking her by the hand, he pulled Macy to her feet. Tess reached out to steady her.

But Macy stubbornly hung back. "No!" Body stiff, face contorted in pain, she locked eyes with Wade. "I don't care if lightning strikes me. Don't you see, Dad? Mom died because of me. And all this time I've been afraid to tell you about it. I just tried to forget."

Tess felt so sorry for Wade and Macy, and powerless to do anything useful as she stared at them. What could she say or do to help? *Should* she say anything, or should she mind her own business? Wade had told her over and over she wasn't Macy's mother and not to interfere. This conversation was obviously highly personal, not to mention bizarre. Tess couldn't begin to imagine what Macy meant by her self-accusations.

Tess made a decision, and hoped she was doing the right thing. "Macy, listen to me." She slipped her arm around the young girl's shoulders and gave her a small shake. "I have no idea what you're talking about, and it might be none of my business. But young lady, if you think I'm going to stand here and let you get struck by lightning, you'd better think again. Now, put your butt in that saddle and let's

get out of here before this storm gets any worse."
She pointed firmly at Amber, staring Macy down.

She didn't dare glance at Wade. He was likely
furious with her. But she didn't care. Her one concern right now was Macy's safety and well-being.
Not only did the lightning pose a danger, but it
couldn't be healthy for her to sit in the rain at the
site of her mother's fatal accident.

Before Macy could utter further protest, Tess
crouched in front of her and looked directly into her
eyes. "You know what? I take that back. This *is* my
business. I'm making it so because I care about you
more than you can even begin to know, Macy. You,
and your dad, and Jason. And I won't take no for
an answer. So get on your horse, honey. Now."

Tess pulled in a breath and dared a glance at
Wade from the corner of her eye. His face was a
mixture of emotions, making it hard to gauge his
reaction. No matter. She'd said what she felt, and
she wouldn't apologize for doing so. She stood up,
intending to take Macy by the hand. Instead, she
swayed on her feet as the effects of rising too
quickly and the blow she'd suffered to the back of
her head gripped her. Black dots swam before her
eyes, and for a moment Tess thought she might
faint. Fighting the sensation, she stumbled and
groped for balance.

Wade caught her by the arm. "I've got you. Lord,
what am I going to do with the two of you?" He
shot a scowl from her to Macy and back again. "Are
you all right, Tess?"

"You *are* hurt," Macy accused, her small face
scrunched with worry.

Tess shook her head to negate Macy's assertion

and to completely clear her vision, but it only made things worse. Cringing, she blinked. Rain pummeled her hat brim. "It's nothing," she told Macy. "Just a bump on the head. Plus, I got the wind knocked out of me, so that's probably why you thought I was hurt worse than I am. I couldn't breathe, much less move. Now, are we going to stand here debating the issue, or are we going to get out of this storm?"

Macy sighed. "All right, but only because I don't want you fainting on us." She managed a small smile, and Tess smiled back.

She squeezed Macy's hand, then reached to cover Wade's where he still held her arm. "I'm fine. Really. I just stood up too fast."

"You can ride back okay?"

She nodded. "But we'd better hurry, before we all become human lightning rods."

MACY'S WORDS HAUNTED Wade all the way back to the fairgrounds: *Don't you see? Mom died because of me.*

He couldn't have been more shocked if Macy had suddenly announced she'd robbed the bank. What on earth had she meant? She'd been five years old when Deidra had gotten killed. What blame could an innocent child hold in her heart? But then, kids had a way of thinking like that sometimes.

Guilt rushed through him. He'd taken the kids to see a grief counselor after Deidra's death, and he'd thought that, plus the loving attention he'd given them afterward, was enough. But then he'd gotten caught up in trying to run the ranch on his own, working long, hard hours to make himself tired enough to sleep at night—a habit that had become ingrained in him as the days passed.

He had to admit he'd never gone to great lengths to discuss what had happened to Deidra with the kids. Not outside the counselor's office, anyway. Macy and Jason had been so young he hadn't thought more talk was necessary. He'd felt that moving past what had happened was most important. And somehow, as time went on, the pain began to fade, leaving him unwilling to bring up the accident anymore.

Had he been wrong in not doing so? He'd put all photographs of Deidra away, hurting too much to look at them. Though he hadn't stopped the kids from possessing photos of their mother, neither had he encouraged them to display them in their rooms. Instead, the pictures had been tucked away in Macy's and Jason's dresser drawers. He knew they got them out now and then, but he'd never asked any questions. All because he'd stupidly left that task to a counselor…a stranger.

Again, Macy's words echoed in his mind: *I can't remember her face.*

Good Lord, what had he done?

They reached the fairgrounds, and Wade realized the rain had all but stopped. The gymkhana events had come to a halt while everyone waited out the storm, but now, as the sun peeked out from behind the clouds, horses and riders began to stir once more. The arena was muddy, but not muddy enough to stop the show. The announcer's voice boomed over the loudspeaker, informing everyone that the events would continue as soon as the tractor could work over the arena and the footing could be deemed safe.

Wade barely heard him. He was no longer interested in the gymkhana, and he doubted Macy was, either. He hated to spoil Jason's fun, however. He spotted his son standing just outside the truck and trailer.

"Is Macy okay, Dad?" Jason frowned, staring at his sister.

Wade swung down from Spur's back and handed the reins to Jason. "I need to talk to your sister, son. Why don't you go ahead and keep riding for a while. Give us a few minutes alone, okay?" He clamped his hand on Jason's shoulder and gently squeezed. He needed to talk to his son, as well, and planned to do so once they got home. He had to make sure both kids were indeed okay.

"Sure, Dad."

"Fix your stirrups," Wade called as Jason led Spur away. Then he turned to Tess. "You should have those paramedics look you over again."

She nodded. "I suppose so." She glanced at Macy, who'd swung down off Amber's back and now sat at a nearby picnic table. "I know you want to talk to her alone," she said. The expression in Tess's eyes left him longing to tell her he wanted her to stay while he talked to his daughter. "But if you want my help for anything, don't hesitate to ask. I'll be close by." She gave him a smile and caressed his cheek.

He caught hold of her wrist and kissed the back of her hand. "Thanks." His gaze held hers for a long moment. She likely wanted an answer to what was behind Macy's statement.

"You're welcome. See you in a few." Tess turned and walked toward the ambulance, and Wade made his way over to the picnic table.

He slid onto the bench next to Macy and studied the serious expression on her face. She'd been quiet on the ride back to the arena, which wasn't like her at all. But at least she'd stopped crying.

Wade took her hand and cradled it in both of his. "Honey, what's going on?" He gestured over his shoulder. "What was all that about back there at the railroad tracks?"

The sadness in Macy's eyes nearly undid him. But he kept quiet, waiting for her answer.

"I know why Mom was in a hurry to get home the day she died," Macy said. "Why she tried to beat the train."

"You couldn't possibly know that," Wade said, squeezing Macy's hand in a comforting gesture. Surely this had to be an underlying part of her grief, coming out in some sort of self-blame. But why now? "Honey, you were only five years old. Well, almost six." Deidra had been killed just prior to Macy's birthday.

The date hit him like a rock to the head. The anniversary of Deidra's death was tomorrow. He hadn't forgotten; he just never made a huge fuss over it. But he took flowers to her grave every year. He hadn't tried to hide the date from Macy and Jason, but he had tried to de-emphasize it, simply because it was so close to Macy's birthday. He didn't want honoring Deidra's tragic death to overshadow celebrating the birth of his adored daughter.

"Is all this coming out and troubling you because of what tomorrow is?" Wade asked.

Macy shook her head. "No, Dad, that's not it." Her eyes swam with tears once more, though she held them back. "It took me a while to really remember something I'd sort of blocked from my memory. At least, I'd mostly blocked it out, though sometimes I've had nightmares about it." She sighed. "Mom was in a hurry that night because of a promise she'd made to me. She told me she'd hurry home from work that day so we could go shopping for stuff for my party. She wanted to bake me a cake, too, but I remember she didn't have much time. Mom said she had a lot of work to do at the kennel, and that she'd have to hurry if we were to get everything done before bedtime."

Sorrow gripped Wade. He'd always loved the fact that Deidra had worked by his side on the ranch, and he'd admired the way she kept up with that and her part-time job at the boarding and grooming kennel in town—a job Deidra had insisted on having in order to buy the kids extras they otherwise couldn't afford on a rancher's salary. But she'd never once complained.

Wade laid his hand on Macy's shoulder and gave her a reassuring squeeze. "Oh, honey, is that what you thought all this time?" Knowing his daughter had suffered with misplaced guilt sickened him. Kids had a tendency to view things out of perspective, but it had never once occurred to him that his little girl would blame herself for Deidra's naturally driven ways. She'd always tried to fit too many things into too few hours.

"Listen to me," he said, staring hard at Macy. "What happened to your mom was an accident. It was no one's fault." *Except maybe Deidra's own, for taking such a foolish risk.*

Wade pushed aside the resentment he'd never been completely able to shake. Deep down, he knew what he felt was not right. Deidra would never purposely have done anything to put herself in jeopardy, or do anything to risk hurting her family. But the pain he'd suffered at the loss of Deidra—and the pain he'd seen his kids endure—had caused that resentment to fester and turn to near anger. And now, to find out that Macy had also been carrying the weight of guilt was almost too much to bear.

"But it was my fault," Macy insisted. "If she hadn't been in a hurry to come home to take me shopping, then she wouldn't have been hit by the train. And today when Tess got hurt, that was because of me, too. Because I let her ride Diego when I shouldn't have." She cast her eyes downward. "I knew Diego wasn't ready. He's too spooky. But I wanted so badly for him to be ready that I got excited and went ahead and said yes to Tess when she offered to ride him. And then he threw her, and I saw her lying there on the ground, all still and pale and I thought..." She took in a deep breath. "I thought it was happening all over again."

"So you ran to the railroad tracks?" Wade asked softly.

Macy nodded. "I felt so helpless and horrible that I wanted to scream. At first I just rode without knowing where I wanted to go. And then I started thinking about how I couldn't remember Mom's face or voice anymore, and how she should've still been with us all this time. I thought about how unfair it was, and about the nightmares I'd been having. It was all too much, Dad." She stared solemnly at him. "Then I remembered how Grandpa Darland always taught you to face your fears. So I rode to the tracks, thinking if I faced up to what had happened, then maybe the nightmares would end. And maybe somehow, Tess would be okay, too."

Wade closed his eyes and silently berated himself. The railroad crossing where Deidra had been killed was located on a shortcut road that led from their ranch to the fairgrounds and on into the town of Ferguson. A back road that Deidra, who loved discovering shortcuts, had often driven.

After her accident, Wade had avoided the road, unable to bring himself to drive where his wife had died. Unwilling to relive the images of twisted metal and flashing lights that were burned into his memory. Determined that his kids would never see the place again. It was bad enough that they'd been subjected to whispered rumors in town about the real reason Deidra was hit by the train.

"Come here, honey." Wade opened his eyes and wrapped Macy in a bear hug, and as he did, he looked over her shoulder and saw Tess standing there, not far from the picnic table. The sad expression on her face told him she'd overheard some of his conversation with Macy.

But something besides sadness filled Tess's eyes. She also looked distracted. Wondering what was on her mind, Wade motioned her to come forward. Tess walked over and slid onto the picnic bench next to Macy, draping her arm around Macy's shoulders.

"I couldn't help but hear part of what you said." Now her eyes filled with concern. "Sweetie, none of what happened was your fault. Not with your mom, and not with what happened today. I made the choice to ride Diego.'' She reached out to straighten Macy's damp pigtails. ''Things just happen with horses—you know that. Any horse can spook, even the most well-trained one.'' She gave Macy a smile. ''Besides, I've taken enough hard knocks on horseback to withstand a few more.'' She tweaked Macy's chin.

Wade looked at Tess, his heart melting at her words. He'd known all along that she cared about his kids; watching her with Macy, though, made him realize that Tess had been right all along. Macy needed a mother in her life. Someone like Tess to care about her. But could he ever get past his reservations and fears? Could he willingly open up his heart and his life completely? Even to Tess, whom he'd fallen in love with?

Before he could dwell on the thought, Tess spoke to him. ''I just ran into Seth,'' she said. ''He came out here to find me with some not so good news. My mom's been put in the hospital with pneumonia.''

An overwhelming need to protect Tess gripped Wade. Concern for both her and Macy bounced myriad thoughts through his mind, leaving him not knowing what to do. He wanted to offer Tess a shoulder to lean on, but at the same time his daughter needed him now.

''I'm sorry to hear that,'' he said, rising from the picnic bench. ''I'd hoped she'd get to feeling better.'' He reached out and pulled Tess into a hug, and she folded so easily, so naturally into his arms that a comfortable warmth poured through him. ''How bad is she?''

Tess pursed her lips. "Not good, that's for sure. I have to go see her right away. Could you look after my horse for me? Take her back to my place or something?"

"Sure." He massaged circles against her shoulders.

"Your mom's still sick?" Macy stood, too. "I'm sorry, Tess. You never did tell me what's wrong with her."

Tess pulled Macy in to share their hug, and Wade stood there, wishing he could take away the pain from both of them.

"Well, maybe it's time I did," Tess said. "How about I come over to your place after I visit my mom? Then we can talk…about whatever you want." Wade knew she was inviting Macy to open up to her, as well, and for once, he appreciated rather than resented her offer.

Macy nodded. "I'd like that."

"Okay, then." Tess moved slowly away from his embrace. "Thanks, Wade. See you later?"

"Absolutely. Are you sure you're okay to drive on your own, though?" Again, he felt torn. "I could ask if Sharon will watch the kids for a bit if you're still feeling dizzy."

She shook her head. And as quick as that, he could envision the shield she erected between them once more. The one that wouldn't quite let him share every aspect of her life. The one that stood in the way of his being able to love her completely. Had he been guilty of the same thing? A voice inside his head said yes. But if so, he was beginning to realize the error of his ways.

"I'll be fine. I promise. If I feel even the least

little bit dizzy, I'll have the E.R. doctor check the bump on my head." She managed a smile, but he could tell her mind wasn't on her injury. In her mother's fragile condition, pneumonia could not be a good thing at all. Alzheimer's patients were more susceptible to going downhill with such an illness. Oftentimes they never recovered.

"Drive careful," he said as Tess turned and hurried toward her truck.

Then he looked at Macy and knew exactly what he had to do. The rest of the gymkhana was not as important as making things right with the people who mattered most in his life. "I think you and me and Jason should have a heart-to-heart, honey. What do you think?" Jason needed to know what his sister had been dealing with all this time, and he himself needed to make sure his son didn't harbor any such feelings or pent-up grief that he'd never talked about. Who knew what might not have come out in their counseling session?

His family meant everything to him. And Tess had become a part of his family without him even fully realizing it.

Macy nodded. "That's fine by me, Dad. I don't really feel like riding anymore anyway."

"Okay, then. Let's find your brother and go home, and after that, I'm going to go to the hospital to make sure Tess is okay and to see how her mom is doing."

Macy gave him a smile that lifted his heart. "I think that's a good idea," she said. "I mean, Tess is strong and brave, but I think deep down she really needs someone in her life besides her animals."

Out of the mouths of babes.

"I think so, too, honey." And he knew how to get through that wall Tess had put up between them.

He'd simply have to smash his way right through it.

CHAPTER SIXTEEN

TESS DROVE to the hospital with her heart in her throat, denial her only companion. Her mother couldn't have pneumonia. She'd suffered enough having Alzheimer's.

Cold reality set in as she made her way through the hospital entrance. While Tess had hoped against hope that the bacterial infection would clear up, she'd known there was every chance it wouldn't. Raelene's body didn't have the ability to fight off sickness the way a healthy person's did.

Tess hurried down the corridor to the elevator and punched the up button. Impatiently, she waited.

"Hey, sis."

Tess whirled around at the sound of Zach's voice. He stood there, looking as miserable as she felt.

"Zach." She couldn't hide the surprise in her voice. "What are you doing here?"

He fidgeted, glancing down at the toe of his boot. "I'm not that much of a jerk," he said quietly. "Even though I've been acting like one. Mom needs us all here."

Quickly, Tess moved forward and hugged him. "I'm glad you came," she said.

The elevator doors slid open and they stepped inside. Tess's dad was already in Rae's room when they arrived. He sat at her bedside, holding her hand.

The sadness in his eyes broke Tess's heart. He looked up at her and Zach and blinked back emotion, removing his grief with a swipe of one hand across his face.

"Glad to see you, son," he said, giving Zach a half hug, half pat on the back. He embraced Tess, then turned sadly to Raelene once more.

She slept fitfully. With an oxygen tube attached to her nose and an IV in her arm, her body looked even more frail. She frowned in her sleep and moved her head back and forth on the pillow.

"Has she been asleep long?" Tess asked in a near whisper.

"About an hour or so. She hasn't been resting well lately, from what the nurses at the care facility told me." Lloyd let out a tired sigh. "Things aren't looking good for your mother, kids."

Fear gripped Tess by the throat. It wasn't what she wanted to hear. Her dad appeared tired beyond his years, more so than she'd ever seen him. Feeling helpless, Tess eased onto the edge of her mother's bed and laid her hand on Rae's forehead. "She's hot," she whispered.

At that moment, Rae murmured in her sleep. Then her eyes slowly opened. For a split second Tess could have sworn her mother was completely lucid. Raelene looked right at her, her face clear of all confusion. She smiled and breathed a word that sounded remarkably like Tess's name.

"Did you hear that?" Tess turned to face her dad and brother. "She said my name, didn't she?"

Lloyd pursed his lips and rested one hand on his belt loop. "I don't know, hon. Almost sounded like it."

But already Rae's eyelids were fluttering closed once more. "W-w-w," she mumbled, trying to form a word. She strained, screwing up her facial muscles with the effort. "W-wh-h..."

Where?

Was that what it was she'd tried to ask? Where was she, perhaps? Yet, Tess doubted her mother was truly asking where she was, though she wished she could believe that somehow Rae's ability to reason had returned. Her mom could be asking anything. Where were her goats? Or she might even be muttering one of her nonsensical sentences.

Tess bit her lip. "It's okay, Mama." She took Rae's hand. "I'm here, and so is Zach." She glanced up at her father. "Where's Seth?"

"He went to get flowers. He was determined your mother should have some."

Tess could tell by the words he left unsaid that her dad realized flowers would make no difference to Rae one way or another. She'd likely not even be aware of them. Still, Tess loved how her family had come together to stand strong. To battle Rae's illness in whatever way they could.

For the next two hours, Tess sat at her mother's bedside, but Rae had fallen asleep once more and did not wake up the entire time. Tess was torn between feeling relief that her mother was finally resting and wishing she would awaken so they'd know she was okay. Zach left just before suppertime, promising to come back later with Donna. Seth had been and gone, reassuring their father he'd look after the feed store for as long as Lloyd needed him to. They'd all pitch in.

The room grew quiet with only Tess and her dad

there. "I could use a cup of coffee," Lloyd said. "You want anything, sweet pea?"

She shook her head. "No, thanks, Dad."

"I'll be right back." He left the room, walking as quietly as he could so as not to disturb Raelene.

As the door creaked shut, Tess was left with only the noise of beeping monitors. She stared at the woman on the bed who barely resembled the mother who had raised her. And ached for Raelene's release. She wanted nothing more than to have the doctor come into the room and announce he'd found a miracle cure, not just for the pneumonia, but for the Alzheimer's, as well. But of course, that wasn't going to happen.

Fear gripped Tess as she wondered just what her mother's chances of recovery were. And recovery to what? The same sad existence she'd lived for what seemed an eternity? Cursing the fates that had put Rae in such a state, she tried to focus, instead, on the fond childhood moments she'd shared with her mother. She'd give everything she owned to see her whole and healthy once again.

The door creaked partway open, and Tess turned, expecting to find her dad or one of the nurses. Instead, she saw Wade.

He stood hesitantly in the doorway, his expression apologetic. "I had to come," he said quietly. His gaze begged her to tell him it was all right.

The genuine compassion in his eyes melted Tess's heart. She'd been protective of her mother for a long time now, unwilling to let outsiders see her this way. But Wade was no longer an outsider. She motioned him to come in, and he walked over and stood near Tess's chair. Reaching down, he took her hand.

"How is she?" He spoke so softly Tess could barely hear him.

"She's finally resting." Tess swallowed over the lump in her throat. "But I'm not sure if that's good or bad." Worry assailed her again. What if her mother didn't wake up? She'd been asleep a long while now. She told herself it was simply exhaustion that had pulled Rae into such a deep slumber.

At that moment, a nurse came into the room to check Rae's vital signs, and Lloyd returned with a cup of vending-machine coffee. He greeted Wade and shook his hand. "Good of you to come, Wade." Lloyd watched the nurse. "She doing okay?"

"As well as can be expected," the nurse said. "Her blood pressure's good. At least she's finally resting." She peeled the blood pressure cuff from Rae's arm and left the room.

"Have you eaten anything?" Wade asked.

Tess shook her head. "I'm not hungry."

"You have to keep up your strength. I could take you to get a bite to eat, or bring you something if you'd like. You, too, Lloyd."

"I'm fine, Wade, thanks," Lloyd said. "Tess, go eat something, honey. Wade's right. You've got to keep up your strength."

"So do you, Dad," she said. "I'll eat later."

"I've got my coffee. I'll get something else after a while."

Suddenly, Tess recalled her promise to Macy to go over to the Darlands' and talk to her. "I'll be right back, Dad." She motioned Wade into the hall-way.

"How's Macy?" she asked as soon as they were outside Rae's room.

"She's okay," Wade said. "We had a long heart-to-heart. Macy, Jason and I."

Tess yearned to be a part of that strong family circle Wade had created with his children. She wanted more than ever to reach out to Macy. The little girl's words, blaming herself for Deidra's accident, still haunted Tess. She wondered what that was all about and truly cared enough to want to find out. But her mother needed her now. Besides, Wade seemed to have taken care of things.

"I'd like to come see her," Tess said, "but I can't leave Mom right now. I don't know how long…" She let the words trail away, and Wade placed his fingertips gently against her lips.

"You don't have to explain," he said. "I understand." He slipped his arms around her and held her in his strong embrace. One that made her want to be a part of his life. She'd love to have him sit with her and hold her. But of course, he had his priorities and she had hers.

He spoke again, interrupting her thoughts. "I hope you don't mind my coming here, but I had to be sure you were okay. And your mom." Sadness filled Wade's eyes. "I'm really sorry she's so sick. What do the doctors say?"

"Her prognosis isn't good. That's why I need to stay. Will you please explain to Macy for me? Tell her I'll be by as soon as I can."

"I told you, don't worry." He massaged the back of her neck. "Do you want me and the kids to feed your animals for you?"

Tess raised her eyebrows in surprise. "Would you?" She'd been wondering what to do, afraid to leave her mother's side but knowing the animals needed taking care of.

"Of course." He leaned his forehead against hers. "I'm not that mean, Tess." He brushed a kiss across her lips, and Tess's heart raced. *If only...*

She pushed her fantasy wishes aside. "I guess you aren't," she said, attempting to lighten the mood. "Not if you're willing to feed the cats."

He heaved an exaggerated sigh. "Only under duress." He gave her a teasing wink, then sobered. "Call me if you need anything. I don't care what time it is."

"All right. Thanks." Tess kissed him, then turned and walked back into her mother's room, conflicting thoughts running through her mind. It felt good to have Wade in her corner, yet at the same time she was afraid of letting herself lean on him.

TESS AWOKE in the middle of the night and sat straight up in the chair. Disoriented, she wondered where she was for a moment. Then the dim light at the foot of Rae's hospital bed came into focus, and Tess saw her father slumped in a chair on the other side of the bed. His cowboy hat rested on one knee; his booted ankle was crossed over the other.

In her sleep, Raelene coughed and moved restlessly. Tess rose and took her hand. "Mama?" she whispered. "Are you all right?"

Rae made an indistinct sound but didn't open her eyes. As the fog of sleep cleared from Tess's brain, myriad feelings raced through her. Fear that her mother would not pull through gripped her and would not let go. What on earth would it be like not to have her around anymore? Looking out for her mom had been such a major part of her life for so long now, Tess couldn't imagine anything else.

She thought of Wade and Macy and Jason. Her life had seemed complete. Then Wade and his kids had worked their way into her heart. Lately, she'd begun to feel more and more as though something was missing from the world in which she existed. When she was with Wade, she felt a joy unlike any she'd ever known. He'd become a big part of her routine lately—a routine that had involved only her family and her animals.

She'd liked her life as it was and hadn't felt a thing lacking. But now Tess questioned her own judgment.

At first she'd tried her best to keep Wade at a distance. After making love with him, though, deep down she'd begun to realize there was no turning back. When he'd shown up at the hospital last night, it had suddenly felt right to let him come into her mother's room. He belonged there. If she could only let herself take that final step and tell him how she felt.

Her dad awakened a short time later, looking completely exhausted. "She didn't wake up in the night, did she?" he asked, moving to stand beside the bed.

"Not that I'm aware of," Tess said. Her throat felt hard and dry and her eyes burned. She ran her hand lovingly over Raelene's arm. "God, Daddy. What if she doesn't wake up?" She clamped a hand to her mouth, suppressing a sob. "I'm not ready to let her go. I haven't had enough time with her. Not near enough."

Lloyd moved around the foot of the bed and took

Tess into his arms. He hugged her tight, then stood her back. His own eyes swam with unshed tears. "You listen to me, sweet pea. You spent more time with your mother these past several years than most folks would in a lifetime." His expression intent, he gave her shoulders a firm squeeze. "You gave to her without complaint." He shook his head. "Not enough? Honey, you've done more than your share, believe me. In fact, you gave too much, Tess, and for that I blame myself."

"Dad—"

"No, I mean it. Your mother's sickness tore me up inside. I couldn't face what was happening to her, and I pushed a lot of her care off on you when I shouldn't have. For so long now you've given so much of yourself to everyone and everything around you. Think about it." He gestured with one hand. "Your mother, me and your brothers, your rescue horses." The look on his face softened. "Raelene may not wake up again. We have to face that. But it's not too late for you to wake up, honey. Any fool can see that Wade Darland is plumb crazy over you." Gently, he shook her. "Go to him. Give yourself something for once. And allow him to give something back to you."

"I can't." Tess shook her head. She didn't know how to stop giving. And she really didn't have a clue about how to truly let Wade into her life. Even though she realized now that she loved him. For so long, her family and her animals had been her world. Neat and orderly, as much in control as she could make things be. She'd filled every inch of her life, her time, with those things.

Now, suddenly, she felt as though her world was

spinning out of control. All order, all routine, gone forever. Again she wondered how she could possibly live without her mom in her life. Knowing what an empty space Rae's absence would leave had her shuddering.

"You can," Lloyd insisted. "And you will." Pride filled his voice, coupled with a protectiveness that was no stranger to Tess. "I'll stay here with your mother. I married her for better or worse, till death do us part. And I meant it."

Still, Tess hesitated. "I hate to leave you here by yourself."

"I'm not by myself," Lloyd said. A sad smile tugged at the corner of his lips. "Your mother's here—you can bet on that. Her body might be a shell, but her spirit is here with me. She's my partner, Tess. We'll lean on each other."

Tess hugged her father close, drawing on his strength. Willing him to draw on hers. Then she bent over and placed a kiss on Rae's forehead. "I love you, Mama. I hope you can hear me. Please find some peace." Tears squeezed from her eyes as she gently hugged her mother's frail body, then turned and left the room.

WADE LEFT the hospital and went straight home. He'd wanted to ask Tess to let him stay, but he knew she needed some space, some time alone with her family. And besides, he had work to do. Something so important it couldn't be put off for one more minute.

He'd done a lot of contemplating lately, and he'd come to a conclusion. Deidra had been older than him, and he'd admired her maturity and steady way

of thinking. Her strong family values and beliefs
were a large part of what had attracted him to her
in the first place. And their difference in age was
the reason he'd initially thought Tess young and
foolish. As well, he'd believed he'd already lost the
one woman in life who could ever truly be his partner. For a long while, that belief had caused him to
deny that his feelings for Tess ran far deeper than
he wanted to admit. Deeper than he'd ever thought
possible.

But slowly, he began to realize something. When
he'd married Deidra, it had been because he'd confused love with friendship. He'd been so determined
to avoid the sparks that had inflamed his parents'
marriage—negative sparks—that he'd reached out to
the one woman with whom he had everything in
common. The one woman he could feel comfortably
safe dealing with, who thought like him and acted
like him and agreed with him on pretty much every
issue. He and Deidra had not been the two halves
of a whole as he'd once believed. Instead, they'd
been two separate wholes.

He'd loved her, and shared his life with her, but
what they had did not begin to compare with what
he had with Tess. *She* was his other half. The one
missing from his life for longer than he cared to
acknowledge. Never had he loved a woman the way
he loved her. Tess, with her wild and crazy ideas,
and her fiery nature that made every moment fun
and unpredictable. Tess, who'd do anything for
those she loved. He'd never known he could feel so
close to someone, in spite of their differences.
Somehow, those differences no longer seemed to

matter. He and Tess had enough in common to make life all it should be. And more.

To see things for what they were had taken him a while, but now that he had, he wasn't about to let her get away from him.

With that thought in mind, Wade saddled his horse. Minutes later, Macy and Jason mounted their horses and joined him in the task at hand. One they'd performed together many times. But now they weren't simply driving cattle from one pasture to another, or moving them to holding pens for the chore of branding calves.

This move was a permanent one. One that would change his life forever.

"All set?" Wade called.

"Ready, Dad," Macy shouted.

"Head 'em out," Jason hollered. He let out a cowboy whoop and began to drive the cattle from the pasture, down the road.

Wade rode at the front of the herd, sitting tall and happy in the saddle. Smokey and Bandit traveled somewhere in the middle, keeping the cattle in line.

Heading for Tess's ranch.

CHAPTER SEVENTEEN

TESS THOUGHT she was dreaming. She'd come home from the hospital and cried herself into an exhausted sleep. Her father's words had stayed with her, whirling in her mind.

Go to Wade. He's crazy about you.

And now, as she awakened to the sound of her dogs barking, Tess made her way to the front door and stepped out onto the porch. Certain Wade was just plain crazy.

Cattle milled about her yard, dozens and dozens of them. Herefords, Charolais…bawling cows and half-grown calves. Frowning, Tess shook the sleep from her mind, standing there in her stocking feet.

"Wade, what on earth are you doing?" She moved to the edge of the porch, watching the cattle form a cluster in her yard and driveway.

Wade rode over on his blue roan and halted at the foot of the steps, looking so good she wanted to pull him from the saddle and wrap him in her arms. "I'm giving up ranching," he said. He gestured over his shoulder toward Macy and Jason, who waved from the backs of their horses as they worked to keep the cattle under control with the help of Smokey and Bandit.

Tess's own dogs slipped into the fray, Duke's challenging bark echoing above the din of the cattle, along with Bruiser's frantic yips. Sasha whined and darted in and out among the herd, eager to help, her cow dog instincts incited.

Tess shook her head again. Surely she was still asleep. "I don't understand."

"Then let me spell it out for you." Wade leaned on his saddle horn, his face serious. "I've been debating for quite some time now whether or not to sell all of my herd. Working the Circle D has taken a lot of effort, more than I have to give. I can't keep up with it and still be the best parent possible to Macy and Jason. That's why I started Cowboy Up."

Tess stared at him, unable to connect what he was saying with the chaos in front of her. "And you've brought your cows to me because…?"

"I didn't bring them to you. I'm just stopping by on my way to Jed Sanders's place." Jed owned a ranch a few miles down the road. Tess knew him as a regular customer of the feed store.

"Why?"

"Because I want you to see firsthand how serious I am, Tess. Jed made me an offer a while back on my herd, and I'm taking him up on it." He swung down from his horse and tethered Dakota's reins to the porch rail before climbing the steps. "I'm not just doing this for the kids. I'm doing it for you…for us."

"Me?" Tess felt like a sleep-deprived zombie, her brain refusing to kick into gear. He was making no sense. Surely he wasn't selling his cattle because she disapproved of raising meat animals. That would be a big step for him. One he'd only be likely to take if…

Her mind began to clear, and her heart raced as

she realized exactly what he meant. "Wade, you can't do that."

"Oh, yes, I can." He pulled her into his arms. "I can't raise cattle and ask you to be a part of my life while I do it. And I can't spend enough quality time with my kids and be a rancher, either. Sure, I'm taking a gamble on Cowboy Up. It's doing great so far, though I realize that could change." He shrugged. "If it does, well, I'll worry about that when it happens. I'll find another way to provide for my family if I have to."

Stunned, Tess could only stare at him. "Wade, I never expected you to change your lifestyle to please me. I may not like the idea of raising meat animals, but at the same time, if that's what you want to do, it's your business."

He held her away. "You're not listening. I don't want to raise cattle anymore. Like I said, that's what I stopped by to tell you." He headed for Dakota and untied the horse's reins. "I'll be back as soon as I've moved these cows." He pointed one finger at her and gave her a wink. "We've got a lot to talk about, cowgirl. Will you still be here, or should I meet you at the feed store or the hospital? I'd like to come see your mom again."

Sudden sorrow washed over Tess.

But she remembered what her dad had said to her.

"I'll be right here," she said.

"Then I'll see you later." Gathering Dakota's reins, Wade swung into the saddle, and then he rode away.

Tess watched him for a long minute, emotions warring inside her.

Wade had just proven to her his willingness to

compromise when it came to their relationship and to her feelings. That he'd thought about giving up ranching before, because of the kids, didn't matter. It was no secret that he'd planned to keep a few beef around for family use. Macy had recently told her as much.

But Tess would safely bet the cattle that had just trampled her yard accounted for every single head on the Circle D. Which told her everything she needed to know. Wade *was* doing this in large part for her.

Still, she couldn't let Wade into her life if he was the only one giving. A relationship required compromise. It had to be a two-way street.

Hesitating no longer, Tess ducked inside the house to slip into her boots and cowboy hat, then strode toward the pasture. As she haltered Angel, she thought about the way life truly was a cycle. One full of good and bad, the precious moments so fleeting. Nothing lasted forever. Her father was right, and Tess was determined to enjoy the blessings she'd been given. She saddled Angel and swung onto the mare's back.

Heading down the road at a lope, in the wake of the disappearing herd of cattle, she couldn't wait to catch up with Wade.

WADE DIDN'T HEAR the approach of Tess's horse over the bawling of the cattle and the noise of their hooves on the blacktopped road. So when he caught sight of her from the corner of his eye, he thought his mind was playing tricks on him.

She rode toward him on her paint mare. The one she called Angel, looking like an angel herself.

He called out to her as she drew near. "Tess, what on earth are you doing?"

"I've come to help you," she said, as though it were a given.

Frowning, Wade looked at her. "Why would you do that? I thought all this went against your principles." He gestured in a sweeping motion to the herd of cattle as they moved along the road.

She quirked her mouth. "I guess if you can compromise, then I need to make an effort, too. Not that I'd abandon my beliefs for one minute. But these cattle aren't being driven to slaughter, right?"

"No. Jed will use them for breeding stock. Of course, he'll likely sell most of the calves."

"Still," Tess said, "we're not driving them to market. We're simply moving them to a new home."

He felt his mouth twitch. "I'd say that's treading a fine line. But, yeah, I suppose you could look at it that way."

"Give me a break, cattleman." She grinned at him. "You're doing this partly for me, so I figure I need to do something for you, as well."

"Yeah?"

"Yep. I meant what I said before. That if you wanted to stay in the cattle business, I'd respect your decision. But if you're serious about selling out, then I want to ride with you. Besides, the quicker you get these cattle delivered, the sooner we can talk. I have a lot to say to you."

His heart hammered. Surely what Tess had to say was something good. Why else would she be here, riding beside him?

Hope surged through him.

He had something to say to her, too—or rather, something to ask her.

Wade rode along, keeping the cattle in line. Hoping with all his heart and soul that she'd say yes.

TESS AGREED TO MEET Wade back at her place. It would give him time to ride home with Macy and Jason and take care of their horses while she brushed and unsaddled Angel.

A short while later, after turning Angel out in the pasture, she made her way inside the house. Tess headed for the shower and washed the trail dust from her body. She shampooed her hair twice and blow-dried it, letting it hang long and loose, the way Wade liked it.

Anticipation filled her as she dressed in clean jeans and a T-shirt, then went outside to wait on the porch.

"I thought you'd never come outside." Wade's voice startled her as he spoke from the bottom of the stairs where he'd sat just out of view, scratching Duke behind the ears.

Without time to ponder the reason her dog had suddenly accepted his presence, Tess smiled and started down the stairs. "Eager to see me, huh?"

"Oh, yeah." Wade rose and made his way up the steps toward her. They met in the middle, and he took her into his arms. He'd obviously showered, too. The familiar scent of his cologne...the one she loved so much...drifted around her.

"You smell fantastic," she said. "And you look even better."

"You look pretty good yourself," he said, holding her at arm's length. Then he brushed a kiss across her lips. "I've dreamed of this day."

"That makes two of us." Excitement filled her. Then she smiled and gave him a mock frown. "But I don't know. Do you think it's possible for a vegetarian and a cattle rancher to coexist?"

"A former cattle rancher," he reminded her. "You know, I realized something while I was driving over here. I've got an awful lot of acreage at the Circle D that's going to go to waste now that the cows are gone." He gave a casual shrug. "Of course, it might make a nice place for a horse sanctuary."

Happiness filled Tess. "You're serious?" He *was.* The look on his face was enough to tell her so.

"You bet I am. Now, I'm not saying I'm going to become a vegetarian, and I don't know about having cats in the house. But I've got a nice warm barn, and I can cook my own meals. I can even cook for you, if you'll teach me how to fix carrot-pineapple-guava punch, and noodles with green things in 'em."

Tess laughed. "Oh, Wade. Do you know how scared I've been of making a commitment to you?"

"No more so than I've been," he said, growing serious. "But I've come to realize something, Tess. I love you with all my heart and soul. It's not just Macy and Jason who need someone besides me in their life. They want a mom, yes, and it took me a while to get that through my thick head. But what took an even longer time for me to see was that I need someone in my life, as well. And that someone is you, Tess."

"I love you, too, Wade," Tess said, feeling as if

her heart might burst. "But I've been taking care of my mom for so long now, and my animals, that I thought those things were enough. I thought they were all I needed. Then my dad made me realize that it's not enough. I want someone to share my life with, and my hopes and dreams. I want you."

"Then say you'll marry me." Wade cradled her face in his hands. "Tell me you'll be a part of my life for as long as forever is."

A gust of wind blew across the porch, setting the rocking chair in motion. And in its wake, Tess could have sworn she heard a woman's laughter. A soft, familiar sound...

"I wouldn't have it any other way."

He kissed her, long and sweet. When he pulled back, the love she saw in his eyes warmed her heart. "Let's go tell the kids," he said.

Smiling, Tess took his hand.

No longer afraid of the future.

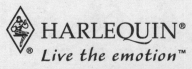

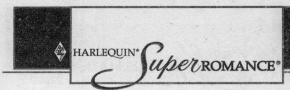

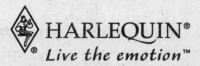

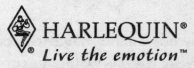

If you enjoyed what you just read,
then we've got an offer you can't resist!

Take 2 bestselling
love stories FREE!

Plus get a FREE surprise gift!

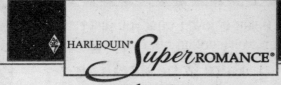

The Target

The action-packed new story by

Kay David

Part of

To some, the members of the bomb squad are more than a little left of normal. After all, they head toward explosives when everyone else is running away. In this line of work, precision, knowledge and nerves of steel are requirements—especially when a serial bomber makes the team *The Target*.

This time the good guys wear black.

Harlequin Superromance #1131 (May 2003)

Coming soon to your favorite retail outlet.

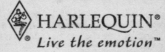

HARLEQUIN®
Live the emotion™

Visit us at www.eHarlequin.com

HSRTGKDM